THE SECRET LIVES OF CHEATING WIVES

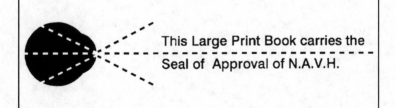

This Large Print Book carries the
Seal of Approval of N.A.V.H.

THE SECRET LIVES OF CHEATING WIVES

CURTIS BUNN

THORNDIKE PRESS

A part of Gale, Cengage Learning

GALE
CENGAGE Learning·

Farmington Hills, Mich • San Francisco • New York • Waterville, Maine
Meriden, Conn • Mason, Ohio • Chicago

GALE
CENGAGE Learning®

Thorndike Press® Large Print African-American.
The text of this Large Print edition is unabridged.
Other aspects of the book may vary from the original edition.
Set in 16 pt. Plantin.

LIBRARY OF CONGRESS CATALOGING-IN-PUBLICATION DATA

Names: Bunn, Curtis, author.
Title: Secret lives of cheating wives / Curtis Bunn.
Description: Large print edition. | Waterville, Maine : Thorndike Press, 2017. |
  Series: Thorndike Press large print African-American
Identifiers: LCCN 2016055508| ISBN 9781410496874 (hardback) | ISBN 1410496872
  (hardcover)
Subjects: LCSH: African American women—Fiction. | Adultery—Fiction | Large type
  books. | BISAC: FICTION / African American / General.
Classification: LCC PS3552.U4717 S43 2017 | DDC 813/.6—dc23
LC record available at https://lccn.loc.gov/2016055508

Published in 2017 by arrangement with Strebor Books, an imprint of Atria Books, an imprint of Simon & Schuster, Inc.

Printed in Mexico
1 2 3 4 5 6 7 21 20 19 18 17

*For my single male friends,
in the hope that you find a wife
made for you — and that you
are made for your wife.*

Dear Reader:

Curtis Bunn peeks at the lives of three couples whose wives decide to venture into the world of cheating after dissatisfaction with married life.

Meet Juanita in D.C. who is bored with her humdrum lifestyle with her husband; Stephanie in the Bay Area whose profession leads her to meet a married man at a conference; and Rhonda in Atlanta whose overweight husband is a turn-off. All three delve into risky adventures and cope with unexpected challenges along the way.

Will these tempted wives find that life is greener on the other side? With relationship drama and steamy scenes, this thought-provoking ride explores the psyche of women in their quest for satisfaction.

As always, thanks for supporting myself and the Strebor Books family. We strive to bring you the most cutting-edge, out-of-the-box material on the market. You can find me on Facebook @AuthorZane or you can email me at zane@eroticanoir.com.

Blessings,
Zane
Publisher Strebor Books
www.simonandschuster.com

ACKNOWLEDGMENTS

God has blessed me in so many ways over my entire life, and crafting this book was another. I love his grace and power.

I am inspired by the memory of my late father, Edward Earl Bunn, Sr. and grandmother, Nettie Royster. I miss them both emphatically. My mother, Julia Bunn, has been my rock all my life. I'm so grateful for my brothers, Billy and Eddie; and my sister, Tammy.

Curtis Jr. and Gwendolyn (Bunny) are my children, my lifeblood, my heartbeats. I cannot be more proud of them. And I'm proud of my wife, Felita, who is wonderful and dynamic to the tenth power.

My nephew, Gordon, has always been like a second son who has grown into a fine young man. And my niece, Tamayah (Bink Bink) and nephew, Eddie Jr. are blessings that I love so much. My cousins, Greg Agnew and Warren Eggleston, are like my brothers. And I am grateful for my Uncle Al and aunts Thelma and Barbara and Ms. Brenda Brown, who has been like an aunt/second mom much of my life, and cousin Carolyn Keener.

My extended family means the world to me: Blake Rascoe, Shirley and Larry Jordan, Ted and Cecilia Baker, Tony, Erika and Eric Sisco, Ashley Darius and Baker Billings, Avant Baker, Zoe, Channing, Rain and Bell Baker.

Again, Zane, Charmaine Roberts Parker and the entire Strebor Books/Atria/Simon & Schuster family have been great, and I am eternally grateful for you. I'm proud to be a part of the wonderful, talented Strebor family.

I enjoy listing by name the supporters because you all mean so much to me: My ace, Trevor Nigel Lawrence, Keith (Blind) and Delores Gibson, Kerry Muldrow, Randy and Flecia Brown, Sam and Maureen Myers, Ronnie and Tarita Bagley, Tony and Raye Starks, Darryl Washington, Leslie Neland, Darryl (DJ) Johnson, Wanda Newman-Johnson, Lyle Harris, Monya Battle, Karen Turner, Star Rice, Tony (Kilroy) Hall, Marc Davenport, Tami Rice-Mitchell, Brad Corbin, Daphne Grissom,

William Mitchell, J.B. Hill and Ericka Newsome-Hill, Clint Crawford, Earle Burke, Robert Diggs, Tony Hodge, Bob and La Detra White, Kent Davis, Wayne Ferguson, Tony & Erika Sisco, Betty Roby, Morechell and Bonita Pryer, Robin and Derrick Nottingham, Kathy Brown, Venus Chapman, Andre Johnson, Nic Mitchell, Tara Ford, Kim Davis, Flecia Brown, Herman Atkins, Greg Willis, Al Whitney, Brian White, Ronnie Akers, Jacques Walden, Dennis Wade, Julian Jackson, Mark Webb, Kelvin Lloyd, Frank Nelson, Hayward Horton, Mark Bartlett, Marvin Burch, Derrick (Nick Lambert), Gerald Mason, Charles E. Johnson, Harry Sykes, Kim Mosley, Steve Nottingham, Joi Edwards, Monica Cooper, Tim and Melanie Lewis, Linda Vestal, Christine Beatty, Ed (Bat) Lewis, Shelia Harrison, David A. Brown, Leslie LeGrande, Rev. Hank Davis, Susan Davis-Wigenton, Donna Richardson, Sheila and Dwight Wilson, Curtis West, Bruce Lee, Val Guilford, Natalie Crawford, Denise Brown Henderson, Nikki Adams, Sherri Polite, Derek T. Dingle, Ramona Palmer, Melzetta Oliver, April Kidd, Warren Jones, Deberah (Sparkle) Williams, Leon H. Carter, Zack Withers, Kevin Davis, Sybil & Leroy Savage,

Avis Easley, Demetress Graves, Anna Burch,
Najah Aziz, George Hughes, Monica Harris
Wade, Nikita Germaine, Yetta Gipson, Mary
Knatt, Serena Knight, Denise Taylor, Diana
Joseph, Derrick (Tinee) Muldrow, Rick
Eley, Marty McNeal, D.L. Cummings, Rob
Parker, Cliff Brown, D. Orlando Ledbetter,
Garry Howard, Stephen A. Smith, Clifford
Benton, Leonard Burnett, Lesley Hanes-
worth, Sherline Tavenier, Jeri Byrom,
E. Franklin Dudley, Skip Grimes, Carla
Griffin, Jeff Stevenson, Angela Davis, Ralph
Howard, Paul Spencer, Jai Wilson, Garry
Raines, Glen Robinson, Dwayne Gray, Jes-
sica Ferguson, Carolyn Glover, David R.
Squires, Kim Royster, Keela Starr, Mike
Dean, Veda McNeal, Dexter Santos, John
Hughes, Mark Lassiter, Tony Carter, Kim-
berly Frelow, Michele Ship, Michelle
Lemon, Zain, Tammy Thompson, Karen
Shepherd, Barbara Hopkins, Carmen Car-
ter, Erin Sherrod, Carrie Sherrod, Tawana
Turner-Green, Sheryl Williams-Jones,
Danny Anderson, Keisha Hutchinson,
Olivia Alston, John Hollis, Dorothy (Dot)
Harrell, Aggie Nteta, Ursula Renee, Carrie
Haley, Anita Wilson, Tim Lewis, Sandra Ve-
lazquez, Angelle Owens, Patricia Hale, Pam
Cooper, Regina Troy, Denise Thomas,

Andre Aldridge, Brenda O'Bryant, Pargeet Wright, Laurie Hunt, Mike Christian, Sid Tutani, Tammy Grier, Roland Louis, April Tarver, Penny Payne, Cynthia Fields, Patricia Hale, LaToya Tokley, Dr. Yvonne Sanders-Butler, Anna Coleman, Alicia Guice, Clara LeRoy, Denise Bethea, Hadjii Hand, Kaira Akita, Petey Franklin, Sibyl Johnson, Shauna Tisdale and The Osagyefuo Amoatia Ofori Panin, King of Akyem Abuakwa Eastern Region of Ghana, West Africa.

Special thanks and love to my great alma mater, Norfolk State University (Class of 1983); the brothers of Alpha Phi Alpha (especially the Notorious E Pi of Norfolk State); Ballou High School (especially the Class of '79), ALL of Washington, D.C., especially Southeast.

I am also grateful to all the readers and book clubs that have supported my work over the years and to my many literary friends Nick Chiles, Denene Millner, Nathan McCall, Carol Mackey, Linda Duggins, Terrie Williams, Kimberla Lawson Roby, Walter Mosley, Eric Jerome Dickey and Caesar Mason.

I'm sure I left off some names; I ask your forgiveness. If you know me, you know it is

13

an error of the head and perhaps aging, not the heart. J I appreciate and I am grateful for you.

Peace and blessings,
Curtis

"There are no good girls gone wrong . . .
just bad girls found out."
— Mae West

THE ONE LEAST
EXPECTED

CHAPTER ONE:
AN ENVIED LIFE

Juanita

Juanita Chandler was embarrassed by all the attention. Supervisors lauded her for her thorough work in helping her firm retain a lucrative multimillion-dollar contract that appeared would go to a competitor.

She took a meeting with the client's president, outlined the value of going with her company, assured that she would oversee the execution of the deal, and the day — and deal — were saved.

That's how Juanita rolled. She got things done. And she did so with grace. She was almost angelic. When it was her time to speak at the company event announcing the new deal after work, Juanita was typically gracious.

"I appreciate the nice words, but they could be said about anyone on this team," she said. "We have a lot of smart and talented people and we love each other.

That is what allows us to be successful. So this thanks goes to everyone, including my husband, Maurice, who gives me amazing support."

Maurice stood near the back of the room and smiled. He'd never expected to win Juanita when they met; she'd seemed too good to be real and as such, too good for him. But she saw the wonder in him, and their two-year courtship had ended in marriage.

"Mommy just got off the stage," he said into his cell phone to one of their two young boys as he stood in the back of the room. "We'll be home soon."

They drove in to work together some mornings, Maurice dropping off Juanita at her marketing firm on K Street before heading to Capitol Hill, where he worked for the city of Washington, D.C.

When they left the office after the celebration and got to the car, Juanita offered to drive. "You've had a long day, honey. Sit back and relax."

Maurice smiled, realizing that he was a lucky man.

At home, Juanita hugged the sitter, who told her, "Your church called. The assistant pastor thanked you for the pies you baked and for stepping in and teaching Sunday

School to the kids."

Juanita thanked her and made a beeline to her sons' room. They were five and seven, Mo and Juan, and had waited up for their mom before going to sleep. She hugged and kissed them.

"When you wake up, I'll be the first face you see." She turned off the light and left the room. "I love you."

She found her husband in the kitchen, opening a beer. "Here you go." She handed him a frosted glass. "I put these in here so your beer can be exactly as you like it."

"You're wonderful," he said. "Thank you."

Juanita smiled. "I'm going to take a shower."

Maurice nodded his head as he flopped in his chair in the family room and searched for ESPN with the remote control.

Juanita retreated to the bedroom, where she dug into her lush leather bag and pulled out her cell phone. A wave of excitement came over her body. *Heat.* She searched her contacts for "Wendy," although she knew no one by that name. It was code. Just in case.

Hey, mister, she started in the text message. *Did you think of me today?*

Within minutes, "Wendy," who actually was Brandon, responded. "I thought about you in bed. Thought about it all day."

Juanita smiled and looked down the hall to make sure her husband was not approaching. Then she responded. *I thought about being with you all day, too. I can still feel you all over me.*

Before Brandon could respond, she texted him again. *What are we doing? What am I doing?*

Whatever you're doing feels great, he answered.

Juanita did not have a response. *Goodnight, B. I have to go.*

She again checked for Maurice before deleting the string of text messages. Juanita lay back on her bed in her clothes and pondered her life. She had a cherished existence, one that her friends and family admired and envied. She was the woman Jill Scott sang about: living her life like it was golden.

But there was some tarnish. She was unhappy. Not deal-breaker unhappy, but heartbroken unhappy. Unfulfilled. *Bored.* She'd never expected this for herself, for her marriage. It was the opposite of what she had anticipated. It ate her up.

And no one knew that but her. *No one.* Not Sandra, her childhood friend and sorority sister. Not her younger biological sister who looked up to her; not her mother, with whom she shared most everything; and certainly not her husband, Maurice, of nine years. It was a take-to-your-grave secret that she trusted *only* with herself. The mere thought of someone knowing she was less than golden petrified her.

And yet, there she was, embroiled in a secret life that, if revealed, would crush people's impressions of her and ruin her marriage. But she engaged in it anyway because it gave her thrills in more ways than one, thrills that she did not get at home. Thrills she *needed.* It also gave her chills, knowing she had fallen short of her purpose. Still, she could not stop herself.

And so, Juanita was riddled with guilt . . . and conflicted. She was so adored and respected, liked and admired, that it bred constant pressure to be the perfect friend, daughter, mother, wife, sister and marketer. It was not an act, either. By all accounts, Juanita was wonderful. And she loved that people loved and admired her.

But she hated that she believed she could not be less than perfect, that she could not misstep, especially to those who loved her the most. She was so magnanimous and giving, so caring and loving, so thoughtful and delightful that any misstep would be viewed

23

as a disaster, a strike against her character. At least that's how she felt about it.

In the beginning, she had found it liberating to sneak around and communicate with Brandon, her old boyfriend. It was exciting, a break from the norm. They were acts outside of what people expected of her. Deep down, she wanted to be a rebel, to go against the "perceived Juanita." She had crafted a genuine image and was unable to free herself of it. That's why she admired Sandra, even as she disagreed with a lot of her actions. Sandra did not show concern about what someone thought of her. Juanita found that audacious. She wished she had some of that in her.

"Girl, please," Sandra said to Juanita when it was common knowledge among some of their friends that Sandra dated two men at the same time. "If I worried about what people said about me, I wouldn't leave the house. They probably wish they had something going on in their lives someone would want to talk about."

Juanita had something going on that would have been the talk for sure. She hadn't planned for it to go as far as it had. It was not her intention to sleep with Brandon. Not at first. But the more bored she had grown with her perfect life and the

24

perception that she was perfect, the more daring she had become and desperate for adventure. She had tried to convince herself that her flirtations over the phone were innocent since she had no intentions of having sex with him.

In her honest moments, she had admitted to herself that her attraction to Brandon had never diminished. They had been lovers years before she'd met Maurice. Indeed, it was years before she blossomed into a woman beyond reproach.

Brandon treated her without concern of offending her. Where Maurice would refrain from using profanity or handle her delicately and sex her irregularly without imagination, Brandon cursed when he felt like it, handled her firmly and was adventurous in bed.

His persona was more like the Juanita her husband never knew. One day, almost twelve years after last hearing from Brandon, she had run in to one of his close friends at the Farragut Square Metro station in downtown D.C. They'd chatted for a moment and she'd reluctantly taken Brandon's phone number.

A week passed before she contacted him. But after a trip to Disney World with the family and resistance from her husband when she was feeling particularly amorous, she had gone into her spacious bathroom and cried. She'd admitted to herself that, despite how it looked to everyone else, she was unfulfilled.

She'd texted Brandon the next day. He'd responded the way she needed him to: *How the fuck are you? Where the hell you been?*

She needed someone to be so indelicate with her. Their weekly flirtations became every-other-day chats on the phone and then every day and then several times a day. Juanita looked forward to hearing from him. And she enjoyed sneaking away to contact him. She enjoyed the adventure, the daring. It provided an edge to her life that was not there. But she vowed not to see him . . . until he challenged her.

"You still can't control yourself around me? That's why we can't meet for a drink?"

That was all it took. She wanted to see Brandon. But she could not be the one who initiated it. And she had to resist when he asked. It had to be work . . . or appear to be work for him to get her to agree. She could not allow him to think she was easy. So she'd resisted, knowing Brandon would persist. And when he did, she'd finally given in.

When she saw him, she melted. Her heart fluttered. She was excited. She tried to pass

26

it off as normal since she had not been in the private company of a man other than her husband in a decade.

It wasn't so much that he looked even better than he had when they were together in their early-twenties. It was that his presence was commanding. He owned the room, from the hostess at the restaurant to the waiter to the bartender when they sat at the bar after dinner. He drew people into him. He showed a different personality from her husband, a lively personality. She felt totally comfortable with him that first night. She was ultra-attracted to him.

He did not try to get her into bed, which made her like him more. He looked at photos of her family — but she did not include pictures of Maurice — and talked about old times, caught up on each other's lives . . . everything other than sex. She was a little disappointed at first; she thought his lack of interest in sex indicated he was not attracted to her. But she quickly dismissed that notion; she kept herself together by being mindful of what she ate and consistently working out. No, Brandon was being respectful — and that turned her on more.

By the end of the month, she was inviting sex. Not with words, but in how she dressed when they met: always in dresses or short skirts with tops that accentuated her body. It became a challenge to make him want her.

Finally, Brandon's discipline collapsed and he kissed her when he walked her to her car after their fifth time together. It was following lunch at the St. Regis in downtown Washington, D.C., near the White House. Juanita did not resist. She closed her eyes and her senses were heightened. She could smell his Viktor and Rolf Spice Bomb cologne. She felt his heart beat up against her chest. He was intoxicating. She was drunk.

"I shouldn't be doing this," she said. "But I want to."

Brandon could have taken advantage of her. Instead, he said, "I'm sorry. But I gotta tell you, my attraction for you is stronger than ever. Can I ask you something? Why are you here with me?"

Juanita did not have an answer. At least not an answer she wanted to share. Brandon had a hold over her, and she told him the truth.

"I should not be here and every time after I leave you, I say it's the last time," she started. "Even though we haven't done anything —"

"Yet," Brandon interjected.

"Even though we haven't done anything," Juanita continued, "I feel bad, like I've betrayed my husband, my vows. The problem is that it's exciting. Seeing you makes me feel alive. I love my life, my family, my husband. I do. But . . ."

"But what?" Brandon asked.

"I need something more," she said. "I can't believe I'm saying this or that I'm even here with you. But it's where I want to be. My husband is a good man. He's a good man."

"When can I see you again?" Brandon asked.

"When do you want to?" That wasn't the answer her head told her to give.

"Tonight. Right here. I'll get us a room and have room service for dinner after you get off work."

Her heart raced from anticipation, and that scared her. She did not consider *not* coming. And knowing she'd have to lie to make herself available excited her. Even though she had never lied to Maurice and did not have an idea of what excuse she'd give her husband, she said, "What time?"

"Six-thirty. I will text you the room number."

The hours leading up to meeting Brandon were long for Juanita. Her anticipation

29

mounted by the minute. She couldn't concentrate on work. The feeling in her stomach was a confluence of fear and excitement. It was similar to the feeling she'd had when she saved the big deal at work. When she realized that, she felt confident. When she had that feeling, she did her best work.

As the time to meet Brandon approached, she exited the office without the requisite small talk with colleagues. She just left. She felt guilty and believed she looked guilty and did not want anyone to detect it.

She could not remember the ten-minute taxi ride to the hotel. But when she got there, she sat at the bar in the lobby and ordered a Dirty Martini. That was the drink she used to have when she was younger and more freewheeling. She sipped only wine with her husband, whom she called from the bar.

"Honey, I tried to get out of it, but I've got to do this dinner with the partners. We're at Mastro's now. I'll take an Uber home," she said. She was shocked that she did not feel guilty about lying.

"Okay, do what you have to do," he said with no trace of suspicion. "I'm taking the boys to Nando's for some wings."

"Yeah, right. I know you're taking them there because that's what *you* like," she said.

Maurice laughed.

"Can't put anything past you," he said. "But they like it, too."

"Okay, have fun. And get me an order of wings for later, just in case."

She watched the high-rollers come and go at the bar and pondered their lives. She wondered if a couple on the couch was married or if they were having an affair. She wondered how far it would go with Brandon. But she knew if she went to that room what would happen.

When she finished the drink, she paid for it and made her way to the sixth floor. At Room 606, where Brandon texted her to come, she stood there several seconds. She teased her hair and made sure her dress laid neatly up against her body. Finally, she knocked.

Brandon answered with a smile. He had darkened the room by pulling the drapes; it was dimly lit by scented candles. A bottle of Grey Goose vodka was in an ice bucket. Rare Essence, a D.C. "go-go" band that originated in the 1970s, played on his iPhone.

"I hope you're hungry," he said. "I ordered dinner. Got you something light, a shrimp dish. Be up in a few minutes."

That impressed Juanita. She was too

nervous to eat, but she liked his initiative. Maurice would not make a decision without asking Juanita's approval.

Before the meal came, Brandon poured her a glass of vodka. Straight. She had wine with her husband because, in her mind, it was more ladylike. He sat on the bed and she sat in a single chair. The drink downstairs got her a little tipsy, so she sipped the vodka slowly.

"So, what did you tell your husband?"

"I'm working on a big client, so I told him I had to do a dinner thing. The truth is that they were in the office this afternoon. I believe that I got it done. They will announce tomorrow night."

"Good luck," Brandon said. "If they are as impressed by you as I am, then you closed the deal."

"How am I impressive?" She took another sip.

"Wow, you're drinking a little too fast," he said. "I don't want you drunk. I want you to make conscious decisions and to remember all this — whatever happens."

"Whatever happens?"

"Yes. Nothing should happen unless you really want it to happen," Brandon said. "I'm single. I mean, I date, but I don't have a wife. And I really don't want to pressure you into anything."

The vodka loosened her inhibitions. She had Brandon pour her more. She kicked off her shoes and loosened a button on her dress, revealing her cleavage. She moved from the chair to the bed.

"This is nice. Thank you for doing this," she said. "I can't believe I'm here. I don't think I've been in a hotel room without my kids in seven years. I'm glad I'm here. I'm glad we reconnected."

Brandon nodded. "Kiss me," she said. "Take me away from my life, at least for a little while."

He was taken aback, but only for a second. She did not have to repeat her request. As he kissed her deeply, he unbuttoned her dress. Juanita did not resist. In fact, she freed her hands and sped up the process — and then began unbuttoning Brandon's shirt. It was like out of a movie, two lovers attacking each other with abandon.

In a minute, they were naked, and Brandon tossed aside the myriad pillows that adorned the bed, almost knocking over a bedside lamp. She pulled back the covers. He intended to reach for the drawer where he had placed condoms, but she was all over him. And then he was all over her.

"You want this dick, don't you?" he said

with arrogance. Such talk made her wet. Her husband was a nice man, a kind man who did not possess the aggression she needed. She believed that he respected her too much. It was a strange position, she knew. But that's what she felt. Worse, she feared that telling him what she wanted, what she *needed,* would make him look at her as some kind of "freak." So she kept her mouth shut, and as a result, suffered through mundane sex for years.

"Please do. Please gimme that dick," she said. She had not used that word aloud in that context since she'd dated Brandon. With her husband, she thought he would think it was unladylike. In reality, for her it was liberating to express her raw feelings without filter.

For the next ten minutes, Brandon and Juanita made love so passionately that Juanita felt dizzy and delirious. It was a level of intensity and passion she did not get at home, that she thought had escaped her for the rest of her life. Brandon tossed her from one position to the next, and even demanded "get on your knees so I can get deep," and she obliged without hesitation. His thrusts made her body feel reinvigorated. Alive.

"You missed this dick, didn't you?" he

said, and Juanita would not lie.

"I did. I did. Brandon, I did," she said with her eyes closed. "I did . . ."

Brandon smiled — but kept stroking. Her words encouraged him to thrust harder, to please her more.

"Oh, my God. What are you doing to me?" she said. "But keep doing it."

There was a knock — dinner had arrived. Brandon yelled toward the door: "We're busy. Please leave it there. I'll get it and sign the check later."

Juanita smiled. And then Brandon continued to make love to her, to reawaken the sensuality in her she thought was dead.

When the deed was done, she lay on his chest in silence. Her body awakened by the passion and physicality. But her heart was saddened.

She had broken her vows, something she never would have expected. It was something no one who knew her would have expected, either. The perfect mother, friend, daughter, sister, cousin was no longer perfect.

But at that moment, her body felt too good to worry too much about it.

■ ■ ■ ■

THE ONE
MOST LIKELY

■ ■ ■ ■

CHAPTER TWO:
THE WEIGHT OF IT ALL

Rhonda

When Rhonda first saw Lorenzo, she was home for several weeks after foot surgery, bored beyond description. She did not like television and was not much of a reader. She liked running, Zumba and line dancing, all of which were off-limits as she recovered.

She happened to walk to the front of the house to check the mail and there he was, taking a walk in her cul-de-sac. It wasn't that he was so handsome. But he was walking, which meant he was considerate of his body, which was something her husband, Eric, was not.

It bothered her that her husband took how he looked for granted. She equated it to him taking *her* for granted. He was lean and together when they first met, six years earlier. It was a personal affront when he told her before they got married that he was concerned she would stop going to the gym after the wedding.

And Eric ended up being the one who got comfortable, who cut back on physical activity and increased his food intake. In two years, he was ten pounds heavier than on their wedding day. Two more years, he added ten more pounds. And, despite Rhonda's semi-regular pleas to stop eating and go to the gym, he added another twenty pounds in the last two years.

Those additional forty pounds looked awful on him. Eric was a handsome man, with beautiful white teeth and a pure heart. But his stomach stuck out as if he had swallowed a beach ball — not a good look.

Rhonda told him as delicately as she could: "Honey, I'm your wife. I'm on your team. I'm the captain of your team, so don't think I'm against you. But you have to either cut back on eating or start working out. Most likely, both. You've gained so much weight, and it's not good."

"I'm still me, the same guy you married."

That alarmed her. So she was direct.

"But all that weight doesn't look good on you, Eric. You've gained more than about forty pounds."

"Oh, so that's it? You worried about how I look? You're that vain?"

40

"I guess I am. And it's not about being vain. It's about being attracted. It's not attractive with all that extra weight."

She knew that was harsh and hurtful, so she cushioned it a little — or tried to, anyway. "But the biggest reason is your health. Eric, I lost my brother to a heart attack. He was overweight and did not exercise. I want you to be around. I'd be devastated if something happened to you."

Still, Rhonda saw no change in Eric's habits. So, when she saw Lorenzo walking, he resonated with her as a man who cared about how he looked and his health.

She watched him that first day and wondered who he was. He smiled and nodded as he kept moving. The next few days, Rhonda watched from the window as he passed by during lunchtime. After four days, she wanted to get a closer look, so she acted as if she had to go to the mailbox as he approached the house. And she liked what she saw.

First, he was fit. Not muscle-bound — she didn't like the overly muscular type. But he looked to be in his mid-forties and well-kept. She smiled at him and he waved and smiled back. She stood there at the mailbox and watched him walk down the street.

That night, when she lay in bed next to

Eric, she was annoyed. He snored like some kind of drunken caveman, so loudly that she couldn't sleep. Frustrated, she got up and went into the guest bedroom down the hall. As she rested on her back, she could still hear Eric's snoring. But the noise coming from his clogged nasal passage was not what kept her awake.

What kept her from sleeping was Lorenzo. She didn't know his name at that point, but she wanted to find out. *Needed* to find out. The next day, Friday, she decided she would wait for him when he came walking by that afternoon.

She still had a cast on her foot, and she came up with a plan: She'd be at the mailbox when he approached and as he circled the cul-de-sac toward her home, she would trip and fall to the ground. He'd see her and come to her rescue. And a conversation would start from there.

It was the cliché damsel-in-distress scenario, but she did not care what scheme she devised. She decided while lying on her back in the dark in their guest bedroom that she needed to meet that man.

Rhonda had grown tired of Eric's complacency and often fantasized about having a man who physically did it for her. She did not consider it vanity. It was merely a fantasy, the way many women fantasized about Denzel or Idris.

Her fantasy was different in that the man was attainable — or at least touchable. She noted that he did not wear a wedding ring. That didn't mean he did not already have a woman, though. In fact, in Atlanta, it was almost assured that he had *several* women.

But, as women were prone to do, she had already played out in her head the kind of relationship they could have — even though she had not met the man.

"What you gonna do after you actually meet him?" her coworker, Olivia, said after Rhonda called and shared that she would fake a fall to get his attention. "You worship the ground Eric walks on."

"I know. I'm curious, I guess. And that ground Eric walks on shakes a little more with every step. But, anyway, this guy has come by the house every day this week at the same time. He apparently lives in the subdivision. Can't no harm come from meeting a neighbor."

"You can tell yourself that if you like," Olivia said.

Rhonda dismissed that notion and let Olivia go back to work. Then she put on a skirt to make it obvious she wore a cast and a sexy top that clung to her body. She had a body that could still turn heads.

At five minutes to noon, she ambled to the mailbox, glancing down the street to catch Lorenzo approaching. She didn't see him. She hung around that mailbox until ten after twelve. He never came. She was disappointed — in herself.

She was a married woman looking to meet a stranger who could have been walking in the neighborhood staking out houses to vandalize. Or he could have been a rapist seeking his next prey. She could have met him and made it easy for him to rob her. It was the middle of the day and all her neighbors were at work. When she looked at it that way, she felt silly about her fantasy.

And she felt guilty when Eric came home, and prepared a nice meal for him as a way of silently apologizing for her behavior: baked trout, steamed green beans and sliced tomatoes. He appreciated the effort but a half-hour after eating, he ordered a pizza. Rhonda was disgusted.

Her friend Olivia came over, which was a welcome reprieve. "I need to get out of this house," she said loud enough for Eric to hear.

"You wanna be one of those people out with a cast on at the club like it's all good?" she asked.

44

"It *is* all good," Rhonda responded. "It's not like I have some disease. And it's not like I want to go to the club and get on the dance floor. I need to be around some people who are living, not sitting around rotting."

"Oh, I ain't people?" Eric chimed in. "I'm rotting?"

"You don't care if I'm here or not."

"What's wrong, Rhonda? You know I want you around."

"Well, I don't want you around. I'd rather you be out taking a walk, getting some exercise."

"Oh, that again?" he said. "Yeah, you're right. You do need to get out of the house."

"Let's go, Olivia."

In the car, they headed from Rhonda's Southwest Atlanta home into downtown.

"You okay, girl?"

"I don't know. Eric knows my grand-parents have been married for fifty-nine years and my parents were married for thirty-three years before my dad died," Rhonda explained to Olivia. "We believe in marriage. My grandmother told me about wanting to leave my grandfather on many occasions. But she said she stayed because of the vow, the covenant and the tradition of marriage on her side of the family.

"Can you believe her parents never divorced? Her aunts and uncles stayed married. None of her four sisters or three brothers ever divorced. And none of her three children ever divorced. I've never heard of a family with that commitment to marriage."

"That's pretty deep, Rhonda," Olivia said. "But I bet all of them weren't happy. Some people stay for different reasons. I couldn't do it. When I saw there was no hope for my marriage, no trust, I had to move on."

"I understand. I told my grandmother about how frustrated I am with Eric and his weight, and she told me, 'Work with him, baby. Marriage is sacred. You're gonna want to take a lamp and crush his head while he sleeps. But you won't. That feeling you have will go away just like the urge to kill him will.'

"She didn't mean literally kill him, but I got her point. But my frustrations with Eric haven't gone away. They've escalated."

"Give it time," Olivia said. "Be patient. Keep talking to him. Better yet, ask him to walk with you. Make it a couple thing."

"I like that; maybe I will."

Olivia pulled up at Suite Food Lounge in downtown Atlanta. It was a hot spot where Rhonda had a good time in the winter when a group of black doctors had a vibrant

Super Bowl party. She left that night feeling sick when Seattle lost in the last seconds, but she enjoyed the event.

They went in and were lucky — two people left their seats at the bar just as they were about to grow frustrated about standing around.

"See," Rhonda said, "it was meant for us to be here."

"Or maybe it was only meant for us to get a seat. What happens next will determine if it's meant for us to be here."

They ordered Moscow Mules, and after the second one, the music either sounded better or got better — Rhonda was too tipsy to distinguish. All around were younger people in high spirits.

And then, like out of a cheesy hard-to-believe movie, there he was. Lorenzo. They had been puffing on a hookah. And when Rhonda saw Lorenzo about ten feet away, she considered that the combination of the drinks, hookah and her imagination produced the illusion of Lorenzo. She could not trust her somewhat glazed-over eyes . . . at first. She'd had Lasik surgery, and, while she was ecstatic with the results, there were times things seemed a little out of focus for a few seconds.

Whatever the case, after literally wiping

her eyes, it was clear: it was Lorenzo, and he was walking right toward Rhonda.

She was so stunned, she couldn't even tell Olivia. She sat on that stool, like an overwhelmed schoolgirl, transfixed. She heard Olivia say something, but it was mere sound, not words. Lorenzo glanced at Rhonda as he got closer and then his eyes shifted to the left, where a server carried above her head a bottle of champagne with sparkles shooting out of it, as if it were the Fourth of July.

Rhonda wanted to turn to Olivia, but couldn't. Her heart pounded like Ricky Ricardo on the congas. In fact, that's all she could hear. All the chatter from hundreds of people in the place and the thumping music went silent, as if someone pushed a mute button on her ears from the outside noise. All she could hear was her heartbeat.

Finally, Lorenzo walked up to Rhonda, who stared into his eyes. His hand came forward and as she began to lift hers, she noticed he was not looking at her anymore. In fact, he reached across Rhonda and . . . tapped Olivia on the shoulder.

"And what's happening with you?" he said to her as she turned around.

"Oh, my God, Lorenzo," Olivia said, extending her arms and nearly knocking

Rhonda over to receive his embrace.

Suddenly, Rhonda's hearing came back. She could hear all the noise again, but only really wanted to hear Olivia and Lorenzo.

"Rhonda, this is my friend, Lorenzo — the gentleman I told you about."

"Huh? Who? When?"

"From the bowling party at the Painted Pen. About three months ago."

"Oh. I remember that."

"Nice to meet you," he said, extending his hand.

"Yes. Nice to meet you."

Olivia then took over, flirting with Lorenzo like Rhonda had never seen her. She crossed her legs, revealing more thigh. She touched him on his arm every time she laughed. Lorenzo, meanwhile, was more than Rhonda realized. He was taller than she thought and nicely filled out his clothes.

But he clearly was attracted to Olivia — he never said another word to Rhonda after the introduction. She was disappointed that he did not recognize her from his walks.

Again, she became angry with herself for her momentary lapse. This time, she was mad because she was jealous that this man she did not know was interested in her girlfriend. She thought: *I am married. Get a grip.*

It wasn't easy, but she gathered herself, recalibrated her thinking and turned her back to Olivia and Lorenzo. Rhonda ordered another cocktail and took her time sipping on it while she people-watched and enjoyed the music.

Finally, Lorenz left.

"Girl, I like him," Olivia said. "We've had a few dates. But we made a date for tomorrow and next Friday. What did you think of him?"

"He's taller than I thought," Rhonda said.

"What do you mean? Why would you think about how tall he is?"

Uh-oh. She had said too much. So she went into straight clean-up mode.

"I should have said that he's a taller man than I have seen you with."

"I don't care about his height — unless he was some Andre the Giant type. It's kinda nice to have a man you have to crane your neck up to look into his eyes."

"So, where do you think it's going?" Rhonda asked. She remained curious.

"It'll go wherever I want it to go."

"Where's that?"

"I will see how much I like him before I decide. But so far I like him."

Rhonda was conflicted. She was mad at herself for having an interest in Lorenzo and mad at Olivia for having one, too. Letting on she felt that way was not an option.

"You're divorced, single . . . you can do whatever you like. Women control men anyway," Rhonda said.

"And you know this," Olivia said, slapping high-five with Rhonda.

The rest of the night was a blur for Rhonda, though. She ordered another drink — her fourth — and tugged on the hookah so hard she almost choked. "Slow down, girl. I don't want to have to drag you outta here."

"That wouldn't be dignified. I'm already in here with this ugly-ass cast on. To be drunk too would be too extra."

They laughed and watched people for a while before leaving. "You don't want to say bye to — what's his name, Lorenzo?"

"I'll talk to him later."

Rhonda passed out on the way home. When she woke up, they were in her drive-way.

"Girl, those drinks hit me hard. Damn."

"Get your drunk ass in the house. Wake up your husband and give him some."

"Some what? Food? Girl, bye."

She made her way into the house and grew more disgusted by the step. There was a plate with remnants of food on it on the

51

kitchen counter. The television was on in the family room, but Eric was in bed. And lights were on in the hallway, guest bedroom and second bathroom.

Worse, when she got into the bedroom, Eric was on his back snoring, with the covers to the side, revealing his ample stomach that protruded under his tank top. A bag of potato chips was strewn on the floor.

Rhonda shook her head and for the first time wondered what her future was with her husband. It was not a good place to be.

■ ■ ■ ■

E-LOVE

■ ■ ■ ■

Chapter Three:
You've Got Mail

Stephanie

"But is it really cheating if we haven't done anything?" Stephanie wanted to know. Her sister, Toya, challenged her.

"What do you think? What would you think if you saw text messages and e-mails back and forth between Willie and some woman? Sometimes it can be worse because you're expressing feelings to each other. When men cheat, most time they can't control themselves and it's no emotion involved. No excuses for that dumb shit. But you and this guy are sharing feelings."

"But I would prefer Willie communicating with someone over having sex with her," Stephanie reasoned.

"You're pissing me off," Toya snapped. "You'll say anything to make yourself feel good about this. I wish Mom were alive. I'd tell her and she'd smack the hell out of you. Then again, she shouldn't see you like this.

The only reason I'm not slapping you is because Mom told me not to hit you like when we were kids. But I have to be honest, Steph: I love you, but I'm really disappointed in you. And I want to smack the lipstick off you."

Stephanie looked away from her older sister by two years and pondered what she had been doing. She understood Toya, but she held on to the notion that "cheating" meant intercourse. Electronic flirting was harmless, she reasoned. She was too intrigued by Charles Richardson to see otherwise.

"I'm disappointed you're not supporting me on something that is important to me," Stephanie said. "I haven't told anyone about this. I told you because I thought you'd understand. But you haven't had a man other than Terry in a while, so —"

"So what? So I should be a married slut fantasizing about some guy who is only setting you up for sex? Girl, you'd better get a grip."

"See a slut, slap a slut," Stephanie dared her sister.

Toya resisted the urge to crash her open hand across Stephanie's face. Instead, she got up and walked out of the coffee shop at Jack London Square in Oakland. She did not look back as she headed to Broadway, where she had found a parking space on the street.

Stephanie finished her tea and walked over to the pier and looked out at the San Francisco Bay.

Before she could think too much, her phone chimed. It was a text message from Charles, who lived in Los Angeles. They had met at an education conference in Sacramento a few weeks earlier. Stephanie was the only woman at the table during a luncheon. Charles sat next to her and they conversed and exchanged business cards.

Two days after they returned, Charles e-mailed her:

Hope you remember me. I'm the one who saved you from being bored at the luncheon a few days ago in Sac. Really enjoyed the conversation. Meeting you was one of the highlights of the conference. Let's keep in touch, if that's OK with you.

Stephanie did not think much of the e-mail at first. But she had eyes; Charles was not overly handsome, but his presence was strong. He was confident and well dressed, and she could smell his cologne over the roasted chicken that was served for lunch.

She responded to his e-mail:

Of course, I remember you. It was very nice to meet you, Charles. I'd love to keep in touch. I definitely want more information about the mentoring program you started at your school. It could be a guide for what I want to do here.

That was the beginning. It was innocent . . . on the surface. But the reality was Charles slipped in his interest when he wrote that meeting her was a "highlight" of the conference for him. And Stephanie was subtle, but let it be known that he had made an impression by writing "Of course, I remember you" and "I'd love to keep in touch." She threw in the mentoring program as a way of keeping it professional. But the fire had been lit. It was only a matter of when it would become an inferno.

From that day, they exchanged emails daily. By the end of the week, Charles messaged her:

I think there is a conference coming up down here on professional development that could be beneficial to you. If you come, I'll be sure you get to see L.A. like you've never seen it.

Stephanie then e-mailed Charles her personal e-mail address. She could sense their messages could become inappropriate for the workplace.

She liked e-mail over texting because she

could say more in less time at the computer than on the cell phone. Charles liked texting because it was immediate. They used both methods as their business meeting rapidly turned into a personal relationship — they hardly ever "chatted" about work.

After twenty-one successive days of texting or e-mailing, Charles decided to make a stronger play.

You never talk about your husband. He doesn't seem to be around a lot, based on how much we communicate. I don't see how he could let that happen.

Stephanie played coy.

What do you mean?

I mean if you were mine, I'd make sure your attention would be on me.

"Oh," Stephanie said aloud, to herself. "I see. I knew it was coming."

Well, he's a busy man, so I get to have some free time or some time to myself. Usually, I'm doing work. But since I met you, I seem to have time to communicate with you. I guess I'm inspired.

#EquallyInspired, Charles wrote back.

Stephanie smiled.

What's your story? Where's your wife?

Did I say I had a wife?

You had on a wedding ring? #DeadGive away

LOL. OK, you got me. That's good that you are observant. Yes, I've been married eighteen years. My wife is actually away a lot. She's a flight attendant. Could've been anything she wanted, but that's what she chose.

Somebody has to do it. You all have flight privileges. You should be seeing the world together.

Stephanie waited with anticipation for a response. It took a few minutes before Charles wrote back.

She travels so much for work, she doesn't want to go much when she's not. Do you like to travel?

She did not completely buy the answer, but she accepted it.

Of course. I travel a lot, but that's still not enough.

What's your favorite place you've traveled?

In the States, I'd say New York. I'm from Minneapolis, but I have always loved big cities. The bigger the city, the better. New York has all that energy. I just get consumed in it.

Charles responded:

And it can be a romantic city, too. Even with the taxis and hustle and bustle, there is romance there with the lights and rooftop bars and seductive restaurants. It's a city, if you're with the right person, that can seduce you.

Charles was seducing Stephanie. She

caught herself that day.

Agreed, she wrote back. *Unfortunately, I have to go. I have my kid visiting from L.A. and a dog. I have to feed them. But you'll hear from me soon.*

The idea of experiencing New York with Charles entered her imagination and excited her. She had enjoyed their back-and-forth, but when she physically could feel her interest rising, she tried to back away.

For a minute.

By the time he texted her when she stood at the pier, they were deep into their electronic courtship. In one sense, it was a tease; they had made no plans to actually see each other. They had not even spoken on the phone. Not once. In another sense, it was a setup: their interest in connecting heightened by the day. The first text after her sister walked out on her at the coffee shop was revealing.

I'm visualizing you right now on the beach with your dress blowing in the wind, revealing your shapely legs, all the way up to your waist. And I didn't see any panties.

How do you know I don't wear panties? I didn't tell you that.

My instincts tell me you're a sexual person who likes to feel sexy.

61

If you didn't see any panties, what did you see?

I saw the light. LOL

LMAO. You're funny. When I'm out like I am today, by the water relaxing, I like to feel the wind rise between my legs.

A smile creased Charles' face. He had been wondering when they would kick up their messages to sex talk. This was it.

You know what makes you sexy? The way you think. Not to say you don't look good. But, honestly, a lot of women look good. But only a few women have a sexy mind.

Well, thank you. But I don't try to be sexy. I'm just me.

And that's the best thing about it. You're not trying. I've seen and know women who go out of their way with what they wear and their body language who are seeking attention and want people to consider them sexy. It's just in you. That's pretty cool.

Stephanie: I don't believe everything you tell me. I'm not calling you a liar. I promise I'm not. But I'm not naïve. I'm not so flattered that I don't understand men — well, as much as a woman can understand a man.

The smile on Charles' face disappeared.

Where is this coming from?

I'm not trying to kill the mood. I'm just letting you know I have my eye on you, mister. You write all these nice things about me, but you're married. I'm married. My point is: Why have you been communicating with me all this time? What do you want from me? When you start telling me I'm sexy, that question comes to mind first instead of being flattered.

Well, that's good. I'm not trying to fool you or even seduce you (yet). I thought we were communicating because we like each other and enjoy hearing from each other. For me, it's good to have a woman I can open up to, get to know. That's it. No pressure. And no need for me to lie or mislead you on anything. But if you'd like me to stop the flirtations, I certainly respect that.

As much as she wanted to tell Charles she wanted the flirtations to stop, she could not pull herself to do so. She enjoyed the attention. She looked forward to it. And, scarily, she had come to need it.

CHAPTER FOUR:
PUSHING THE ENVELOPE

Juanita

After her evening with Brandon, Juanita found it increasingly more difficult to sleep at night. Guilt dominated. She loved her husband, Maurice. She loved her family. It meant everything to her. And yet, she looked forward to her next encounter with her lover.

Her actions and thoughts were contradictions to the woman and wife she had been. At the same time, doing something unexpected and out of character gave her a charge that she could not get in the life she lived and the image she created. She was the epitome of Miss Goody Two-Shoes, a position she coveted but one that limited her.

Juanita loved and hated that image. It was an accurate depiction, but it was not *all* her. It was the part of her that she wanted everyone to know. But it also prevented her from unleashing that wild side of her, which included a free sexual identity that made her feel complete. Maurice, who was conservative and ineffectual in bed, would be taken aback if exposed to Juanita's desire for aggressive sex, perhaps public sex, rap and go-go music, bourbon and cigars.

She knew this because he'd told her. "My brother told me about that woman right there," he said when he and Juanita began dating. They were at his brother's birthday party near Rock Creek Park. "After all he told me about her, I have no respect for her. She's a wild girl. A freak."

"What do you mean?" Juanita needed clarification.

"My brother told me she's like a sex fiend. And he said once she started drinking and smoking, she'd do anything, even engage in sex in the car or in a restroom at a restaurant."

"And that makes her a freak? Maybe she likes a little fun," Juanita said.

"I know you're not trying to defend that kind of behavior," Maurice said. "You're too much of a lady to be like that."

Juanita knew then she'd have to dial back her sexual proclivities. She liked to use a vibrator at times and certainly enjoyed more than basic sex. Maurice was so rigid that

Juanita gave in to his preferences because she saw so much in him as a provider. He was stable and successful and she was convinced he would be a good father and loyal husband.

She'd had her fill of irresponsible men whom she could see would not serve as an ideal long-term mate. Maurice was different. His personality assured her that she could have the life she desired — nice home, supportive husband and darling children. Stability. A storybook life.

She was fine — or accepting of her life — until she reconnected with Brandon. Brandon reminded her of not only who she had been, but who she really was — and how much she missed having her body worked over, how sexually deprived she was. Above all, he reminded her of how important sex was to her.

She missed the excitement of being erotic and feeling sexy and sexually free. She missed using profanity and blasting hip-hop and go-go music. She missed dancing while puffing on a cigar. To maintain the farce, she had to act as if she were perfectly content being basic Mrs. Wonderful. It was not easy.

No one knows what it's like to have to do right all the time. That's a lot of pressure to be perfect, she thought. It was only a thought; she would not dare let anyone know what she really felt. *No one.*

Her indiscretion with Brandon would be her dying secret. She pleaded with Brandon that he not tell a soul — not his pastor, counselor, closest friend, dying confidant — about their affair.

"I'm giving you more than my body," she told him. "I'm giving you my trust."

"It's me and you, baby," he said. "Whatever we do, it's between us — it's no one else's business. You can trust me."

Ironically enough, her biggest concern was whether she could trust herself. She swore that one after-work rendezvous at the St. Regis would be it, no matter how liberating it was to be with Brandon without inhibitions. But Maurice, while he tried hard, did not meet her pleasure-principle standards.

Juanita liked to get her wig rocked.

She trained herself to put aside that passion in her DNA for the betterment of her life and family. Often, even before she reconnected with Brandon, Juanita cursed herself for holding back when she dated Maurice. After his comments, she should have let him know it was OK to be adventurous and sexual, that sex in a public place on occasion was fun and freeing, not an indictment on whom she was. Instead, she shut down what she called her "freak-nasty" to preserve the reputation Maurice had of her.

"You're the only one who knows about my 'freak-nasty," she told Brandon as they rested in bed after their intense sexual session.

"Oh, 'freak-nasty,' huh?" he said. "I like that. And I'm honored. You can get freak-nasty with me any time you need to."

"Yeah, I'm sure that's true," Juanita said. She caught herself sounding like some serial cheater, a floozy, and she did not like that. "Don't think I'm your personal fun package," she went on.

"Come one, Nita, act like you know me," he said. "Act like you know how we always rolled. Much respect. I would never put you out there like that. Nothing but love between us."

As they drove out to dinner one night when they were dating, she listened to her husband tell his friend Manny, "If she wanted you to hit it while y'all were in the park, then she's telling you she's a freak. And you can't trust a freak."

That was more confirmation for her to believe she had to suppress her sexually adventurous nature to prevent judgment from Maurice. She had just purchased a vibrator, which she used in the bathroom after showers and before going to bed. She had to get her orgasms somehow. And while they did not meet the joy that came with enjoying a man's body and his scent and his aggression, it served a purpose.

What's a freak, anyway? she wondered. *I like sex; that doesn't make me a "freak." It makes me a woman confident enough to be how I am. My sexual freedom does not define me. My brain doesn't define me. Neither does my career or my family or any one thing or combination of things. All of those elements together make me who I am. It's sad that I feel like I have to hold back so I won't be judged.*

When she slept, more than once she dreamed of how devastating her parents were to learn of her infidelity and how angry and humiliated Maurice was. She also dreamed of laughing with Brandon and having her body pained and pleased at the same time by him. She would wake up either relieved that she was dreaming or craving Brandon's touch.

Perhaps worse was that she had no one to share her thoughts, no one to solicit advice. There was no one to reel her in, no one for her to share in her excitement about Brandon. And there was no one to share her disappointment in herself. There were girlfriends who shared their darkest secrets with Juanita. Many sought her advice, support and encouragement. She was desperate they never know of her outside-the-marriage activities. So she suffered in silence, trapped in her own obsession with being perceived as perfect.

All that, and she found it nearly impossible to pull away from Brandon. She tried, though. After that night of passion, the guilt kept her from answering his text messages or returning his calls for three days.

In fact, when the weekend came, she had her sister keep her kids that Saturday night. Maurice had not shown any interest in sex — which was OK with Juanita because she could still feel Brandon all over her — but she believed intimacy with her husband would move her closer to him and farther away from Brandon.

So, with the kids gone, she set up a night of passion with her husband by preparing a nice meal followed by champagne. She suggested they sit on the deck, where she had a candle burning and soft music playing on her iPod dock.

Maurice resisted. He was so disconnected from his wife that he did not notice that she was trying to set a romantic mood. He was so into the routine that he said, "What's the point of sitting out there? The TV is in here."

It took all her strength not to bellow like an opera star. "But we always sit in there in front of the TV," Juanita reasoned. "Let's do something different."

"Why fix what isn't broken?" he responded.

Growing angry more than disappointed, Juanita snapped.

"Who said it isn't broken?"

"You didn't hear me say it?"

"I heard you, but you apparently didn't hear me."

"I heard you."

"No, if you heard me you'd get the clear message that something *is* broken."

"What? What are you talking about? What's broken, Juanita? *What?* We have two beautiful kids, a beautiful house, money in the bank. We don't have any worries."

"You don't take your wife saying something broke as something to worry about?"

"Worry about what? We have the family you said you wanted? We have everything. Don't we?"

Juanita's stomach turned because Maurice was not being flip or sarcastic. He was dead serious, which was a dead giveaway that he saw their marriage as fine when she was almost catatonic in it.

"Mo, honey, we should talk," Juanita said. It was bad enough her night to make amends — to herself — was derailed. It was worse that Maurice derailed things.

"And turn off the TV."

"I'm trying to watch —"

"I don't give a damn what you want to watch," Juanita yelled. "I told you we need to talk. That should have meant something to you."

"What is it, Juanita? What is it?"

His tone was condescending and dismissive, making Juanita more livid.

"Maurice, it's not okay to mock this situation," she started. "This is serious, goddammit."

That last word made her husband take notice. He turned off the television and tossed the remote control on the couch.

"What's wrong?"

"What's wrong? You. Me. Us."

"Explain that."

"Everything seems fine to you?"

"Yeah. Tell me what isn't."

"We haven't had sex in two weeks. You haven't touched me. And I try to set up a romantic evening for us — get the kids out of the house — and you want to sit in here and watch sports?"

"This is what we've always done."

"I don't want what we've always done all the time. And you shouldn't, either."

"Now we're back to if it's not broken, don't fix it."

"You still don't get it. Oh, my God. It *is* broken, Maurice. I'm not happy."

She was astonished she said the three magical words: *I'm not happy.* But she was relieved, too. Juanita wanted her marriage to work. But she was desperate for Maurice to do his part.

"You're not happy because of sex?" he asked.

"Not because of it," she answered. "Because of the *lack* of it."

"That's kinda shallow to me," he said. "We have all that we have, all we have built together, and that's your focus?"

"My focus is on feeling closer to you. All this stuff you seem to believe is so important is nothing if we don't love each other and show that we love each other."

"Oh, now you don't love me?"

"I love you very much — and making love is a way of showing it."

"The way you're coming at me is not cool," he said. "It's kind of sad to me to pin our marriage on sex. It's like sex makes the world go 'round."

"I think it can make the marriage go 'round for damn sure," Juanita said. She was not going to back down.

"I'm not getting any response from you that I hoped for," she went on. "Let me try this: Are you still attracted to me?"

"Of course, I am."

"Do you still enjoy sex with me?"

"Of course."

"So why have we gone two weeks without being intimate? I'm no sex fiend. You know that. But I'm thirty-eight. I'm in the prime of my sexual life. I love my husband. It doesn't make sense to me that you'd be okay going that long without making love to me."

"It's not that, Juanita. I really didn't think about it. I thought we were both working and kinda fell into this pattern of —"

"I don't want to fall into any pattern, Maurice. That's dangerous."

"Dangerous?"

"Yes, dangerous to a marriage. I know you don't always get or even like Chris Rock, but he said something in a movie once. It was something like 'the most dangerous time in a marriage is when the couple accepts that they're not having sex.' I would agree with him. We can't do that. It would make everything stale. We promised we wouldn't let that happen."

Finally, Maurice seemed to get it. "I know the movie you're talking about. It was called, *I Think I Love My Wife.* You're right. I'm sorry. It's easy and comfortable to get into a routine and let things go. I could sense it, but I thought you were okay with it. I'm sorry."

Juanita was relieved. Maurice hugged her and she kissed him on his face. He took a deep breath. "I love you, J."

She smiled and kissed his face again. "I love you, Mo."

He took her hand and led her to their bedroom. They stripped and met each other in the middle of the bed. He kissed his wife with all the passion he could muster. She closed her eyes and freed herself to let Maurice take command of her body.

All the while, she thought of Brandon.

Chapter Five:
How Lo' Can You Go?

Rhonda

Before Rhonda could express her disgust with Eric, he told her the next morning: "I'm sorry. I went in the living room and realize I left the house in a mess. I was so tired. After you left, I got on the treadmill. I walked for thirty minutes."

"You did?" she said, delighted. "I'm so happy you did, Eric."

"I did it for you."

"Thanks. But you should do it for yourself."

"If I did it for me, it would have been a thirty-second ride. So, even though I didn't want to, I did it for you. It doesn't seem right that you're judging me by my weight. Underneath everything, I'm the same person."

"I don't want to make this about vanity," Rhonda said, "because I'm not vain. I accept you for who you are. I do. But let's be honest. People like what they like, whether you like it or not or whether it's vain or not. I like my husband to look like the strong man I met and fell in love with.

"I used to look at you and see this really attractive physical specimen. And don't think that's what I fell for, because it's not. I fell for the complete package. The physical and the mental — how you made me feel when I thought about you, when I looked at you. Everything is important in figuring out a life partner. I looked at everything. And I still do. You should, too. Whatever you'd like to see me improve, you should tell me."

"Oh, really. Okay, great. Well, improve on your need to complain. What you're doing is complaining about your husband who is here every day, not out chasing women or wasting money at strip clubs or treating you bad. Our bills are paid. We don't have any extreme worries. And yet you're complaining."

"Because I have the right to complain. I don't take what you said for granted. We have a comfortable life. But is comfortable good enough for you? It's not for me."

"What do you want then?"

"I want everything. I want to feel like my husband cares enough about himself that he works out and eats right too, and first and foremost, make sure he's healthy. Don't make it about me. It's about you. This isn't that hard. I didn't ask you to replace a transmission in your car or build a computer. Or to wash dishes, for that matter. I'm asking you to take care of yourself. That would take care of a lot of things."

It was not like Eric did not understand Rhonda's issues with him. He understood completely. What she didn't understand was that Eric did not have the requisite willpower necessary to reshape his body. He loved to eat, and eating made him sleepy. So, that's what he did: eat and sleep. He also gained weight.

"Okay, honey, let's not make this a big deal," Eric said. "I'm going to do better. Eat better, get some exercise and see what happens."

"Oh, I love you for saying that," Rhonda said. "So, we should get a scale so you can weigh yourself and set goals. When you write down goals, you're more likely to accomplish them. I read that somewhere. I can walk with you sometimes. And I can make some meals that are more friendly to your body and —"

"Hold up. Wait a minute," Eric said. "I'm not looking to you to be my trainer or my healthy-eating adviser. I will figure this out the way I want to figure it out. But I appreciate your willingness to help."

"See, that what I'm talking about," she said. "That flip-ass mouth of yours is gonna get you in serious trouble one day."

"To prevent that from coming today, I'm going to stuff it with pizza, some beer and a little pound cake. My mouth can't get me in trouble if it's full of food, can it?"

"That's not funny, Eric," Rhonda snapped. "You should be eating salads only. And drinking water."

"I'm done arguing with you," he said. "You need to love me for me and not what I eat."

"You are what you eat. Ever hear of that?"

"I don't want to hear anything else out of your mouth right now."

The day that started off with so much promise turned indifferent. Rhonda knew she had been too pushy. Eric knew he had been unnecessarily resistant. And yet, neither relented.

When lunchtime came, which was usually when Rhonda made a meal or provided something from a nearby restaurant, she did neither.

"You gonna make lunch?" Eric asked her. He found her in the guest bedroom — reading.

"I'm not hungry," she said. "And I'm not enabling you. If you want a salad, I'll make it. If not, I'm sure you'll figure it out."

Eric stood in the doorway for a few seconds before storming off. He changed shirts, grabbed his keys and left the house. Rhonda fumed.

All the rest of that Saturday and all of Sunday, they did not speak. Monday morning, when Eric left for work, he didn't bother to tell Rhonda goodbye. She was disappointed; inasmuch as she wanted to stand on her principles, she did not like or want to remain at odds with Eric.

All in all, they had a good marriage. They did not have children to distract them, so they were one-on-one their entire time together. Rhonda called Eric on his way to work.

"Um, why didn't you say bye before you left?"

"We haven't spoken a word to each other for about two days. I didn't think you wanted to hear from me."

"So you're going to let this silent treatment go on forever?"

"I figured you would end it when you got tired of it."

"You know what? We need to go to counseling because this isn't going to work. So by the time you come home, you'd better be ready to talk about counseling or talk about leaving. Your choice."

And then she hung up. Rhonda was proud that he took a strong stand. She made her way from her bed to the kitchen, where she poured two painkillers out of a bottle and washed them down with water. Since she had been home following foot surgery, Rhonda had started her day when Eric left around eight o'clock. But she instead got back in bed and pondered her life. Before long, she drifted off to sleep.

It was not until her cell phone rang that she woke up. It was twelve minutes to noon. She was momentarily delirious.

"Girl, what's wrong with you?" Olivia said into the phone.

"Damn. I'm so out of it. What time is it?"

"Time to get your lazy ass up."

Rhonda yawned and ran her fingers through her hair — an attempt to get her bearings. "Shit. Is that right? It's almost twelve o'clock? Damn."

"I can't believe you're still in bed."

"Me, either. I'll call you later."

The lack of sleep over the previous few days had caught up with Rhonda. She usually felt guilty when she slept past nine o'clock. Sleeping all morning had her

81

chaotic . . . for a minute. She realized she did not have anywhere to be and no responsibility that required her up in the morning — except to take care of her healing foot. And so, she relaxed.

She showered, checked her e-mail on her laptop and made a cup of coffee. Finally, about ninety minutes after waking up, Rhonda dressed and made her way out of the house to grocery shop.

She was somewhat dejected that Eric had not called or texted her, but also angry for the same reasons. When she entered the garage from the kitchen, she smelled the garbage that had sat there over the weekend. Eric usually took the trashcan to the corner on Monday mornings, but he had not.

So, now irritated, Rhonda pulled the large plastic barrel toward the street — until she heard, "Can I help you with that?"

To her astonishment, she turned around to see Lorenzo. Startled and happily surprised at the same time, she was not sure how to react. He seemed surprised to see Rhonda.

"Oh! You scared me," she said. She wanted to say more but could not come up with the words.

"I'm sorry. Let me get that," he said, grabbing the trashcan and toting it to the street.

Rhonda used those few seconds to tease her hair and straighten her clothes.

"Thank you."

"Sure. Anytime," he said. Then he blew her mind.

"You're Rhonda, right?" he said with confidence.

"Yes, I am. But how do you know that?"

"Wow, I thought I made an impression," he said. "I guess not. We met Saturday at Suite Lounge. I'm Lorenzo. You're Olivia's friend, right?"

Rhonda lit up. "*You remember me?* I mean, I remember you."

"Yes, I saw you on my walk at least once."

"Did you know that was me the other night?"

"I did."

"Why didn't you say something?"

"Why didn't *you* say something?" Lorenzo asked.

Rhonda didn't have an answer — not one she wanted to share with him, anyway.

"I didn't want Olivia to know," Lorenzo said.

Rhonda was puzzled. "Really? Why?"

"I know that's your friend and I like her," he began, "but I would rather get to know you."

Rhonda thought she was dreaming.

"I saw when you all walked in Saturday night and I immediately felt like I should know you," he added. "It was probably your walking cast that attracted me to you."

He laughed and Rhonda joined in.

"It should come off next week," she said. "But I'm still — I don't know — puzzled. Did you know it was me just now?"

"I didn't. Not until you turned around did I know it was you. It shocked me at first. But I put it all together kinda quickly. I couldn't remember which house was yours until I saw you."

Lorenzo continued to talk, but Rhonda didn't hear him. Her mind was scrambled as she tried to make sense of the moment.

"So, what's going on with you and Olivia? She likes you, you know?"

"That's okay."

"It's okay? Why?"

"Because it's more about if I like her than if she likes me. If I like her in the same way, then we have an issue. But . . ."

"But what?"

"I thought there might be a chance I could like her in that way — and then I met you."

"You know I'm married, right? You seem to be very observant. So you couldn't have missed this ring."

"I saw it — nice ring, by the way. But does

84

the ring prevent us from getting to know each other."

"You're a playa, huh? I'm no kid. And I'm not silly. I know what you mean by 'getting to know each other.' And you don't mean the words you used."

"I could tell right away that you're not silly. But we can still get to know each other, no matter how you define it."

Rhonda was flattered. Lorenzo's body, conversation and self-assuredness were totally opposite her husband's, and she found it all attractive. But she was conflicted about seeing Lorenzo again, even though she'd had all kinds of plans for the man in her head the previous week.

Coyly, she said, "I think we'd better keep it to 'nice to have met you.' That 'getting to know you' stuff sounds potentially dangerous."

Lorenzo smiled, revealing a softer, warmer disposition. "I respect that," he said. "Can I give you my card? I'm opening my first restaurant in three months. Right now, I'm training to become a bartender/mixologist. I don't want to just mix cocktails. I want to be able to create cocktails. My restaurant will be known for drinks with fresh ingredients along with good food."

"Where are you bartending? In fact, where

do you live? You live in this subdivision?"

"Yes, way on the other side and —"

"Too close for comfort," Rhonda said. She surprised herself.

"Or it could be lots of comfort close by," Lorenzo fired back.

"See, you're bad. I'm going in the house. Nice to meet you."

"Same here. But you should be my cocktail guinea pig. I'm experimenting with some different things. I work the bar at the Glenn Hotel Monday through Wednesday, starting at six. The bar downstairs."

"I don't think so, but I will reach out when your restaurant opens to support you. And I'll be sure to bring my husband — and Olivia."

"Everyone is welcome," Lorenzo quipped. They smiled and then laughed, and he went on his way.

Rhonda went to her car and sat there. She was angry at Eric and had a man she was interested in make it clear he had interest in her. She knew she was most vulnerable when she was mad at her husband — their problems seemed bigger when another person entered the equation. The temptation to react out of anger was heightened. But she was proud of herself that she held it together.

But what was she going to tell Olivia? *Would* she tell Olivia? Rhonda once told a coworker that her boyfriend had asked for her phone number. Instead of being grateful that Rhonda was upfront with her, the woman blamed Rhonda, saying she was too friendly and that her friendliness could be taken as flirting. Their friendship ended over Rhonda's honesty and her coworker's response. Of course, the woman broke up with the man less than two months later — because, predictably, she'd caught him cheating.

That history made her refrain from sharing her encounter with Lorenzo. She did not want to risk the friendship. But she was uneasy about her decision. What if Lorenzo told Olivia?

Rhonda fastened her seatbelt, started her car and backed out of the garage and driveway intent on catching Lorenzo. And she did. He had cleared the cul-de-sac and was walking up the street at a brisk pace. When she got to him, he glanced over, noticed it was Rhonda and pulled out his earphones.

"I'm not a hitchhiker," he said, smiling as he leaned into her car from the passenger window.

"I'm sorry to interrupt your walk, but I

had to ask you something. Are you going to tell Olivia that we met?"

"Aren't you?"

"I'd rather not tell her. It's a long story, but basically she hasn't had the best luck with men and I don't want her to feel like I'm coming between something she might want."

"Aren't you noble?"

"Are you going to tell her?"

"If you don't want me to, I won't. I hadn't planned on it; hadn't even thought about it. But I won't. I guess we'll have to act like we didn't have all this conversation if the three of us are together."

"Or I'll never see you again."

"Could be."

Lorenzo smiled and walked on. Rhonda drove off, but her mind and heart were in a tug-of-war.

CHAPTER SIX:
SURPRISE, SURPRISE, SURPRISE

Stephanie

Each morning after they began sharing sexual innuendo, Charles sent Stephanie a text message when she knew her husband had gone to work. It was always something kind or thoughtful, like, *I woke up thinking of you this morning and it made me smile. Have a great day.*

He was careful not to go too far, but far enough to elicit a smile from Stephanie, an emotion. He did not want to push sex too much. Rather, he wanted to build a connection. He wanted her to gain feelings for him. It would make taking the next step not only easy, but also natural.

And it worked. With each missive, Stephanie smiled, and she began to feel like a schoolgirl being courted by the kid all the young ladies liked. She played it as if she were unmoved, though, replying with a smiley face or simply, *Thank you. You, too.*

I can't let him think I'm easy, that this cheating thing is easy for me to do.

The reality was that it may not have been easy, but Stephanie had cheated on Willie before, about seven years into their marriage. It was so long ago that she almost forgot about it. She reasoned that one affair over twenty-four years of marriage was not bad, considering she had plenty of opportunities to do more.

The affair had happened in a similar situation to how she met Charles. She was at a conference in Chicago. Willie was just starting his accounting firm, and it was tax season, so he was buried in work. For Stephanie, it felt like he ignored her. She had been used to him working a nine-to-five and being around the house around the same time each evening. But in building the business, Willie spent countless hours working with contractors to build out the space and worked tirelessly to grow a strong clientele.

Stephanie did not quite understand at the time, and she'd left for the teachers' conference following an argument about it with her husband. Willie was frustrated that she did not grasp the amount of work needed to launch his business. "Can't believe you're being this selfish," he'd said in the argument. That set off Stephanie . . . because it was true.

"I'm doing this for us, Steph, and you're bitching and nagging. I'm not out golfing or partying. This shit isn't going to happen through osmosis. I have to *make* it happen. You need to understand that and stop driving me fucking crazy."

When Willie cursed, and he did not curse a lot, it incensed Stephanie.

"Don't curse at me," she'd yelled back.

"Then get the hell out of my face," Willie had responded.

This was the night before Stephanie was to board the plane to Chicago. That morning, they did not speak to each other before he left work, further angering and disappointing her.

She did not go to Chicago looking to mess around. It was the proverbial, "It just happened." That's what she'd told her sister, Toya, who was livid. "I'm so ashamed of you right now," she'd said then. "This is not who we are."

"We? What did you do? Don't be so dramatic; this isn't about you," Stephanie had said.

"We're cut from the same cloth," Toya had said. "We were not raised like that."

"Like what? Are you saying I should be

perfect? I made a mistake, like a million other people. So don't try to shame me."

"You should be ashamed of yourself," Toya had shot back. "And that mistake you're talking about? Bullshit. A mistake is dropping a glass and breaking it. Screwing around as a married woman for eleven months is a *decision*. A bad one that could ruin your life."

Stephanie was able to break off that affair after almost a year without Willie finding out. She was lucky, though. Once, she'd walked into a restaurant in Sacramento to meet Andre, her sidepiece, and saw one of her husband's close friends sitting at the bar, right next to Andre, who'd smiled when he saw her approaching. Before Willie's friend could see her, she'd turned and left the restaurant.

After a few minutes, Andre had come out to see what was wrong. "That guy sitting next to you is my husband's friend."

They had picked Sacramento to meet because it was far enough away from Oakland that they believed they could be out in the open. From then on, their encounters were either at Andre's place or a hotel.

Another time, Willie had come home early after saying he would visit his family in Vallejo. Stephanie had changed into a sexy dress and heels; she was going out to meet Andre and always dressed up for him. "Why you all dressed up?" he'd asked. She was flustered, but had collected herself.

"I was just trying this on," she'd said. "I might wear it to the company Christmas party. You like?"

She'd had to sneak away to call Andre and cancel. It was then that she'd decided to end their once-a-month rendezvous. Tempted many times since then, she stayed the course, considering herself lucky that her reckless behavior did not cause her to devastate her husband at best, lose her marriage at worst.

Charles, however, presented a real challenge because not even her sister knew that her tendency was to stray. In high school she'd had a boyfriend, but also dated his friend — in secret. Same in college. Before settling down with Willie, Stephanie ran men like men ran women, one after the other. She did not sleep with all of them. But she slept with many. She enjoyed the freedom of being single and the company of several men from different backgrounds.

The problem was, it was more than that. It was something innate in her that prevented her from being wholly faithful. There were multiple excuses that passed as reasons in her mind:

If men can do it, why can't women? I'm single and free to do what I want. I'm not hurting anyone. I like variety.

She did not tell Toya about her adventures. But she thought she could turn it off once she got married. She was wrong. A year after their wedding in Reno, Nevada, she'd found herself flirting with the manager of their apartment complex. She did not let it escalate into infidelity, but she knew then staying committed would be harder than she thought.

Charles presented a significant problem because it was more than about fulfilling her whim. She *liked* him. They had many things in common, especially working in education and a passion for teaching youths. That gave them something to discuss all the time. And because Charles was smart and genuine — and did not pressure her — she embraced him.

Their mostly e-mail and text messaging relationship took a surprising turn when Stephanie had gone to a regional meeting in San Francisco and looked up to see Charles as the featured speaker for the breakfast. She had told him about the event and that she would attend, but he did not share that he would be speaking there.

Stephanie had arrived a little late, held up by traffic clearing the Bay Bridge. But her coworkers had held a seat for her at their table in the middle of the ballroom. They'd chatted over coffee and breakfast. Charles had seen her, but did not come over. He'd wanted the surprise to take shape when he walked on the stage.

Finally, the host had introduced the speaker. When she'd said, "Charles Richardson . . . ," Stephanie was stunned. Outside noise was blocked out.

Charles had risen from his seat at the front of the ballroom and smoothly walked to the podium. He'd made eye contact with Stephanie and smiled. She was more turned on than she was surprised.

He had started by saying, "Good morning. I'm happy to see you here — some more than others."

The people had laughed. She and Charles had stared at each other. It was their private moment in a public setting. Over the course of his thirty-minute speech, Stephanie's attention span had wavered. She'd alternated between hearing him and fading away to fantasies. Her attraction skyrocketed.

Charles had commanded the room. He was smart and humble and engaging and informative. The crowd had enjoyed him.

She'd enjoyed seeing him.

When the breakfast was over, she'd lingered to have a moment with Charles. She'd waited until everyone had spoken to him. Then they'd embraced.

"Good to see you, Mrs. Simmons," he'd said, knowing people were watching. "I remember you from the conference in Seattle."

"Yes, good to see you, too," she'd said. "I enjoyed your speech."

When all the people were out of earshot, Stephanie had said, "I can't believe you. Why didn't you tell me you were speaking here?"

"You look good. Real good."

"Focus, Charles."

"If I had told you, we wouldn't have this moment we're having right now. And I wouldn't have gotten to see the look on your face when I stepped to the mic."

"I must have looked like I had seen a ghost — a quite handsome ghost."

Charles had blushed. "Well, I'm headed back to L.A. in a few hours."

"Really? That's it?"

"It can be more. Much more."

"I'm here at this conference all day."

"My flight leaves at four. Why don't you skip the conference lunch and have lunch with me?"

"My coworkers are here."

"They won't be in my room."

Stephanie tried to resist . . . for about five seconds.

"What's your room number?"

"It's 1906. I have to meet with a few people, but let's meet there at twelve forty-five. Deal?"

Stephanie didn't answer, as if not answering was better than saying "yes." Her smile had told Charles all he needed.

So she'd gone to a pair of sessions that seemed like torture. She had been completely distracted and could only think about getting to Charles' room. She'd dismissed thoughts of Willie; they would only make her feel guilty.

When the time came to head to his room, she'd told her coworkers, "I'm going to do some shopping instead of going to the lunch session. Willie's birthday is coming up and I think I should take advantage of being in the city while I'm here."

They'd bought it and off she'd gone. Before she could knock on Charles' door, he'd opened it. She'd stepped back, startled.

"Oh, wow. Perfect timing," he'd said. "Come on in. I'm going to get some ice."

Stephanie had walked in and gone straight

to the window, which offered a majestic view of the Bay Bridge. Looking out at it and the sailboats in the water had calmed her. So did the glass of chardonnay Charles had poured her.

"I don't see any food," she'd said.

"Did you really come here to eat?"

Stephanie had made up her mind and was not about to play coy. "I came here to work up an appetite."

Charles had digested that with ease. He'd stood in front of her and extended his hands. She'd grabbed them and he'd pulled her away from the window and into his arms. He'd looked down on her with caring eyes, and she'd looked into them almost as if hypnotized.

He'd leaned in and kissed her deeply and passionately. She'd closed her eyes and enjoyed the softness of his lips and the firmness of his body.

"I've been wanting to do that for a while now," he'd said.

"I'm glad it finally happened," she'd replied.

From there, it was like they were dance partners in sync to the rhythm of their desires. With little effort, she'd unbuttoned his shirt and unfastened his pants. He'd unzipped the back of her dress in an instant, and they'd stood before each other with only their underwear between them.

Charles had considered asking Stephanie if she was sure she wanted what was to come, but he was dissuaded from doing so when she'd unfastened the back of her bra with a flick of a finger.

He'd kissed her shoulder first, and then her neck and then her lips. Stephanie had kissed him back before pulling away to get into the bed. Charles had followed her between the sheets and she'd broken the silence.

"Do you have a condom?"

As if by magic, Charles had displayed one in his right hand. Stephanie had been wowed by that, but more impressed with what she'd felt between his legs.

"This is what I came for right here," she'd said, his rock-hard manhood in her grasp.

He'd kissed her again, and she'd aided him in applying the condom. She'd spread her legs and Charles had maneuvered between them. Stephanie had wasted no time. She'd held her breath and flinched when she inserted Charles' dick. It was full enough and long enough and exactly what Stephanie wanted. Exactly what she *needed.*

He had been too anxious at first, going deep and hard. She'd slowed him down.

"I'm here. I'm not going anywhere," she'd whispered into his ear.

Charles had slowed his tempo and made love to Stephanie — measured, deep strokes that took her breath away and pleased her at once. In no time, she was begging for that aggression he had shown, thrusting forward as he pumped harder.

He'd held her legs up by her ankles and thrust into her in rapid-fire succession, drawing sustained moans from Stephanie. The sound of their bodies colliding had filled the room. The pleasure of it all got to Charles sooner than he'd wanted. The harder and deeper he'd pounded, the closer he'd come to climaxing. She could feel him swelling inside her, the sign that he was about to cum. "Come on, baby. Give it to me. Give it to me."

The combination of the pleasure and her words had sent Charles into a frenzy until he'd filled the condom. He'd let down her legs and kissed her deeply, but not long, as he'd sought to catch his breath.

"Oh, my God," he'd said as he lay on top of her.

"That was . . . oh, my God."

After a few minutes, he eased off Stephanie and lay beside her.

"That's it," he'd said.

"What?"

"I need you to get a divorce."

They'd laughed.

"You know what's crazy — or sad? Or both?" Stephanie had asked. "I don't feel guilty. I hope that doesn't sound ugly. What I'm saying is I'm so pleased right now that I can't think of anything negative. And I didn't even cum."

"Well, we have to fix that," he'd said.

"I didn't expect this to happen when we met."

"Neither did I. I'm not going to lie; I noticed that you were attractive. But sometimes things do just happen."

"I don't feel guilty, but we can't keep this up. The good news is that you live in Los Angeles. If you lived here, this would be trouble. Right? Tell me, do you feel guilty? Are you thinking about your wife?"

"I don't think we should be talking about that right after what we just did. I really don't."

"You're right. That's kind of morbid, huh?"

"I wouldn't say morbid. Let's say inopportune."

"You know what? Now I will have that lunch," Stephanie had said.

They'd ordered room service and dined

by the window. When Charles had gone to take a shower, Stephanie had joined him.

"We're here now, might as well maximize it," she'd said.

"Like the alcoholic who's going to rehab the next day, so he drinks the night before."

"Yeah, like that."

Stephanie had taken the soap and washed Charles' body, paying special attention to his groin area. She'd cleaned and stroked it until it was no longer flaccid. He'd told her where to find the condoms and she'd stepped out of the shower to retrieve one.

With the water pouring down his back, Charles had bent over Stephanie, who used both hands to support herself up against the wall. It was a position that invited intense passion, and he'd discarded any notion of sparing her, penetrating her from various angles with violent thrusts.

She'd held the wall and took the aggression, and had screamed when her body was overcome with sensation. Charles had pumped and pumped until Stephanie had reached the ultimate pleasure.

After gathering herself, she'd embraced Charles as the water covered their bodies.

"That was so good," she'd said, "that it's trouble. It's trouble."

CHAPTER SEVEN: I'LL HAVE ANOTHER

Rhonda

It did not get any better for Rhonda when Eric came home with the same attitude that he'd left with. But at least he wanted to talk.

"Look, we need to set something straight," he began. "I'm a grown-ass man. And I'm your husband. We don't have any children, so don't think you can try to treat me like one. You don't think I know about my weight issues? I don't need you hounding me. I need you encouraging me."

"What do you think I've been doing?" She was angry. "As a matter of fact, grown-ass man, you shouldn't need anything from me. Men do what they have to do."

Rhonda was particularly weight-conscious because she'd lost an older brother she adored to the effects of obesity when she was a teenager. Lavon was big all the way through college. When his college football career ended, it took him less than two years

103

to go from 310 pounds to 450 pounds. With the weight came diabetes, back problems, and high blood pressure. They added up to him seldom in good health.

She was devastated to see him so sickly at such a young age — all of it a result of being so overweight. Lavon did not mean for it to happen; it just did. With no incentive to exercise, he instead ate. And ate. When he came to visit the family one Thanksgiving, she was astonished at his size.

But she did not say anything, although she heard him wheeze as he ingested his meal and saw him struggle up a flight of steps that their parents negotiated with ease. Rhonda practiced what she wanted to say to Lavon: *Big brother, you have to slow down. We want you around. Let's figure out a way to get this weight thing under control. We love you too much to see you like this.*

She thought that would be sensitive enough to share. Her parents had a talk with their son, but Rhonda believed coming from her, the concern would especially register because he knew she looked up to him. Still, she never said a word.

Six months later, Lavon was dead. His body's vital organs had collapsed. He was twenty-six. Rhonda carried guilt with her the rest of her life that she did not urge her brother to take better care of himself. Her parents and others had told her it was not her fault. It was on Lavon, they'd told her. Those words never eased her pain or guilt.

All these years later, she was not going to let her husband have a similar fate. Not without saying anything.

"If you want to let your health go downhill, you can do that," she told Eric. "But as your wife, I have a responsibility to you. I've seen it before. I told you about Lavon."

"I'm sorry about your brother, Rhonda," Eric said. "But I'm not him."

"You can't disassociate yourself from him because you have two things in common: me and being overweight. If I'm worrying too much, I'm sorry. I can't help it. I can't let this happen again and not say anything."

"Okay, you've said enough. I hear you. Now let me deal with it the way I want to and in my time."

"Is your time now, because it should be?"

"Okay, I'm done with this. You've said what you needed to say. I've said what I needed to say. That should be it."

"It should be about action, not words."

"Give me a fucking chance to do something. We're discussing it right now. Damn. I said I will handle it."

"You think cursing at me is the way to go?"

"I sure the fuck do. You're getting on my nerves."

"Okay, it's like that, huh? Curse at me like I'm some trick off the streets? Okay. Remember that."

And with that she promised herself that if she did not see improvement in Eric's eating and workout habits, she would give leaving him strong consideration. She preferred leaving over cheating, but she also said she would not rule out infidelity if she were pushed beyond her level.

This was new thought territory for Rhonda. Their marriage had been one of routine — a routine she approved of, but one that left her wanting more. She was disappointed Eric found their patterns acceptable — dinner at home during the week, a movie on Saturday or a visit to his mother, church on most Sundays and sports on TV in between.

Rhonda's niece, Anna, who was like the daughter she never birthed, had gotten married two years earlier, and Anna's marriage was replete with travel to exotic islands and fun events. She was a dozen years younger than Rhonda but doing more in two years of marriage than her aunt had in fourteen years. That frustrated her as much as being an attendee at three friends' weddings over the summer, friends that married men who were hell-bent on living exciting lives.

She hoped being aggressive with Eric would ignite something in him to do better. But change was slow — too slow for Rhonda. A week passed and Rhonda's walking cast was removed, but she wanted to boot her husband. Eric showed little effort in modifying his food choices and a lack of an exercise regimen.

Exasperated, she remembered Lorenzo said he was bartending a few nights a week. Rhonda put on a pair of Spanx under a flattering dress and made her way to the Glenn Hotel. She almost always hung out with Olivia. But she did not want Olivia to know her business, especially since she liked Lorenzo, too.

When she arrived at the hotel, she hesitated at the entrance. She felt silly, strange . . . weak, even. She had never pursued a man, adhering to her father's edict shared with her when she was fourteen: "Pursue a man and he will have all the power. Let him pursue you and you will deal with him from a position of strength, not weakness."

Rhonda decided to return home, her

father's words permeating her thought process. But before she could turn to leave, Lorenzo emerged from an elevator to her right. He stopped in his tracks and smiled.

She wanted to move, but it was as if her pumps were cemented in the floor.

"Glad to see you," Lorenzo said as he approached. "I had to take something to the upstairs bar on the roof. How are you?"

He seemed so genuinely happy to see her that her concerns eased by the minute. Still, she felt compelled to lie.

"I'm waiting on my girlfriend — not Olivia — who picked this place to meet. She works across the street, at Turner."

Usually, Rhonda detested lying. Actually, she detested *liars*. She did believe in telling a lie in extreme circumstances.

"Cool. I'm glad she did," Lorenzo said. "Come on over. Let me make you a drink before she gets here."

"I don't know," Rhonda said, extending her deceit. She *needed* a drink.

"No reason not to," he said. "You can sit at the bar and watch me make it."

Finally, she put one foot in front of the other and followed Lorenzo to the right side of the bar, which was empty.

"So what do you like to drink? Tequila? Vodka? Gin? I would suggest vodka," Lorenzo said. "Tequila is good too. But gin? Had my last sniff of gin about nine years ago. Let's say I woke up in somebody else's room in someone else's house and didn't remember how I got there or where my left shoe was. Searched this strange house for ten minutes for my other shoe.

"My body felt like I had been in a giant blender. My stomach was queasy. My head was throbbing. It was one of those times that you bargain with God: 'Make me feel better and I won't drink again.' It was bad."

Rhonda laughed and felt more at ease. Lorenzo's consideration and humor comforted her. She liked to laugh, but she hadn't been getting many at home. It felt reinvigorating and made her body feel vibrant.

"You know what?" she said. "I will let you make what you want me to have. That's a big responsibility, you know?"

"I think I can handle it."

He began the process, all the while explaining to Rhonda what he was doing.

So, you slice the fresh ginger thinly and then muddle it to bring out the flavors . . . Then you muddle some fresh lemons and then some fresh mint . . . Put in an ounce of vodka and a half-ounce of agave nectar, a natural sweetener . . . Add some ice and then shake it really good.

Rhonda appreciated the undivided attention, and she found herself smiling at Lorenzo as he vigorously shook the concoction.

He placed a martini glass in front of her on a napkin and strained the liquids into it. Then he added a mint leaf that floated on the top of the drink.

"This drink will change your life," Lorenzo said, smiling.

Rhonda smiled back and thought to herself: *Great, because my life needs changing.*

She sipped it and a smile creased her face. The martini was refreshing — not sweet, not alcohol strong. It had the ideal blend for her.

"Wow, you're good," she said. "This is delicious."

He nodded his head. "Great. Glad you like it. I'm relieved."

Lorenzo excused himself as he tended to other drink-seekers. Rhonda sipped on her cocktail, all the while watching with admiration as he engaged customers and fashioned drinks.

By the time he got back to Rhonda, she had already consumed her entire martini.

"You were thirsty, huh?" he cracked.

"What actually happened is I spilled most

of it — you know how hard it is to handle these martini glasses."

"Yeah, spilled it right over those sexy lips," Lorenzo said, and Rhonda blushed. The attention was flattering and needed. Eric had not only become complacent about his appearance, but also about complimenting his wife. She didn't consider herself insecure. But she *did* need to feel appreciated by her husband, at least some time.

"What makes my lips sexy?"

The alcohol took hold.

"Their shape. They are nice and full. The lipstick makes them look moist. I bet they're soft."

"Wouldn't you like to know?"

"You want me to know, don't you?"

"I do," she said. Those two words made her realize she was tipsy. She'd said those words when she married Eric. Now she was saying them about another man kissing her. The realization sobered her up.

"I'm sorry. I'm *way* out of line. I shouldn't be talking like this as a married woman."

"A little flirting never hurt anyone," Lorenzo said. "I know you're a respectable woman."

"If Eric saw me flirting, he'd be hurt," she said.

"I'm glad he's not here," Lorenzo added.

Before Rhonda could respond, a customer at the other end of the bar caught Lorenzo's attention. She was an attractive woman who projected an air of familiarity with him. He raised a finger to Rhonda as if to say, "Be right back," and went to take her order.

He shook the woman's hand when he got to her and she smiled the way women do when they want to show their interest in a man. And Rhonda was surprised at herself. She was jealous.

She could not take her eyes off them, and in her mind crafted a story that the lady was Lorenzo's girlfriend — or at least someone he had invited to see him, as he had invited Rhonda. After a few minutes, during which time her angst grew to virtually a boiling point, Lorenzo returned, smiling.

Before Rhonda could say anything, he said, "I'm sorry I left you like that. But that's my brother's wife. She and my brother thought they'd drop in and surprise me. He's parking the car."

All the tension in Rhonda oozed out as if released from a balloon. "Oh, really," she said, managing a smile. "That's nice."

"Since your friend hasn't come yet, I'll make you another drink, if that's okay. These drinks are on me, by the way."

"I don't know where my friend is, but I'm going to call her now. But, yes, another drink sounds great."

Rhonda pulled out her cell phone and pushed some buttons, feigning as if she called someone. She felt silly about it, but that was the problem with lying: She had to advance the lie, keep it alive, for it to be convincing.

A bar-back told her that the bathroom was upstairs, and she went to it as Lorenzo made her second drink. There, in front of the mirror, she stared at herself and wondered how far she would go with this man. Her attraction to him heightened, while her displeasure with her husband rose. She tried to stay on an even keel about the situation. But she made a decision while looking into the mirror: If Lorenzo did not blow it, she would blow him.

She freshened up in the bathroom and made her way down the steps and back to the bar. Lorenzo had another drink waiting for her — and a proposition.

"My shift is over in a few minutes; I wasn't scheduled to work today, but I wanted to get in a little more time behind the bar. Why don't you and your friend join me on the rooftop for a drink? There's a beautiful view from up there and it's a nice night."

Who was she to resist? "That sounds nice. But I don't know where she is. I have called and texted her."

"If we're in luck, she won't come," Lorenzo said.

Rhonda gave him a look.

"But I do hope she's all right."

"Yeah, I'm sure you do, Lorenzo. I'm gonna have to watch you."

"Please do," he said. "We can watch each other."

Rhonda pretended to send a text and accompanied Lorenzo on the rooftop, called the Sky Lounge. The combination of the view — she could see the standout structures of Atlanta's sprawling skyline: the lit-up Ferris wheel, the prodigious Bank of America building with its gold, pointed top; the cylinder-shaped Westin hotel and virtually any other Atlanta site. It was breathtaking. And the drinks made her more and more aggressive . . . and less the lady she valued being.

"It's kinda romantic up here, Lorenzo. Is that why you asked me up here?"

"Well," Lorenzo started, not knowing how he should answer, "it *is* romantic. I know you're married, though, so I wasn't sure if this view mattered to you or not."

That was the best he could come up with

that would not put off Rhonda.

"Everyone likes romance, right?" she said. "I can use a little romance in my life."

It came out before she could stop herself. That's what drinking did to Rhonda. She became blunt, flirtatious. That's why she tried to drink heavily only when she was with Eric.

Lorenzo hardly was Eric. "I'll order us some drinks," he told Rhonda. "I have to catch up with you."

She waited by the railing that overlooked the city. That was the last thing she remembered before waking up at 3:50 a.m. — in bed with Lorenzo.

Chapter Eight:
Meeting of the Minds

Juanita

The frank discussion and making love to Maurice gave Juanita a foundation to ward off her affections for Brandon. Maurice was trying, and she had told herself that if he put in the effort, she would do the same.

Brandon seemed to get that Juanita had ended things when she did not respond. It took twelve days, but he finally settled in his mind that Juanita wanted a fling to scratch a sexual itch. He convinced himself that she used him, and built up enough animosity to not care if he heard from her again.

For all her efforts, though, Juanita remained unfulfilled. At least that was what she thought. But she couldn't figure if her discontent was about her husband or her interest in Brandon. Or both. Or something else.

"I'm confused," she said to Maurice. "You want to go to counseling because *you're* not happy? What are you talking about?"

Juanita had invested so much effort and heart into being the ideal wife and mother — at the expense of her own peace — that she could not fathom that he did not feel privileged, not to mention happy.

"We should talk it out with a neutral person," Maurice said. "If we try to do it, we'll likely end up arguing and end up nowhere. I'd rather us get things under control before they get out of control."

Only because she was eager to hear what Maurice had to complain about did she agree to see the counselor. A few days later, they showed up at Dr. Cynthia Fields' office in Southeast D.C., where they were surprised and disappointed to see white women walking dogs and pushing baby carriages in a part of the city where that had never occurred in the past.

Maurice picked a female therapist because he didn't want Juanita to feel ganged on if the doctor were a man.

Dr. Fields was highly regarded and came highly recommended. "It's nice to meet you both," she started the session. "I'm sure you know but I have to say it anyway: Anything we share in this room goes no place else. Period. And I say 'we' share because my method of counseling is to be personable.

So, there may be instances where I will give my clinical analysis *and* my personal analysis — if I believe it will help us get the most out of our discussion.

"That said, what brings you in? How long have you been married?"

"It was my idea," Maurice said. "We've been married nine years. We have two great children, boys. We have no bills. We're both accomplished in our professional lives. And yet, my wife recently told me we had a problem.

"That threw me for a loop because I think I have been a model husband. Like I told her, I don't gamble or waste money. I don't hang out at night. I don't go to strip clubs. I'm about my family. But that's not enough for her, she tells me."

"Well," Dr. Fields said, "let's first understand that it's important and Juanita should be commended for being honest about her feelings. I have been in relationships in the past when I wanted to say something and didn't, and I paid for it. So, it's a good job by her to reveal what's really on her heart. Your response could have been, 'Thank you for being honest. Now, what's wrong?' But if we get on the defensive, it almost always turns what could be a revealing talk into an argument."

"And that's pretty much what happened," Juanita said. "I told him that because I see our marriage a little differently than Maurice. We do have two great children and we've done well with our money and have this ideal family — to the average person. But —"

"Oh, what are you, above average?" Maurice jumped in.

"Please, Maurice, let Juanita finish. One of most couples' biggest issues is knowing how to communicate when you disagree. Go ahead, Juanita."

"Thank you. I was saying that we do have a lot of wonderful elements to our lives, our marriage. But, for me, what I'd like is more excitement, more adventure."

"She's talking about sex," Maurice interrupted again.

"There's nothing wrong with sex," Dr. Fields said, "but there is something wrong with you interrupting her."

"I'm sorry."

"Juanita, please continue," the therapist said.

"I agree with you, Dr. Fields; there's nothing wrong with sex. But that was not even what I was getting at. I think we're in a rut. We don't do anything unpredictable. And when I tried something as simple as asking him to sit outside with me and have a drink, he complained that the TV was inside.

"He's a good man and I love Maurice. He's a good father and husband. But he's also complacent. He does not covet me. I'm taken for granted and it makes me uneasy because it's unfair. I've given everything I can to this marriage and I feel I deserve to get more out of it than a mundane routine."

"Can I speak now?" Maurice asked. "Okay, thanks. What's mundane is her placing sex as an issue that's making her unhappy. We have been in what I thought was a happy marriage all this time, and now doing what we've always done is mundane? I don't get it."

"Juanita, explain to him what you mean by 'mundane.' "

"I mean we went two weeks without sex. There's nothing exciting about that. It's mundane. During those two weeks, we did not go to a movie, a play, a concert . . . nothing. We came home and I cooked, we ate, dealt with the kids and he camped out on the couch with the remote control in his hand.

"Even that wouldn't be so bad if he said, 'Honey, let's find a good movie we can watch together.' Instead, it's sports, sports and more sports. I get no consideration at all. And as for sex, because I love my husband, I think making love is a natural way of showing it. So I try to set a romantic mood and he's dying to get back to watching sports. There's nothing loving about that. All that is mundane."

"But all of a sudden, this life we've lived all this time is a problem," Maurice said. "We've gone two weeks without sex before. Didn't hear a peep out of her. Now it's a problem."

Dr. Fields jumped in. "Do you think it's possible that she didn't say anything before because she wanted to keep the peace and that she reached a point where she needed to speak up now?"

"You can ask her that," Maurice cracked.

"That's exactly right, Dr. Fields," Juanita interjected. "It's happened *many* times over the course of our marriage. I didn't say anything because I have been intent on being this perfect wife. And each time I figured would be the last time. But it's a pattern — a nine-year pattern that's gotten old."

Dr. Fields: "Why is it, Maurice, that you seem to be fine with going two weeks without making love to your wife?"

"It's not that at all. I don't even pay attention to the number of days in between. I don't think our marriage should be based on sex. That's so shallow."

"See, Dr. Fields. He's not addressing the question."

"I don't see going two weeks without sex as right or wrong," he said. "I see it as normal for our relationship."

"But it shouldn't be normal," Juanita said. "I take the blame for us only now having this discussion because I let it go for so long. But this is the most blatant example of taking your mate for granted. You don't see the need to be intimate with your wife? You see intimacy as something that happens when it happens? I see it as necessary for a marriage to have a heartbeat."

"Wow, I like that, Juanita," Dr. Fields said. "You get that analogy, Maurice? For your marriage to have a pulse, you need intimacy. The good news is that this is a common concern in marriages. Most of the time it's the husband complaining about a lack of sex. Juanita is not concerned only about sex. She's concerned about intimacy. Sex is physical. Intimacy is all heart. It's better than sex. Your love comes out, so the pleasure is more intense."

"But he can't see that," Juanita said. "And with the way our lives are — working hard, raising two boys — we should use each other's passion as fuel. We have to deal with the children and the ebb and flow of our jobs that will tire us or frustrate us or challenge us. We should be overflowing with passion with each other to help us keep our sanity."

"Okay, okay," Maurice said. "Everything is duly noted. I can admit when I'm wrong. I have to do better. I kinda fell into this thing where our lives are set and we have this thing figured out. But what I'm hearing is that I can't be that way, that I have to give up some of the things I'm used to like watching sports all the time to make Juanita feel special and needed. See, I'm a quick study."

"That's really good to hear, Maurice," Dr. Fields said. "I respect when a partner accepts responsibility. It's mature and it shows you care about your spouse, which always is good."

"I do have something else to say," Maurice added. "I'd like to talk about some things that bother me. I brought up this sex thing because she brought it to me. But I have some things in the marriage that bother me."

Juanita was anxious to hear.

"I'm sure you do," she said. "But I can't imagine what they can be."

"Well, for one, I often feel like she takes

me for granted," he started. "I mean, I do as much or more with the boys as she does. We both have demanding jobs, but she's the one who always works late under the assumption either that my job isn't as important or she simply doesn't care about my job. So I never get to stay late in the office and get ahead or dig a little deeper.

"And here's the worst part: She comes home two, three hours after I have worked, picked up the kids, made dinner for them, got them through their homework and in bed. It's almost nine o'clock and she comes in and it's quiet in the house and I have a chance to get some work done. But she comes in and immediately starts talking.

"I'm on my laptop, working. She kicks off her shoes, makes a plate and sits on the couch with me and eats and talks and sips on wine as if I'm not there trying to work. And it's always about either her job or the most mundane stuff, to use that word again. It's so annoying. But mostly it's disrespectful of what I have to do. You stay at work late to get your work done. I bring mine home, but I can barely do it because you won't stop talking. Now how is that fair?"

Juanita was thrown. She had not even considered Maurice's position. It wasn't that she disregarded his job.

"That happened because I hadn't seen you all day and wanted to connect with you at least a little bit," she said. "I'm so sorry, Maurice. I am. I had no idea. I wish you had said something."

"I thought not responding, not saying anything as you went on and on would deliver the message. Instead, you continue to talk. And I can't really focus. I'm not talking to you, but I can't center my thoughts on what I was working on, either, because I'm hearing you. Not the actual words, but the noise."

Juanita was embarrassed. She prided herself on being everything to her husband. Maurice's revelation revealed a flaw, something she prided herself on not having.

"I apologize again," she said. "And I mean it."

"That's good, Juanita. Mature," Dr. Fields said. "But do you really understand his point, which is that you have to respect his job as much as he respects yours? This is another area where couples can have troubles. You cannot look at your career or job as more important than your spouse's. All things being equal, there has to be mutual respect and support of each other's jobs and careers. That's how you grow together — and avoid animosity."

Juanita and Maurice nodded their heads, Maurice more aggressively than Juanita, who wondered what other areas of work she needed. For someone who had been lauded — by so many people that she started to believe it — as this saintly "perfect" woman, Maurice exposed flaws she did not know existed.

Before their time was up, Dr. Fields said: "I think this was a really good opening session. A lot of honest feelings were shared, which is a good thing — if you receive them with love. You all have the love you must have to be successful. Now it's all about how you put that love — and all the information learned tonight — into practical usage. You care, which gives me real optimism that you will find a balance."

Maurice and Juanita agreed not to schedule another appointment before seeing how the upcoming weeks would play out. With Brandon out of her life, and awakened to her imperfections, Juanita centered her thoughts on her husband and family. Her night of infidelity faded into an afterthought as the days went by. But she remembered.

CHAPTER NINE:
GUILT TRIP

Stephanie

Stephanie's afternoon delight with Charles turned into trysts every chance she could. She even told Willie she was traveling for work one Friday and had him drop her off at the San Francisco airport. She kissed her husband goodbye, exited the vehicle and walked into the terminal.

Five minutes after Willie drove off, Charles pulled up in a rental car, and off they went for two days of fun in Napa Valley.

"It's making my marriage better," she told her sister, Toya, as they sipped cocktails at District, a popular lounge in downtown Oakland.

"What is?"

"Charles."

"Tell that crap to someone who is stupid enough to believe it," Toya said. "Why would you tell me about what you're doing? It's none of my business. Better than that, I don't want to hear it."

"You're my sister; I should be able to share stuff with you."

"No, not this. I don't want to know you're being unfaithful. You told me years ago what you did and I feel now as I do then — you're a better person than this."

"This doesn't make me a bad person."

"I didn't say you're a bad person."

"It doesn't make me a better person if I didn't have an affair. It's not right. But I need it."

"You *need* it? Why?"

"Because after so long with one man, it's not exciting anymore. That's not to blame Willie. I know he's a good man. He's, overall, been good to me. But we don't have that spark anymore. His interest is in his business. Not me."

"Most women who are in marriages that lose their spark don't try to find it somewhere else. They work at it. Sacrifice. Talk to their husband. Anything other than cheat."

"I don't feel good about it. But you tell me: You'd rather be at home in a stale marriage or would you rather have someone add life to your life?"

"I'm in a marriage that could use a little spark," Toya admitted. "My marriage isn't perfect. Terry seems complacent at times. But we work at it. I have not considered running around with another man. Are you crazy?"

"We're different people. You're no better than me because you haven't done what I'm doing."

"I'm not a better person, but I'm a better wife. I'm loyal to my husband."

"I could argue that I'm better to my husband because since I've been seeing Charles, I'm in a better mood, and my husband benefits from that. So he's probably happier than Terry."

"You always cross the line, Steph. You can't judge my husband's happiness."

"Let me ask you a question, big sister," Stephanie said. "Do you think Mom ever cheated on Dad?"

"I *know* she didn't. I know she wouldn't."

"What if I told you that I had proof that she did cheat? Would you think of Mom as a bad person?"

"My mother didn't have the same morals as you. You know how I know? Because you don't have any."

"That's what you've always done when I challenged you."

"What?"

"Get personal. I don't have any morals?

Wow. Do morals only matter when it comes to your marriage? Or do they matter in every part of your life?"

"Every part, of course."

"Good. I thought so. So let me ask you something: Is it immoral to use my address to get your daughter into the school in my neighborhood? Everyone does it, but is it right? No, it's not right. But you did what you needed to do to get your child in the best possible school. And you know what I said when you did that? Nothing. I didn't judge you. I praised you for doing right by your kid."

"That's not the same thing," Toya said.

"I didn't say it was the same thing. I asked if it was *immoral,* and you acknowledge that it was. No one got hurt by it — except a kid from my neighborhood who needed to be in that school more than yours who didn't get in because a child from outside the district took his place."

"Now you're trying to make me feel guilty?"

"No more than you've been trying to make me feel guilty," Stephanie responded.

"I need another drink," Toya said. "I can't get over you trying to justify your behavior."

She flagged down a server, who took orders for another round of Lemon Drop

130

martinis.

"And as for Mom, you know how much I love and miss her," Stephanie said. "But you and I have different fathers. And neither of them were married to her. So . . ."

"So what are you saying?"

"I'm saying I'm probably more like Mom than you are."

"I get it: You want me to throw my drink in your face tonight. Our mother broke her back raising us, teaching us to be respectable women. And you're gonna sit here and throw around innuendo about our dead mother like it's nothing? You think I'm okay hearing you desecrate my mother's name with this nonsense?"

"Don't get your bloomers in a bunch. As far as I'm concerned, Mom was an angel. But there were circumstances in her life when she did what she had to do."

"You'll say anything and shame anyone to make yourself feel better about your crap."

"That's not it. It's —"

"No, we need to have something else to talk about," Toya insisted. "The last three times I saw you, all we did was talk on the subject of your cheating. I hope to God you aren't talking about this to anyone else."

"No. Of course not. I only talk to you about it because we're supposed to be able to share everything with each other. But I see you've been holding back. I didn't know you were bored in your marriage, bored with Terry."

"I didn't say that and I'm not going to talk about it. It's my marriage. It's sacred."

"That doesn't mean you can't vent or share with your sister. It helps to talk about it."

"I've said enough. We're fine. We work on our marriage. I don't go sleeping around with men when it gets tough. That doesn't help."

"Don't make me out to be some whore; it's one guy. And now with my husband, we're happier. He even asked me the other night: 'What do you want?' I asked him why he asked that. He said that because when we were first married, when I was this happy, I was setting him up to ask for a new coat or a pair of earrings. Something. We laughed about it."

"Bet he wouldn't be laughing if he knew you were sleeping with someone else."

"I bet he won't find out — unless you tell him. That's the only way he would know."

"You don't get it that you could tell him without knowing you're telling him. Your actions can be a giveaway. Don't take for granted that he won't notice when you're missing in action. Willie is no brain surgeon. But he's not a dummy."

"I won't be missing in action."

"So you're going to answer the phone when he calls, even though you're with this other man?"

"First of all, Willie doesn't call me much; I call him. And if he did call, yes, I'd answer."

"I'm going to ask you this and then leave it alone," Toya said. "What if he finds out? What then? And forget about what it would do to your marriage. What about how hurt Willie will be? You love him, right? You know he loves you. He'd be devastated. That should be enough for you to cut it out."

Finally, Toya's words gave Stephanie pause. She was not excited about the state of her marriage, but she loved Willie and did not want to hurt him. And she knew finding out about her infidelity would wreck him.

Willie was a strong man, but he was fragile, too. He'd cried the first time he told Rhonda about his parents' divorce — and he was twenty-three years old. He'd talked about his disappointment in their breakup and how it changed *his* life.

"I'm glad we won't have to go through that," he'd told Stephanie at the time.

His fragility would not allow him to accept Stephanie's reckless behavior. He would walk. Stephanie was certain of that. And as much as her fling with Charles reinvigorated her, she surmised that it was not worth losing the man she had been with for nearly thirty years.

"Willie and I have built something," Stephanie said.

"That's what I'm saying," Toya chimed in.

"I'm not trying to lose that; I'm not. I'm trying to save us, really. I know Willie better than anyone. I know us. The spark is gone. I'm not sure he knows how to get it back. Shit, I'm not even sure he realizes it's *gone*. I can't do it alone. But this thing with Charles — I know it's wrong — but it makes me go back to Willie feeling free and alive."

"Maybe," Toya said, "but it's wrong. It's wrong in your eyes. It's wrong in my eyes. It damn sure would be wrong in Willie's eyes. And you know it's wrong in God's eyes."

Stephanie was a spiritual person but not religious. It was another point of contention between her and Toya, who was steeped in Christianity.

"Don't start with the God stuff," Stephanie said. "If your God was so . . . whatever . . . Mom would still be here."

"You cannot blame physical issues on God, Steph."

"Why not? He can do everything, right?"

"You have to have faith that God knows what's right. That's the difference between you and me. I don't question Him. I know what He does for me every day."

"And I know what He didn't do for us — spare our mother. I was okay with God before losing Mom. I thought He was testing me at first. That was bad enough. Awful. But Grandma, too? And Aunt Mildred? That's cruel. He didn't have to do that to us."

The combination of the drinks and Stephanie's still-raw emotions converged to make her fight back tears.

"I don't want you to get upset," Toya jumped in. "But I do want you to be happy, and to do what's right. That's all."

Toya put down her drink, slid across the couch and hugged her sister. "Don't be all empathetic now," Stephanie said, smiling. "You know, cheating is contagious. You don't want to be this close to me."

The women laughed and waved over the server for another drink. "I have a lot of thinking — and drinking — to do," Stephanie said.

CHAPTER TEN:
WHERE DID THE TIME GO?

Rhonda

When Rhonda woke up, she was disoriented, confused, scared. And she was naked.

It was like out of a movie: Women drinks away her sorrows, wakes up in an unfamiliar place in bed with a man without a clear memory of what happened. Only it was Rhonda's real life.

Lorenzo tried to help.

"Calm down. I can see the look on your face. You're in a panic," he said. "I've been where you are. What do you remember?"

"Oh, shit. Where are we? What time is it? Where's my phone?"

She held the bed sheet up to her neck. She struggled to get her eyes to focus.

Lorenzo, who was dressed in shorts and a T-shirt, found her cell phone on the floor next to her shoes.

"It's going on four o'clock? Oh, my God. Look, I have six missed calls and seven text messages — all from my husband. *Shit.* What happened? Why am I naked?"

"Calm down. It's going to be all right. We —"

"Going to be all right? I don't know where I am. I'm naked. And it's almost four in the morning. And —"

"I know, but let me tell you what happened because you clearly don't remember."

"What can you tell me that will make this better?"

"You spoke to your husband when we were on the rooftop. You told him you weren't coming home. You said you were hanging out with Olivia and would stay with her."

"I did? Why would I say that?"

"That, I can't explain. You were feeling the drinks, that's for sure. You had about six or seven and —"

"Six or seven? Are you serious?"

"Yes. I made you two and we stayed on the rooftop — you remember going up there? — and had four or five more. I lost count."

"Why would you keep getting me drinks?"

"Me? Twice I went to the bathroom and when I came back, you had ordered another round. You don't remember any of this?"

"I remember being up there and seeing

the skyline and the Ferris wheel. I remember dancing. Did we dance?"

"*You* danced almost the whole time we were there. And you kissed me."

"Oh, no. I'm so sorry."

"Don't be. I liked it."

"So tell me about how we got here. I'm guessing this is your house. And can I have some water?"

"Right there," Lorenzo said, pointing to a glass on the nightstand. "I brought it in before you woke up."

Rhonda gulped the water.

"What are you laughing at?"

"I wished you remembered what happened. You were a real trip."

"Go ahead. Tell me."

"We closed the bar on the rooftop, and on the way to the bathroom, you took me into one of the conference rooms. It was called Risk. For some reason it was open. I'm like, 'What are you doing?' You started dancing like you were a stripper. And if I hadn't stopped you, you would've taken off your dress."

"Stop lying. And why don't I have a bad hangover?"

"Could be because everything we drank was high quality. No mixes with all those chemicals. Fresh cocktails. Anyway, I found out that you parked across the street instead of through the valet. So we get to your car — which I was not going to let you drive, by the way — and it had a boot on it."

"What? Are you serious?"

"You insisted you couldn't leave your car there. So I called the company and the guy was on the other side of the lot. We left my car and I drove your car here, to my house."

"What if my husband sees my car?"

"My house is on the other side of the subdivision. He has no reason to come by here. Plus, I parked your car in my garage."

"But he called me six times after I spoke to him. What do I tell him now?"

"Call him in the morning and tell him you went to Olivia's house, had too much to drink and fell asleep. That's reasonable."

"It *is* reasonable. Why are you helping me? And how did I get naked, mister?"

"You took off your clothes. I was making some tea for both of us — I was pretty trashed, too — and when I came in the room, you were in my bed and your dress was on the chair."

"And nothing happened?"

"A lot *could* have happened. But you wouldn't have remembered it. I tucked you in, lit that candle over there and got some sleep, too."

"Sorry you had to sleep on your couch."

"Couch? That's funny. It's my house and I needed to stretch out. I was right beside you. We had a snoring contest."

"Oh. I can't believe I was so tipsy."

"Tipsy? Come on. You can say it: You were drunk. *Really* drunk."

"Wow. Can you leave the room for a minute so I can put some clothes on? And you're telling me we didn't do anything?"

"If we had done something, your body would tell you. You'd feel it."

"I heard that."

"Here." Lorenzo handed Rhonda a toothbrush, toothpaste and washcloth. "Be right back." Lorenzo left the room and went downstairs to the kitchen to make coffee. Rhonda slipped into her dress, but could not find her panties. Suddenly, she remembered that she had not worn any and wondered what message that sent to Lorenzo. At that point, it did not matter. She used the bathroom and brushed her teeth.

When she came out of the bathroom, Lorenzo was sitting on the bed with the coffee.

"Can you zip up my dress?" He did.

"You had a lot to drink, so hopefully this will help you come down."

"Did I embarrass you? More importantly, did I embarrass myself?"

Lorenzo smiled. "You didn't embarrass either of us. Considering how many drinks you had, I was impressed. But not enough to let you drive."

"But tell me again how I got out of my clothes. I woke up naked, Lorenzo."

"I should have recorded you so you could see for yourself."

"Since you didn't, will you tell me?"

"You took your clothes off yourself. You politely asked me to pull down your zipper. And then you asked me to watch. But I left the room."

"What? Oh, my God. That's not what you said at first. I don't remember any of that."

"You might not remember it, but I won't forget it. That's what happened."

Rhonda looked at her cell phone and studied the messages from her husband. "I should go home. Wait. We're at your house, around the corner from my house?"

"Calm down. Yes, but I put your car in my garage to be safe. Your husband has no reason to come down this street, but it's in the garage. That doesn't mean you shouldn't go home. But you told him you were spending the night with Olivia. Sounded like an argument. I gave you some space so you

141

could talk to him. When I came back, he was calling you back. You said, 'I will deal with him tomorrow.' Then you put your phone in your purse and finished your drink.

"I'll be honest: I wasn't sure what to do. Definitely wasn't going to let you drive. You know I'm attracted to you. But I couldn't even consider taking advantage of you."

"I'm so embarrassed."

"Don't be," Lorenzo said. He slid closer on the bed to Rhonda. There was a tenderness in how he comforted her, and as Rhonda's head began to clear, her reason for coming to the bar resurfaced.

"Thank you for taking care of me," she said, "and not taking advantage of me. But I have to be honest with you. I wasn't meeting a friend at the bar. I came down there to see you. I made that up when I got cold feet. Before I could leave, there you were. So I had to say something — I couldn't tell you I was there to see you. I'm sorry I lied."

"I'm flattered that you came. I'm glad you came."

He slid closer to Rhonda and put his arm around her.

"You should stay. I want you to stay."

Rhonda pondered her life for several seconds. Lorenzo had treated her with more empathy, concern and consideration than her husband had in what seemed like years. She looked around the room — it was orderly, neat. On a dresser was a photo of Lorenzo after he crossed the finish line at the Peachtree Race, Atlanta's popular annual July 4th run. Rhonda had pleaded with Eric to train so they could run the race together. He had laughed at her.

That memory was enough for her to dismiss whatever reservations she had about sex with Lorenzo. She stood up and turned her back to him. "Can you unzip me, please?"

Lorenzo smiled and obliged her, and Rhonda let her dress fall to the floor. "You've already seen me naked," she said.

"I like this better. You know what you're doing," he responded.

Rhonda's mindset was clear: Take advantage of me. Her love life had diminished from good enough to not enough, with a lot of it having to do with her loss of attraction to Eric as he gained weight. Her body needed a working over.

She straightened up the ruffled bed sheets and then pulled back the covers as Lorenzo pulled his T-shirt over his head and slipped out of his shorts. Rhonda had her hand on the lamp to turn out the light, but not before inspecting Lorenzo's body, focusing on his body part she now craved. It was already erect — full and long with a slight curve to the left. In Rhonda's mind, inviting.

She flicked off the lamp, leaving only an illumination from another room as the sole light source in the room. Immediately, she thought: "This is romantic."

Rhonda lay back on the bed, and Lorenzo assumed a position beside her. They turned on their sides, and he hugged her and ran his hand along her back. She closed her eyes, as she was pleased by his touch and physicality. Lorenzo was different from Eric — he was athletically built, and Rhonda explored his body eagerly, excited that there was not the excess mass that she had become used to with her husband.

Lorenzo kissed her left shoulder and she closed her eyes. As wrong as the moment was, his lips on her body felt sensual and right, and the moisture between her legs increased. She had totally submitted. In those moments, her need for passion superseded any moral obligation. *I need this,* she told herself, *to keep my sanity.*

While she talked to herself, Lorenzo was about the business of pleasing her. He did not know at the time, but his attention to detail and commitment to making sure she felt good drew Rhonda closer to him. But he was being who he was — a sexual being not only interested in what he got out of intimacy.

Lost in the passion, Rhonda did not feel Lorenzo slide down and take her breast into his mouth. His kisses went from her shoulder to neck to face to lips, to the other side of her face, neck and shoulder and down to her nipples. She panted at the pleasure she received, and admired his diligence at giving each nipple ample time.

She rubbed his strong shoulders and closely cropped head and breathed heavily as Lorenzo caressed and sucked her nipples that were nearly as big as a thimble.

The anticipation of her feeling Lorenzo inside of her was almost unbearable. "Please, put it in," she said in a voice that surprised her. It was breathless and sexy, ways she had not felt in some time.

Lorenzo stopped. "What's wrong?" Rhonda said in a desperate voice.

"Everything is right," he said. "Just need to get something. Be right back."

She exhaled — from the release of his weight from her body and in pleasure. Before her mind could wander too far, Lorenzo was back, with condom in hand.

As if auditioning, he stood to the side of the bed — his dick erect as a spear — and methodically unwrapped the condom and eased it on as Rhonda watched with her mouth watering.

"Oh, my God," she said.

Lorenzo leaned over and kissed her and then eased down, between her legs. "Please, put it in," she said.

He kissed her lips again and then reached down and eased the head of his hardness into her wetness. The opening of her pussy lips with the insertion almost made Rhonda dizzy. Size mattered, and clearly Lorenzo was working with more than Eric. And she learned quickly that Lorenzo knew what to do with it. That excited her.

She braced herself as he slowly eased more of his manhood into her, and the feeling was hypnotic. The more he gave her, the more she wanted, and so she went from bracing herself to opening her legs wider and asking for more.

Lorenzo followed her directive and progressed from being careful and tender to forceful and purposeful. His thrusts were long and precise, strokes that caused splashes of Rhonda's secretion to splatter inside his thighs.

She managed to say something amid the

stroking, but it was unintelligible. Lorenzo took it to mean he was doing a good job, and so he thrust deeper and harder as Rhonda's once sexy voice became primal screams. The longer he stroked her, the more emphatic she got.

Don't stop. Don't stop. Oh, my God. Fuck me. Please. Don't stop.

Lorenzo smiled to himself, but kept pumping. Rhonda threw her head from side to side until he slowly eased out. She was about to ask why, but he showed her before she could inquire.

He turned her by her waist so she could get on her knees. It was a position she used to love — doggy style — but had not experienced with her husband in too long to remember. Lorenzo was not interested in her history or her reflections. Rather, he nestled between her legs, and reinserted his manhood that was wrapped in a condom covered with Rhonda's juices.

She flinched at entry; the angle allowed him to penetrate deeper. Lorenzo took it easy to start, but pumped more emphatically and almost violently as Rhonda, her face buried in a pillow, insisted he "get it."

Caught up in the moment, Lorenzo instinctively smacked Rhonda's ass. She was stunned. Neither Eric nor the several men she had dated before getting married had ever smacked her ass during sex. *She liked it.*

Lorenzo could tell by her movements, and so he smacked her on the other cheek. Rhonda began to buck like a wild horse, and Lorenzo gained a rhythm of smacking her ass and stroking her as the combination intensified the pleasure for her.

He held her waist firmly and took different angles as he banged on, sweat dripping down his face and neck. Rhonda perspired, too, and it felt like a refreshing shower to her. She had not had her body appreciated and pleased and handled in too long.

Lorenzo felt the pleasure rising in him, but he was not ready to climax, so he rubbed Rhonda's ass as if to calm it down. Then he pulled out and lay on his back, his heart racing from the activity.

Rhonda was exhausted, but not done. He pulled her on top, and she reached down and put his erection back into her womanhood that was on fire. All Lorenzo had to do was hold on; Rhonda rode him like she would a mechanical bull, bouncing up and down on it, rotating her hips — anything to feel his bulge in all parts of her vagina.

She found a groove and stuck with it, closing her eyes and concentrating as a burst of pleasure filled her body. Lorenzo could sense she was about to cum, and so he thrust upward, giving her more to feel. And in an instant it happened: the overwhelming sensation from all parts of her body exploded between her legs, sending vibrations through her body that made her feel suspended in air.

It was a scary but exciting pleasure, one that caused Rhonda to scream and uncontrollably gyrate. This was a significant climax, one that she knew, when she finally calmed down, meant trouble for her marriage.

Before she could think too long about that, Lorenzo rolled her on her back without coming out of her and stroked her more. It was his turn to climax, and he went for it. Rhonda invited his strokes by spreading her legs and whispering, "Come on. Give it to me, baby. Come on."

And several deep strokes later, Lorenzo gasped loudly as he filled up the condom with his sperm. He all but collapsed on top of Rhonda, and she cradled him as she would a lover.

They lay there in silence for a few minutes, before Lorenzo delicately moved to her side.

Neither of them said a word for another few minutes. Finally, Rhonda said: "You're in trouble."

"*I'm* in trouble?" Lorenzo asked.

"Yes, *you*. You have awakened the sleeping sexual beast in me. This was amazing. But you don't even know the best of what I'm about. I hope you can hang."

"Damn. It's like that?" he said. "Don't mess around and sleep on me. You may find yourself turned out."

"I love a challenge, Lorenzo," Rhonda said, while reaching down and clutching his testicles. "So, we will see."

"Yeah. Should be fun."

CHAPTER ELEVEN: TURNED TABLES

Juanita

For three weeks, Juanita resisted the urge to contact Brandon. There were times when the urge grew into a need, but she held it together. Meanwhile, Maurice upped his game and paid more attention to his wife and less to ESPN. Juanita appreciated the effort and felt optimistic about the prospects of her married life.

When Maurice's birthday arrived, Juanita planned a dinner party for five other couples at Del Frisco's Double Eagle at CityCenter in downtown D.C. She considered it more than a celebration of his birth, but also a monumental moment in the rebirth of their marriage.

Juanita had avoided spending time with others as they worked on fixing their union. She did not want to have to put on a happy face when she was sad. But the therapy and Maurice's notable change brought Juanita to a comfortable place.

While getting ready for the party, Juanita sipped on a glass of chardonnay as she applied makeup while wearing her bra and thongs. She smiled in the full-length mirror as she maneuvered into a form-fitting little black dress that her conscientious eating habits and consistent exercise habits allowed her to wear with pride. She felt sexy and carefree, ready for a wonderful night with friends she enjoyed.

Maurice emerged from the other bathroom looking tall, handsome and happy. They smiled at each other the way they used to when they had first married, before kids and long work hours.

He extended his hand. "Let's go have some fun, wifey."

Juanita's heart fluttered; he had not called her "wifey" in years. She clutched his hand and they walked down the steps smiling. Juanita was relieved that she had survived her cheating episode without any noticeable damage to the marriage.

The party was a surprise — Maurice thought they were having a quiet dinner for two. But he was ecstatic that Juanita thought enough of him to organize the event.

Their friends greeted Maurice with hugs and gifts, and he embraced Juanita with as much gratitude as he had ever shown her. "Can't believe you did this for me," he said. "Thank you, 'Nita. I love you."

"I love you, too, Mo."

He kissed her on her face and they took seats in the middle of the long table. They enjoyed lively conversation and laughs . . . and many drinks.

"I can't eat another thing," Juanita said. "But I can take another drink."

"Oh, really?" Maurice said into her ear. "Don't drink too much now. Don't want you getting drunk."

"You should. It's easier to take advantage of me," she said, rising from her seat.

"Going to the bathroom?" Wanda Coleman, a friend from their neighborhood, asked. "I'll go with you."

"Me, too," Diana Murray, one of Maurice's coworkers, said.

The ladies made their way from a table on the lower level, beyond the bar and up the stairs to the bathroom.

"Really glad you invited us, Juanita," Wanda said. "We don't get to go out much anymore. No one invites us to anything. I guess because our kids are five and six, people think we don't want to have fun anymore. But we need fun the most."

"I know that's right," Diana said. "You've

got to make the time. Hire a sitter. We're blessed because my parents live nearby and they are excited to have our kids spend the night or even the weekend. So we get our social life in. If we didn't, we'd fall into a rut. I can see it. And the way these women are out here, they don't care if your man is married or not. They go for what they want. So you'd better keep things exciting."

Juanita took in their perspectives as she reapplied her lipstick. She agreed with their positions and reasoned she would suggest more one-on-one time with Maurice. She had been so committed to building the family, that interest faded in keeping her husband-wife relationship strong. In that moment, she realized the more excitement she built with her husband, the less she would have urges for Brandon.

"Let's get out of here," she said. "We need to do a birthday toast to the birthday boy."

The ladies filed out of the bathroom, with Juanita last. As she came out of the bathroom, she noticed the other ladies' heads turning at a man who was entering the men's room. When she looked up to see Brandon, her heart skipped.

His did, too.

"Well, she lives," Brandon said.

"Hi," was all Juanita managed to get out.

"You know him?" Wanda asked.

"We go way back," Brandon said. He turned to Juanita. "Haven't seen you in — what — ten, twelve years?"

"Something like that. How have you been?" Juanita said. She was relieved that Brandon did not blow her up with her friends.

"Good. Real good. And you? Y'all hanging out tonight?"

"It's Maurice's birthday and Juanita had a surprise party for him," Diana interjected.

"Yes," Juanita added. She was not comfortable, but tried hard to be smooth. "We're downstairs. Who are you here with?"

"Oh, I'm with a young lady I'm dating," he said. Juanita's heart raced. "You all are all married and happy and shit. I'm trying to find that right one."

"I can't imagine you have troubles finding a woman," Wanda said.

"The good ones are already taken," he said, glancing at Juanita. "So, the search continues."

"We have to go," Juanita said. "It's good to see you."

"Nice to meet you ladies," Brandon said. Then he leaned in to hug Juanita. She hugged him back. "And really good to see you after so long," he said. Brandon squeezed Juanita's ass before letting her go. She did not flinch. Rather, she was turned on.

That kind of risk-taking and show of attraction excited her. She looked back with a sly smile at Brandon as they walked away. En route to the table, Juanita scanned for women sitting alone to see who might be Brandon's date. There was only one woman sitting by herself: She was young and elegant, pretty and poised. Immediately, Juanita became jealous.

She worked hard to mask her distraction, and everyone was so tipsy and conversational that they did not notice Juanita maintaining an eye on that table. Finally, after a few minutes, Brandon joined the woman, and Juanita's distraction turned into spying. She glanced at him and his date every thirty seconds or so, somehow believing she could gauge his interest in her. She almost hyperventilated when he moved from across the table to sit beside her. They faced Juanita now, but she could not focus on the woman's face — only Brandon's, and her spastic mind told her Brandon moved beside her to make her jealous — or so he could see what she was doing.

Either way, the fact that she could see him whispering into her ear and making her smile and rubbing her back and commanding their space — all the things about him that she loved — made her sick. Literally.

She gathered herself enough to make the toast and lead the Stevie Wonder "Happy Birthday" version to her husband, but her mind was about thirty feet away at another table. After nearly thirty minutes of faking as if she were interested in the conversations around her, Juanita became nauseous.

"I'll be right back," she told Maurice.

"You okay, dear? You seem a little — I don't know — flustered."

"Not sure the champagne is agreeing with the crab cakes, spinach, butter cake and martinis," she said.

In reality, it was seeing Brandon with another woman that upset her stomach and messed up her head. She knew he saw other women — he was single and a catch. She had left him hanging without expressing why. She had focused on her marriage and put her indiscretion in the far recesses of her conscience. She had tried to make it like Brandon did not exist.

But seeing him made her dismiss all that.

As she passed his table on the way to the bathroom, he looked up and smiled. She did not smile back. She was angry: angry that he was with someone else and angry at herself for being angry. It did not help that she got a good look at his date. The woman was clearly younger than Juanita and she appeared smitten with Brandon, which, to Juanita, meant that he had slept with her.

He heard them laugh as she walked by, which she took as them laughing at her. Her night that represented so much promise for her marriage ended up registering as a clear and present indicator that all was not well with her, no matter how much she ignored Brandon or dismissed him. What he provided was far different from Maurice, and the difference made a difference for her.

In the bathroom, she cursed herself. "Are you fucking serious?" she said aloud, looking into the mirror.

Right then, a woman came out of one of the stalls to answer and startle her. "I didn't think anyone was in here."

The woman said, "It's okay. I curse at myself all the time. Feel better afterward, too."

Juanita did not feel better. All the ignoring of Brandon and counseling with Maurice and working to bring things together with her husband collapsed like a popsicle-stick house in a windstorm.

She took a few minutes to gain her composure and let her queasiness subside before vowing not to dignify Brandon and his friend by acknowledging them. But when she stepped out of the bathroom, there was Brandon, arms folded.

"How long were you going to make me wait?" he asked.

"I didn't know you were out here," Juanita said.

"I wasn't talking about tonight."

"Forever then."

"Really? Why?"

Juanita looked around. "I'm married, remember," she said in a low voice. "It couldn't go on."

"I thought we were at a point where you'd at least say that and not ignore me. You made me feel like you used me for sex, to fulfill a fantasy or something, and then move on."

"I'm sorry. I didn't mean for that to happen. I needed to get back to my life."

"The life that drove you to me in the first place?"

"Yes, that life, but only better with some work."

"I squeezed your ass a little while ago. Did you like it?"

"That doesn't matter."

"Sure it matters. If you didn't like it, you would have made it clear. But you liked it.

You *loved* that shit."

"Why do you think you know me so well?"

"Only because I do. Trust me, as I've always said, I don't want to cause drama in your life, in your marriage. But you know we have something between us that's not normal, not regular."

"That didn't stop you from being on your date with fake Beyoncé down there."

"Jealous, are we? She's not Beyoncé, but the fact that you would bring Bae into the conversation says you see how beautiful she is. She's smart and sexy and, for some reason, seems to really like me."

"So why are you here talking to me?"

"Because she's not you. You and me . . . we have something. We don't have to work at it. Never had that with anyone else. So, I see you out tonight — your husband seems like a nice guy, by the way — and there's no way I can't at least let you know I miss you and I wish the best for you."

He said it with sincerity, which threw Juanita. She expected that he would make her feel awkward.

"Thank you. I apologize again for not being up front with you. But I thought cutting ties cold turkey was the easiest way for me to move on. I needed to do that. And it seems you've gotten over me pretty quickly."

"What, you want me to sit at home in the dark, flicking the lights on and off? I moved on — had no choice. But I didn't get over you. Never got over you from way back when."

Brandon smiled, and Juanita, despite all her efforts, smiled back. "You'd better get back to your people," he said. "Good to see you. Oh, and you look sexy as fuck in that dress."

She shook her head and smiled as she went in for a goodbye hug. Brandon kept his hands to himself this time, and Juanita was disappointed. So she squeezed his ass.

"You're a bad girl."

"Not as bad as I wanna be," Juanita replied.

"Remember I'm your partner in badness," Brandon said. They laughed and he watched her walk toward and then down the steps. "Don't be a stranger."

"What took you so long?" Maurice asked when Juanita made it back to her seat. "You okay?"

"I'm better now. Should not have had that champagne," she said. Brandon made it back to his seat. "But I feel like continuing the celebration now."

Wanda and Diana waved for Juanita to come to the far end of the table to take photos. The server took five versions of the same pictures with five different cell phones. Then Diana suggested Juanita and Maurice pose for photos.

Everyone began snapping. Juanita smiled instinctively, but she worried how it looked to Brandon, who sat in a perfect line of vision to their table.

"Okay, enough already," Maurice said, ending the succession of clicking phones. "We're not Princess Diana and Prince Charles. But my wife is a princess. Thank you, baby, for this night with great friends, good food and good drink. Really appreciate it."

Juanita, distracted, said, "Okay, you're welcome, husband. It's my pleasure to do something like this for you. You deserve it."

They hugged, and she looked over his shoulder for Brandon. But he was gone. And despite all the cheer and joy around her, Juanita felt a little empty.

Chapter Twelve:
The Untruth of the Matter

Stephanie

For all the pushback she gave her sister on validating her reasons for cheating, Stephanie's guilt surfaced. So, she went online and did research on wives' infidelities and learned some numbers that lessoned her culpability.

A poll on a website called womansavers .com, which called itself "the world's largest database of rating good and bad men," talked to 55,000 married ladies, and 49 percent of them said they had cheated on their husbands. Just as significant was that 29 percent more indicated they would cheat on their spouses.

Those numbers comforted Stephanie — or at least made her feel as if she were not alone. She studied the article, which went into reasons why wives cheat. One point struck her: That the couples become too familiar, which led to indifference or boredom.

Willie fit the negative, obligatory stereotype of an accountant: money-focused, unenthused, regimented. As the wife, she followed her man's lead, and he led them to financial stability. But he seemed to consider that enough.

Stephanie could not recall the last time Willie complimented her on how she looked or attended one of her events at school or surprised her with . . . *anything.*

Charles paying attention to her ignited a light in her that was dim. That's what she feebly tried to explain to her sister. She was not cheating for kicks. She needed to feel cared for, to be coveted, to be desired, to *matter.* She wanted it from Willie, but got it from Charles.

So, in a rare case of following her sister's advice, she planned a heart-to-heart with her husband. But first, she made sure it was in a setting that would allow him to be receptive and open. Stephanie cooked dinner — rib eye, baked sweet potatoes and spinach. Because Willie was so predictable, she had the food ready at half-past eight — the time he almost always walked into the door.

She also had an ice-cold Chimay — a

gourmet beer he loved, but she disallowed him from frequently having. The house was cleaned and the dining room table beautifully set with sparkling China and tall candles.

Two minutes before he arrived, Stephanie received a text from Charles:

I have had a good day in one sense: I thought about you all day. Didn't get any work done, but I had a good feeling. I thought about Sunday and about my trip there this weekend. I hope you can find some time for us to be together.

Stephanie had not prepared to end things with Charles. She didn't want to end things with him, so she avoided thinking about it. But if Willie handled the night the right way, she decided she'd figure out how to let go of Charles.

Before Willie made it home, she returned her lover's text:

You . . . I don't know what to do with you. But I'm glad you're coming here this weekend. Not sure what my availability will be, but I will do my best. You know that.

Then she put her phone on silent; she didn't want any distractions. She made sure to wear the dress that Willie seemed to last notice her in — almost a year earlier . . . a red number that hung off her shoulders and hugged her ample hips.

Willie came in a moment later and stopped in his tracks when he saw the table.

"What's this?"

"Dinner for my husband," Stephanie said, smiling. "And here — here's your favorite, Chimay."

Willie smiled, but it was not a smile of excitement or joy, which alarmed Stephanie.

"What's wrong?"

He put down his bag, took the Chimay and sipped. "Ah, this is good. Thank you. But I'm trying to figure out why you've done all this today, a Monday."

"Trying to break the routine, that's all. You're not happy about this?"

"That's the reason? No other reason?"

"No. That's it. Why?"

"I thought it would be for my birthday. But — *oh, that's right* — that can't be it. And you know *why*? Because my birthday was *yesterday.*"

Stephanie's smile vanished. Her shoulders dropped. Her heart pounded. She felt numb. She had spent the previous afternoon and early evening — her husband's birthday — in a room at the W hotel in San Francisco with Charles, making love like horny teenagers.

"So, you made this nice meal because, but you couldn't remember my birthday? Listen, I'm no kid. I'm not going to pout. But if I had forgotten your birthday, you'd never let me hear the end of it. And the way I look at it, it says to me that you're going through the motions in this relationship, this marriage. After this, that's all I'm left to believe."

Stephanie was at a loss. She had nothing of substance to add. So she threw herself at his mercy — and sprinkled it with lies.

"Willie, I'm so sorry. Oh, my God," she began. "Please forgive me. You know I never forget your birthday. But I got caught up in my sister's troubles. Toya and Terry are having problems and she's relying on me to help her get through it."

"Since when? I talked to Toya yesterday; she called to wish me Happy Birthday. She seemed fine to me. And she didn't say a word about any problems at home."

"Well, you aren't her sister, Willie. She's trusted me with all the private stuff she doesn't tell anyone else."

"What's that got to do with you forgetting my birthday? She's worried about her marriage, but she thought enough of me to at least call me. But my wife didn't remember? And you think you saying you were helping Toya make this excusable?"

Stephanie had not seen Willie so upset and disappointed in years. After so long together, they had found a groove where arguments were infrequent, if at all. One of them would acquiesce, and any potential blowup would be averted. This was different — and Stephanie could sense it.

"There is no excuse, Willie. No excuse. I don't mean for it to seem like I'm offering one. Nothing should prevent me from remembering and celebrating your day with you. You're my world and I'm really sorry. What can I do to make it up to you?"

"You can tell me what's really going on with you. That's what you can do. I'm as busy as the next man, but I know you. We've been together for too many years not to know when you start acting different from the norm. And for a few weeks, you've been different."

Stephanie took that opening as an opportunity to flip the momentum of the argument. *"Wow,"* she said in exaggerated disgust. "I *have* been different. I realized I have a good husband and so I have been more loving and attentive. I have been more in tune with you, more romantic. And that's a problem? See, that's a real issue for me.

"I love you, make love to you, make sure you're satisfied, and you don't like it? You

168

think there's something wrong with that? How do you think that makes me feel?"

"I'm not trying to make you feel anything," Willie said. "I'm trying to figure you out. You act different, more loving, as you put it, but then you forget my birthday? There's a disconnect with that, Steph."

She knew then she had wiggled her way out of danger. Whenever Willie called her "Steph," it was in moments of endearment. He never called her that while in angst.

"What do you want from me, Willie? You want me to be this stale wife or do you want more? 'Cause I can be what you want me to be."

"I want you to be happy," he said. Stephanie smiled to herself. She had turned the subject to what she wanted instead of Willie's concerns.

"You know what would make me happy now?" she asked. "Letting me make up for my mistake. Arguing about it isn't going to get us anywhere. I made a major mistake, Willie. I can't believe it. And Toya didn't say a thing to me. She bent my ear about her issues and what she's planning on doing about her marriage."

In her moment of desperation, Stephanie was unrepentant about lying about her sister's marriage. It was the first thing that came to mind, and she ran with it.

"So what's going on with them? Toya and Terry always seemed happy to me."

Stephanie had to make a split-second decision on how far to carry the lie.

"She's thinking about having an affair."

"What? Come on. Not Toya. She's as ethical as they come. She talks consistently about the downfall of marriage is about infidelity. And she's thinking about cheating? With who?"

"She wouldn't say his name. But it's some guy she met recently while walking along Lake Merritt. Said he stopped her because he thought he had met her before. They ended up talking and staying in touch."

"But why? You don't cheat because some guy hollas at you? What's wrong at home?"

"You have to promise not to mention any of this to Toya or Terry. None of it, Willie."

"Of course not."

"I'm serious. You can't act any differently. Toya can't know I told you any of this."

"I said okay."

"All right, well, apparently, their love life has fallen off," Stephanie began. She knew she had to take the lie to the mountaintop to convince Willie and to keep his mind off her not being home and forgetting his birthday. "She said their life is boring, that

Terry doesn't have any interest in doing anything but work and visiting his mother. She wants to get pregnant and he's not ready for a baby and —"

"Wait. What? Terry told me last weekend at the Warriors game that he wanted Toya to get pregnant. I thought I told you that."

Stephanie realized she had messed up. Willie *had* told her what Terry had shared. In her zest to lie, she'd forgotten.

"You did tell me that. But some time since then, he changed his mind, I guess, because Toya said they have been arguing about it."

She felt bad about lying so much, but she could not break the axiom that one lie leads to another and another and . . .

"Bottom line, they have troubles. But I'm tired of talking about their issues. That's what got me all twisted up yesterday."

"Yeah, okay."

"Really, I'm sorry, baby. Let me start bv making up with this nice meal — look I made you a rib eye, which you know I don't normally do because I don't want you eating too much red meat. But I'm trying to be out of the box and not predictable. I don't want the troubles Toya and Terry are having."

She walked up to her husband and hugged him. Willie reluctantly hugged her back. She laid her head up against his chest and breathed a sigh of relief.

"Come on, finish your Chimay and then wash your hands. I'm going to get dinner ready. Can you light the candles for me?"

Willie did so and they eventually sat down at the table. "You look nice. You know that's my favorite dress."

"That's why I wore it. See, I'm trying to do the things I know you like. I guess seeing what Toya and Terry are going through makes me realize we have to keep it fresh and new. We've been married going on twenty-five years. So we have to really work at it, almost as much as we did when we first got married because after a certain point, it gets harder for it to stay exciting."

"I give you credit because I work so hard that sometimes I look forward to the end of the day, visiting my mom, dinner and bed so I can do it again the next day," Willie admitted. "So I do appreciate you wanting to keep things going for us."

"Thank you, baby," she said, grinning more from relief than anything else. And then her cell phone chimed, indicating she had a text message. She thought she had turned off the ringer.

"I know you're not going to get that now; we're at the dinner table," Willie said.

"I was only going to get it because I texted Wilhemina earlier and I hadn't heard back from her," Stephanie said. "You know how your daughter is. She keeps that phone in her hand, but she didn't respond. So I have been looking to hear from her since it's been so long."

"I spoke to her on my way home," Willie said. "She's fine. She's trying to figure when she's going to come home for a visit. I told her we weren't going anywhere. She can come whenever she likes. Think she's talking about driving up this weekend."

Their twenty-four-year-old daughter lived outside of Los Angeles. She wanted to be in the film industry, so she needed to live in L.A., New York or Atlanta. Willie and Stephanie were glad she'd chosen to stay in California.

"This weekend?" Stephanie asked. For all she had avoided and despite her pledge to cut Charles out her life, her close call gave her a charge to keep up her shenanigans instead of the opposite impact. The close call scared her, but excited her, too. She liked the adrenaline rush. It invigorated her, made her feel vibrant — all elements that allowed her to embrace her erstwhile uninspiring existence with Willie.

"Yeah, Saturday afternoon. Think she's

talking about bringing some guy with her she's dating. So, I hope she does. She's been spending a lot of time with this guy and I — we — need to check him out."

Saturday was the day she and Charles had planned to go to Sausalito, a quaint town in Marin County on the shore of the Richardson Bay with a charming hotel — The Inn Above Tide — right at the pier where ferry boats docked. Charles told her of the spectacular views of the San Francisco skyline, Golden Gate Bridge and Alcatraz, rooms with fireplaces, sunken tubs.

"We can walk to the village of Sausalito and have dinner on the water, in a booth in the back, in the corner, in the dark. We can do anything we'd like there," Charles had said.

The notion of it all was enchanting for Stephanie.

"Maybe this isn't the best weekend for her to come home," she told her husband. Willie gave her a curious look. "I'm thinking about Toya and Terry. First of all, she asked me to go someplace with her on Saturday afternoon. Second, you know Wilhemina will want to see them, and I don't want her to be worried about how they are doing."

"What? Wilhemina is a young lady, a grown lady. And maybe with her around,

174

they will be on their best behavior and find whatever is missing."

Stephanie knew better than to fight it, so she gave in, knowing she would call their daughter and make up an excuse to come another weekend. "You're right. What am I thinking? I need to see my baby. It's been about three months."

Willie enjoyed his meal and took a seat on the couch in the living room. The thought of her rendezvous with Charles was all Stephanie could think of, so she took her cell phone into the bathroom, sat down on the toilet and texted him.

I'm in my bathroom right now with panties at my ankles, thinking about two things: Last weekend and this coming weekend. I can't wait.

Charles responded: *Where is he?*

Not in here with me. Where is she?

Who cares?

Let me ask you: Does this thing with me make your life better at home?

To be honest, maybe. I don't know. It makes me feel better. And when you feel better, you act better.

That's how I feel. I know this is wrong. But the only way to keep my sanity is to have you. This is crazy to say, but you're saving my marriage, Charles. You are.

CHAPTER THIRTEEN:
DÉJÀ VU ALL OVER AGAIN

Juanita

Juanita found herself weak to Brandon. Again. She was doing fine . . . until she had seen him at the restaurant with another woman. That broke her down.

So, she called him — he didn't answer. She texted him — he didn't respond. His silence made her desperate. After two days of not hearing from Brandon, she decided she would take drastic measures to get a response from him.

Before she could take that step, though, she had to endure another counseling session with Maurice.

Dr. Fields got right to it. "So, how do you feel about things since we last met?"

"You can go," Juanita said, looking at her husband.

"It's actually been better, I think," Maurice started. "She —"

"You mean, Juanita, your wife?" Dr. Fields

interjected. "You should refer to her by her name or 'my wife' or 'sweetheart' or 'baby.' Do you ever call her affectionate names?"

"Yes, I do."

"You apparently say them to yourself," Juanita cracked. "I don't recall hearing anything affectionate for years."

"Years? You're exaggerating . . . *honey."* Dr. Fields smiled.

"I have not heard you call me 'honey' in who-knows-when," Juanita said.

"Well, he did now, so the best move for you is to embrace it. It's a show of affection. It's an effort."

Juanita smirked. She viewed Maurice's "affection" as condescension.

"What I was going to say," Maurice continued, "was that my *baby* threw me a birthday dinner over the weekend that was really nice. There were friends we hadn't seen in a long time, and it was nice to be around people and have a good time."

"Very nice," Dr. Fields said. "What made you throw him a party, Juanita?"

"It was his birthday. That was enough reason."

"I have had a lot of birthdays when you didn't do anything."

"I always did something for you. Are you kidding? Last year, the kids and I baked cupcakes and sang to you on the back porch. You don't remember? See, this is what I'm talking about. We put a lot of time and effort into that celebration. And yet, it didn't mean anything to you."

"I remember; I don't have dementia, *darling.*"

"My point is, Maurice, that I have celebrated your birthday every year in different ways. And it bothers me that you seem not to remember that."

Dr. Fields asked: "Why did you do a party this year, Juanita? What was the message you were trying to send?"

"I was trying to do something different. We came in here last time talking about trying to make things better. I thought we should do something without the kids, be around some adults. And I'm glad I did. It felt good."

"I enjoyed it. I did. And I thanked her for it. But I was surprised by one thing."

Juanita held her breath. Could Maurice have known about Brandon?

"I felt like Juanita drank too much, especially as the night went on. She was fine, but then, later, she had two glasses of champagne after two other drinks. That's not like her. And I wondered why she was drinking like that?"

"Did you ask her?" Dr. Fields said.

"I knew we were coming here so I thought I'd wait to ask now."

"See, I don't think that's right. I'm right there with you; why not ask me? Also, I was not drunk, if that's what you're insinuating. I was having a good time — that's it. But then, you're not used to seeing me have a good time, so I guess it *was* a surprise to you."

"What's that supposed to mean? I hadn't seen you drink that much, that's all."

"And you couldn't talk to me about it? You had to wait until we got here to bring it up? That's a punk move to me."

Before Maurice responded, he looked at Dr. Fields, who interjected. "Name-calling never helps to bring a couple together. It only causes animosity."

"But am I right, Dr. Fields? Isn't it punk-ish to hold back on something so insignificant to bring it up here, like 'Ah-ha. I got you'? I don't appreciate that."

"Was that your intent, Maurice? Or was it —"

"Wait, Dr. Fields. Don't help him by putting words in his mouth. Let him answer."

"I'll be glad to answer," Maurice said. "Juanita, I love you. You're my wife. You're wonderful. But you're not perfect. And I

179

think that's what all this is about — me realizing that she's not perfect. It's all right that you have flaws, make mistakes. But you seem to think it's some fatal strike against you."

"That's not it, Maurice. I'm not God, so I know I'm not perfect. I have tried to be a perfect wife to you and a perfect mother to my — our — children. And that's not easy. It hasn't been easy to be a good wife because you didn't put much effort into being a good husband. For me, being a good husband is more than providing and being there. It's being engaged. It's understanding me. If you were really in tune with me, you would know . . ."

Juanita caught herself. She wanted to talk about how displeased and disinterested she was in having sex with him, that their love life was less than exciting and that those facts drove her to another man, a man who coveted her body and appreciated her sexual expression. Instead, she held it in.

"If I were in tune with what, Juanita? Say what you want to say."

"I'm saying you did not know I was unhappy about some things."

"You weren't aware that I was unhappy, either, Juanita. So I guess you weren't in tune to me."

"Let's not make this a tit-for-tat," Dr. Fields said. "You're here to understand each other and to build from that knowledge."

"And that's why I had the party," Juanita said. "I wanted us to do something fun and not the same old same old. I don't know about for you, but it was great for me."

She sat back and crossed her legs — a show of sass Maurice had never seen.

The rest of the hour-long session was uneventful, with neither Juanita nor Maurice making significant inroads in getting their positions across. And that left Dr. Fields disappointed.

"I have to tell you," she said, "I came into this session feeling like we would end on a high note, with you all feeling closer to finding common ground on some key issues. My notes said that. And I felt it. But what I felt most of this session was animosity — or at least discord that should not be present in a healthy marriage.

"So, this is what I hope you will accomplish by the time we meet next week: Maurice, I want you to make a concerted effort to compliment Juanita at least twice a day. Whatever compliment it is that you feel, share it. I'm asking you to do this because expressing compliments shows that you appreciate her, that you recognize how wonderful you say she is.

"Juanita, I want you to do the same. Tell Maurice twice a day something you appreciate about him. Not something out of the blue, but something that he does during the course of the day that you might not have acknowledged in the past.

"The goal here is to help you identify the good in each other, and that can only come from each of you making the other feel appreciated and loved. This is the easiest homework you'll ever receive. I'm looking for two As from this assignment."

Neither of them felt excited about the challenge, but each agreed that expressing compliments would be a nice start to them showing consistent affection. "This will be interesting," Juanita said.

"You have time to go to lunch?" Maurice asked.

"I wish I did. I have to get back to the office," Juanita lied. She hugged her husband and he went to his job on Capitol Hill and she went the other way. After she saw him drive off, Juanita called Brandon. When he did not answer, she sent for an Uber that would take her to Bethesda to Massage Envy, where he worked as a massage therapist.

The ride there was torturous. She was

worried because she took the rest of the day off and hoped Maurice would not call her office looking for her. What would she do then? But she was mostly worried about how Brandon would receive her showing up on his job.

She did what she considered the right thing: She made an appointment for a massage . . . under the name Renee Rice — her middle and maiden names. She hoped Brandon got her clue and knew she was coming. But would he be upset that she showed up at his workplace? That was a concern.

Her biggest fear, however, was that Brandon would reject her. She had never faced rejection in her life. At the same time, she had not put herself in a vulnerable position, either. This was a significant step for her, one that crystalized how much she needed change in her life. It was an indictment against her husband and against *herself.* And she did not care.

When she arrived at the business, she walked in with trepidation, worried that Brandon would be in the lobby and shut her down before she got started. It was fifteen minutes before her appointment. The receptionist greeted her with a smile, confirmed her appointment and offered her something to drink as she filled out paper-work and waited for Brandon.

"He will be with you in a moment."

Juanita went from concerned to nervous then. *What am I doing? I'm a married woman? I shouldn't be here.*

But she could not move. The need for passion in her life was overwhelming. She was scared because she did not believe she could get it from her husband. Before she could torture herself with more unpleasant thoughts, Brandon emerged from the massage rooms to the right of the front counter.

He did not look up. He took the clipboard that had the list of clients to be served. He looked at his watch. Juanita looked on with a mix of excitement and fear. She crossed her legs and straightened her dress.

"Renee Rice," he said, without looking up.

Juanita did not move. Brandon placed the clipboard back on the counter and turned toward the lounge area.

His eyes met Juanita's, and they both had a confused look on their faces: Juanita because she was trying to read his look and Brandon because he couldn't believe she was there.

"Miss Rice," the receptionist said, "Brandon is ready for you."

Juanita uncrossed her legs and rose from

her chair. Brandon scanned the length of her body and finally said, "Miss Rice?"

"Yes."

"Miss Rice?"

"Yes, I'm Mrs. Rice."

Brandon made a small smile, which eased Juanita's mind.

"How did you get referred to me?"

"My husband."

"Your husband?"

"Yes, he sent me here."

"Okay, great. Let's go this way."

Believing others could hear, he said, "I see you're having a deep tissue massage today. We're going to be in this studio right here. You can get undressed, cover yourself with the sheet on the table and I will come in shortly. Would you like something to drink?"

"I'm fine, thank you," she said as she walked into the room.

Brandon went back out to the lobby to examine her paperwork. He also looked around to see if her husband was there. He wasn't.

He gave it a few more minutes before knocking on the door and slowly opening it. He closed the door and let out a sigh of relief. He knew the walls were thin, so he spoke in his regular voice and in a low voice.

She was lying on her back, naked.

"So, Miss Rice, do you have some areas I need to work on in particular."

She pointed between her legs. "Yes . . . right here needs the most work."

Brandon smiled and shook his head. "I can feel the tension."

He stood on the side of the table, leaned in and he whispered to her. "So what's going on with you?"

"I need your services," she said. "You wouldn't call me back so I came to you."

"You're bad."

"Why didn't you call me back?"

"Okay, let me know if this is too much pressure," he said in case anyone could hear.

Then he leaned in and whispered. "Because I saw you with your husband and I felt guilty. It was one thing to do what we did and not know who he was. He was a phantom. But to see him . . . he became a real person. And I don't want to hurt anyone."

Juanita was moist the moment she undressed and became more amorous as Brandon stood in front of her.

"No one's going to get hurt. But I need you to take care of me."

Brandon weighed not sexing her for about ten seconds. Then he said, "Turn onto your stomach. Let me give you a massage — and more."

Juanita obeyed his commands and Brandon turned on some soothing "music" that sounded like a bubbling brook. He then lathered his hands with lavender-scented oil and removed the sheet to reveal half of her body. He slowly ran his hands over the left side, concentrating on the shoulder and neck at first and then the center of her back and the small of it. He added more oil and massaged it into her ass, which was exposed. He let his hand "slip" between her legs, where he could feel the heat coming from her insides.

Brandon moved along, rubbing oil slowly and firmly down her thigh, to her calf and feet. She moaned at the pleasure of his touch and the anticipation of his passion.

He covered the side he had finished and took the same, deliberate approach that almost made Juanita climax on the table — from his hands on her body and the anticipation. After he finished the right side, he said, "You can turn over now."

When she did, she noticed Brandon's bulge stretching out his pants. She reached for it and he backed up.

"Come here," she said in a whisper. "Please come here."

Brandon obliged, and Juanita moved to her side and immediately reached for his belt, which she unfastened. She unzipped his pants and they fell to the floor.

"Wait," he said, before stepping out of his pants and locking the door.

Juanita tossed aside the sheet and got off the table. When Brandon came over to her, she grabbed his erection as they kissed.

"I'm sorry," she whispered. "I'm sorry."

"For what?"

"For denying myself this dick. I miss it. I *need* it."

Brandon's ego was stroked, but he worried about what that meant. Was she going to be a pest? Was she going to stunt his social life? Was she going to become a stalker?

Those thoughts flooded his mind as he looked down on the top of Juanita's head as she took him into her mouth. She seemed famished, going up and down on it with a passion he had not seen since she used to blow him many years before she was married.

She gazed up into his eyes as she performed and the contorted look of pleasure on his face excited her — and made her suck harder. Before he could explode, she got off her knees and leaned over the massage table. Brandon eased his way over and she reached back to get a handful of his penis.

He leaned over and whispered, "I don't have a condom with me at work."

Juanita did not care. "I had my tubes tied."

Brandon took that to mean she wanted him inside her, and he went for it, entering her from behind and forcing himself deeper and harder while somehow managing not to sound like two bodies colliding in heat.

Juanita fought back tears throughout the session. The pleasure and guilt overwhelmed her. When they were done, Brandon held her in his arms.

"It's okay, Juanita. It's okay. Come on. Lay on the table. Let me finish the massage."

She got herself together and he moistened towels at the sink so they could clean themselves. He pulled out a can of air freshener to dim the aroma of sex that hung in the air.

Juanita lay on her stomach, her face in the opening at the head of the table. Brandon lit another candle, washed his hands and covered them in oil. Then he rubbed Juanita's shoulders and arms and back and legs — meticulously and lovingly. Her body felt reinvigorated — but not from his hands.

CHAPTER FOURTEEN: WALKING TALL

Rhonda

When she came home, Eric was in the kitchen waiting for Rhonda. And he was not exactly welcoming.

"Where the fuck you been?"

This was out of character for him — yelling and cursing. He hardly ever raised his voice, unless at the TV as he watched a sporting event. He was so loud and angry that he scared Rhonda.

"Why are you screaming at me?"

"Rhonda, where the fuck have you been?"

"I told you I was staying at Olivia's."

"Well, you didn't tell Olivia that."

"What are you talking about? I called her several times and she didn't answer."

"Because I told her not to. I didn't answer your calls, either. I didn't want to talk to you."

"You think that's okay? To go out and spend the night somewhere and not answer when I call you?"

"Well, looking back on it, it probably wasn't right. But at the time, I was pissed off at you and I didn't have anything to say to you."

"You're not fucking single, Rhonda. Pissed at me or not, you don't go out and spend the night somewhere and you don't ignore my calls. If I did that to you, you'd lose your mind."

"I told you what I was doing. You didn't want to accept it. I felt like I needed a break, some time away to think."

"That's not the way to go about it."

"Okay, okay. You're right about that. And I was thinking this morning that I shouldn't have put Olivia in the middle of our marriage. I apologized to her about that. She doesn't need to know our business."

"Well, she does now. And you made me look like some sucker, not answering your phone and telling her not to answer hers. That's wrong and rude and disrespectful. What do you think she will think of me now? And look at you. You look a mess."

"I told you I had too much to drink. I feel like I need some more rest. I want to take a shower and go to bed."

"That's fine. But don't ever fucking do that again."

"Can you please stop cursing at me?"

"Fuck no. I'm pissed."

"See, that's not right. That's —"

"Don't talk to me about what's right. What were you going to say, that I'm being disrespectful by cussing? Well, good. I don't give a fuck right now. Everything isn't about you. What you did last night was reckless, disrespectful and you'd better not do it again. Period."

Then he stormed out of the kitchen, knocking over a chair along the way.

Rhonda picked it up and sat in it. She was disappointed that she made Eric so mad, but she did not regret her time with Lorenzo, who made it easier for her by being all her husband was not: attentive, thoughtful, affectionate. She needed that.

But Rhonda was concerned about how to coexist with Eric so angry. It was two days before they had a real conversation. She came into his man cave as he watched TV. He picked up the remote control and hit "mute."

"Look," Eric said, "I'm not trying to go around here not speaking to you. But I needed some time to process what's been happening. The bottom line is that you're not happy, and as your husband, I should take that as a cue to do something about it because I don't want you to resent me. So I'm going to do better, starting with my weight."

Rhonda was stunned. It was as if Eric had read from a husband's guide on how to communicate with the wife. She appreciated that first, because his pattern of communication had devolved into mostly short sentences and grunts. And his acknowledgment of his weight issues *really* inspired Rhonda, who, in that moment, decided she could end it with Lorenzo before the cheating picked up any more momentum.

"Well, Eric, I really appreciate you saying those things. I mean, I *really* appreciate it. And I'm really sorry about the other night. It won't happen again. I was mad and hung out with Olivia and I had too much to drink. My car got booted downtown and it was best that you not see me like that. But it won't happen again. I promise."

Eric nodded and Rhonda went over to him and they hugged. She felt grateful that he vowed to make changes, but mostly relieved that he moved beyond her night with Lorenzo. She had moved past it, too, and vowed not to cross the sexual line with him again.

She had another week off before she had to return to work, and she planned to use her days reading and relaxing and mentally preparing to go back to the job. Rhonda also decided there was no way she would tell Olivia — or anyone — about her night with Lorenzo, so she had to keep her from her house, fearful Eric would ask her about the night she supposedly stayed with Olivia.

Three days after getting things calmed down with Eric, while sitting at home reading *Uptown* magazine, Rhonda looked out of her window, only to see Lorenzo on his daily walk. Her mind told her to stay inside, but her legs moved her to the door nonetheless.

As he looped the cul-de-sac, she walked down her driveway. "Were you going to walk by my house without saying hello?" she asked Lorenzo. She could not think of anything better to say.

"I'm glad you were here, but I was not going to ring your doorbell, that's for sure. How are you? You know, I texted you the last couple days."

"I know. I wasn't sure if I should stay away from you or not."

"I understand."

"You do? I'm glad someone does because I don't. I know it's wrong. But I know it's not right for me to deny myself, either."

"Maybe we should go inside and talk

about it."

Rhonda looked around to see if any neighbors were outside. There weren't. She knew she would be taking wrong to another level by allowing Lorenzo into her home.

"I want to, but I shouldn't. Maybe I could come visit you."

"Let me know when."

He kissed on her on the cheek and continued his walk. "I will call you later," she said as she watched him strut down the street.

Rhonda went back into the house and plotted on how she would visit Lorenzo. Seeing him reminded her of their intimacy — and she wanted more. All her notions of dismissing Lorenzo evaporated like steam.

It became a clear plan when she sat down for dinner with Eric that evening after work. She watched in irritation as he breathed heavily while eating. Her husband had vowed to do better about his eating habits, but until she saw a difference, some things about him continued to bother her.

After dinner, she told Eric: "I'm going to start walking in the evenings."

"Walk? Where? And are you up to taking walks?"

"The doctors cleared me last week. I'm taking another week off because I can. Gonna walk in the neighborhood."

She wanted to ask Eric to join her, but her plan to see Lorenzo was to walk to his house on her evening strolls. So, she washed the dishes, put up the food and changed into a pair of black stretch pants, black razorback top and sneakers. She pinned up her hair and dabbled perfume on her wrists, behind her ears and a little on her cleavage.

"I'm going to walk for about an hour," she said. "That should be about two miles."

Eric nodded his head. "Okay."

Rhonda plugged her earphones into her Samsung cell phone and headed out. It was more like a date than a walk.

She left her cul-de-sac and headed right, about a quarter-mile down to the next street and turned right, toward the subdivision's entrance. She turned left and continued down another neighborhood street, passing men mowing lawns and kids playing basketball in driveways.

She was intentionally slow, not wanting to build up any perspiration. But her heart rate increased as she got closer to Lorenzo's house. She texted him: *If you're home, come outside. I have a gift for you.*

She made a right on his street and passed three houses before reaching his. Lorenzo was standing at the front door, hands on hips. When their eyes met, he smiled and shook his head, which gave her relief. He looked happy to see her.

"And what's the gift?" he said, grinning.

Rhonda looked down at her body and back up at Lorenzo.

"Oh, well, you should come in."

He held the door open and Rhonda, without hesitation, walked in.

"Don't you look cute in your workout gear?"

"I plan to walk every day — every day that you are home around this time."

"If that's the case, I will make sure I'm here."

They walked to the den. "Have a seat. Can I get you something?"

Rhonda was purposeful and efficient. She did not engage in small talk.

"Unfortunately, I only have about forty-five minutes. And I didn't come over here to eat."

And with that, their secret affair was set. Up to three times a week, Rhonda would leave Eric at home to walk — right to Lorenzo's house, where they would engage in the kind of intense passion she so lacked at home.

"What's going on with you, girl?" Olivia asked as she and Rhonda had dinner one weekend at Yebo Beach Haus in Buckhead.

"I haven't seen you in about three weeks."

"What are you talking about? I've been back to work for a week and I see you every day."

"I'm talking about us doing this, hanging out. Things must be better at home."

Rhonda did not want to lie, but through her affair with Lorenzo, she realized she could be keen at deception. So, she said, "I will say this: I'm getting some good sex right now."

"Oh, shit. Go 'head, Eric. I knew my boy would bounce back."

"He's trying. He's cut back on eating — at least around me. And he goes to the LA Fitness a couple times a week. That's all I need to see — an effort. I was pissed because he took me for granted, like I should accept him looking any kind of way."

"Well, Rhonda, you actually should. He's your husband. You married him for his looks or the man he is?"

"Both. If I blew up thirty pounds and he found that unattractive, I would understand. He likes to look at me and find me attractive. I get that. It's the same with me. He's my husband and I'm attracted to all the things about him that I love. But I also liked that he was a fine, handsome man with a nice body.

"And, wait — I know you're not coming at me like that. You're the same woman who constantly talks about needing a fine man, eye candy."

"Yeah, but I'm not married. When you're married, it should be about the man, not how the man looks."

Rhonda turned defensive and irritated.

"Who are you to determine what anything should be like for me?" she said. "You manage your life, I'll manage mine."

"Don't get mad. I'm keeping it real."

"It's not about keeping it real. It's about keeping it *right*," Rhonda snapped back. "And I mean Eric has to keep himself right. I have to keep myself right for him. That's it, that's all."

"I'm just saying."

"And I'm saying let's skip the subject. What's going on in your love life since you're so interested in mine?"

"You shouldn't be so touchy. I thought you said you were getting good sex. You're acting like you ain't had none."

Rhonda was not going to be lured into more conversation about her love life or marriage. "Are you getting any?" she asked Olivia.

"I will be, if you must know."

"Really? Who?"

"Remember the guy we saw at Suite Lounge . . . Lorenzo?"

A knot filled Rhonda's stomach. It was hard for her to act casual.

"Oh, that guy? I thought you didn't like him."

"I never said that. Said I had to think about it. I thought about it and I think I'm gonna give him some."

"How do you know he wants some?"

"Why wouldn't he?"

"I don't know. Have you been talking to him? Is he interested in you?"

"You were there — he wants me. I haven't talked to him much since that night, but I did text him the other day and he texted me back."

"So, what did you say? What did he say?"

Rhonda tried to sound as if she were being inquisitive, not nosey. But Olivia picked up on it.

"Why you so interested?"

"I'm asking questions like you do. You told me you were holding out and not that interested in the guy. Now you're throwing it at him."

"I'm not throwing it at him. I'm saying I like the fact that he hasn't been chasing me like most men. He made himself more interesting by not acting too interested."

"And that's it? Sounds like a game to me."

"It *is* a game. You're married — you don't know what it's like out here. You have someone. As a single woman out here, you'd better be up on your game to survive."

"Who has time for all that?"

"It's better than being in a marriage you don't want to be in. I'm not saying that's you. I'm saying that was *me*. I don't like being single. But I didn't like being married to the wrong person, either. So, I have to play the game to control my happiness."

Rhonda's happiness had come to depend on her encounters with Lorenzo, and she did not want it threatened by anyone, especially her friend. So the next ninety minutes she spent with Olivia were torture. She wanted to speak to Lorenzo. Since she couldn't, she got what answers she could through Olivia.

"So what's the deal with that guy, what's his name? Lorenzo?" she asked. "I hope you really like him."

"I always liked him. But I wasn't sure I was going to take it where he wanted it to go."

"Where did he want it to go?"

"He wanted me to be his woman. I wasn't ready for that. I still don't want that."

"But you want to sleep with him?"

"It's a new day. Not a better day for women, but it's a new day. We take what we can get in some cases. In some cases, we take what we want."

"So now you want Lorenzo?"

"I'm going to find out if I want him. If I don't, I'll move on."

"And sex is the way to find out if you want him?"

"It's one way."

"Isn't that the one way that puts you in a no-win situation? Look, if you give him sex without building a relationship, how do you think he's going to look at you? You think he's going to want to build something with you if you give him sex so easily, so quickly? That's the quickest way to lose his respect."

Rhonda was well aware that she had done exactly what she told Olivia not to do. But she had already done it and couldn't take it back. And she didn't want to take it back because it was good and liberating. And she did not want Lorenzo to have Olivia, too.

"I thought about that," Olivia said. "Men can do all kinds of stuff without anyone questioning them. But if a woman decides to play the field or test the waters or what-ever, we're the worst creatures on earth. You know that's been the case for a long time. But that's changing."

Rhonda could not disagree with the double standard. She did not want Lorenzo sexing her friend, though. It was not like she had any right to weigh in or determine anything he did. But she was going to do her best behind the scenes to protect what she considered her territory.

"I don't want you to put yourself out there and have that guy thinking you're some kind of desperate chick who will do anything for sex because there are so many more women than men," Rhonda said. She was almost embarrassed by the statement. She hoped Olivia did not see through it.

"I ain't doing all that thinking," Olivia said. "I'm gonna find out if I really like the guy enough to get with him. It couldn't be long term. He's a bartender, for goodness' sake."

That surprised Rhonda. Lorenzo had told her he would be opening a restaurant. How could Olivia, who knew him before Rhonda met him, not know that? Or was she telling the truth and he was lying? Suddenly, it was no longer about keeping Olivia from Lorenzo. It was about learning about Lorenzo.

"A bartender — not that there's anything wrong with that," she said. "But I thought you said he owned a restaurant."

"Owned a restaurant? He barely owns a

203

car. He's a nice guy, but I met him through his cousin, who used to go to my church. Said Lorenzo is a great guy, but doesn't have nothing but dreams. That's it."

Rhonda suddenly became confused. Did Olivia know of what she spoke? Had Lorenzo deceived her to impress her and thereby get her into bed? And what did it matter; she only wanted sex with him anyway?

She excused herself and went to the bathroom, where she texted Lorenzo.

I'm here with Olivia and she says you want her and she's going to give you some. What's that about?

You're telling me something I never heard from her. I haven't seen or talked to her. But I'm glad you care.

Rhonda cared, but she didn't *want* to care.

Should I care?

I'm glad you do. But you shouldn't worry about Olivia. I'm not interested.

Men don't have to be interested to have sex.

That sounds overly judgmental.

But it's true, right?

I'm sure it is for some men. But I think you should judge me for me.

All I can do right now is judge.

What are you wearing?

What?

Why don't you cum over here so we can work it out.

What time?

And just like that, all the concerns over Olivia and her throwing herself at him and if he was a bartender or restaurant owner . . . all of it rinsed down the proverbial "who cares?" drain. Rhonda wanted to protect what she considered hers.

She returned to Olivia and tried to move the conversation toward work or family or the TV show *Power* — anything other than Lorenzo.

When ten o'clock came, she paid her portion of the bill, placed her wallet and cell phone in her purse and headed for the door.

"You seem anxious to get home," Olivia said. "Must gonna get some tonight."

"Not that it's any of your business, but I will get some. Call Lorenzo. Maybe he'll give you some."

"I think I will. Tell you about it tomorrow."

She smiled, knowing Olivia would be rejected. "Please do. I want to hear all the juicy details."

CHAPTER FIFTEEN: FACING TRUTHS

Stephanie

Wilhemina found the text message from her mom curious, so she called Stephanie.

After the pleasantries, the child went in. "You don't want me to come home this weekend?"

"I was thinking next weekend would be better, that's all. There is an August Wilson play that opens on Friday, *Gem of the Ocean.* I saw it years ago. It's excellent. And I'd like to take you to it."

"What about Dad?"

"Him, too."

Stephanie then took a risk.

"But if this weekend is better for you, then all right."

She knew her daughter — she was an actor who loved plays. So Stephanie attacked her weak spot.

"I actually read *Gem of the Ocean* for a class," she said. "August Wilson is my favorite playwright. I can't wait to see it on stage."

Stephanie let out a sigh of relief. Her date with Charles would not be interrupted, as her lie about having to see Toya through her troubles on Saturday gave her a pass out of the house without question.

To avoid Toya and Willie speaking, Stephanie lied to her sister. "He's all upset and wants to ask you about what's going on with me. I acted like it was fine with me, but it wasn't. I know you probably want to tell him. I know you."

"I do want to tell him, but I won't. It's not my place. And I wouldn't cause that kind of trouble for you. But I also don't want to lie to him. So I won't be calling your home number for a while. And if he calls me, I'm not answering. But you need to do right by that man before this whole thing blows up in your face."

Her words made sense, but nothing Stephanie did made sense at that point. She was deep in an *"I want what I want"* mindset, and critical words or logical thinking were not going to reel her in.

Friday night, after dinner at The Cook and Her Farmer in Oakland, Willie suggested going to a birthday party for the former owner of Geoffrey's, a nightclub that was a stellar staple for years between various locations. Stephanie had her mind on getting some rest so she could look her best for Charles and have the energy to perform the way she wanted.

She knew her husband as well as she knew her daughter, and so she played to his personality.

"If you really want to, that's fine."

Stephanie knew that Willie took "fine" as code for "I'd rather not."

"It was *just* a suggestion," he said. "We used to love hanging at Geoffrey's."

"Yes, we did. Maybe we can find a movie at home and relax. I've had a long week — you have, too. Let's relax. On top of that, I don't know what's in store for me tomorrow, dealing with Toya."

"I feel bad about that," Willie said. "I hope they work it out. They haven't been married as long as we have, but they have a lot of history."

"That's true, but history doesn't hold a marriage together, Willie."

"I didn't say it did; I'm saying they've spent a long time together and it would seem like a waste if they split."

"Nothing in life is a waste. We learn from everything."

"What are you saying? You're cool with

them splitting?"

"No. I'm saying it would not be a waste if they did. They had a lot of experiences together. They both learned from each other and grew. They wouldn't be the people they are if they hadn't grown together and learned from each other."

"They have eighteen years together. We have twenty-four. Those are a lot of years. You get past the early drama, and you believe you should be together forever. That's what I see in them. That's what I see in us. If it doesn't happen, it would be a shame."

"Well, you're right about that — so don't do something to make me leave your ass."

Willie laughed. "What you see is what you have gotten."

Stephanie thought to herself: *And that's the problem. I'd like to see something else. Some energy. Some spirit. Some something.*

"That's true, husband. I hope things are better for them. I will let you know tomorrow night after I see Toya."

"Tomorrow night? I thought you were picking her up at noon."

"I am . . . but I'm thinking this is a time when we could go visit Mama's gravesite, have some lunch, go to a movie . . . I don't know. Sort of keep her mind off their troubles while also talking about them."

"That doesn't mean you have to spend the whole day and night doing that," Willie said. "Baby girl isn't coming home until next week now. So I wanted to do something with you — a movie. We haven't been to a movie since . . . I can't even remember. And we both like movies."

Stephanie considered that an indictment against Willie. He was more of a movie-lover than she, and yet he had not suggested a film in almost a year. That was the activity they had shared the most, and they were not doing that.

"I will call or text you so you know what time I'll be back," she offered.

"Text? You know that's not me. Call me. What's the big deal? It's less effort to call than to push all those buttons."

"Willie, I will call. And I will try to be done early. I don't want to dump her, you know what I mean?"

"You want me to call Terry? Maybe I should see what he's doing and meet him somewhere. Maybe he'll open up to me and I can be of some comfort to him."

That was the last thing Stephanie wanted, so she jumped in with another fabrication.

"Toya told me he was playing golf in the morning with some guys from college, I think. Or maybe it was coworkers. But she asked me to hang out with her to give her something to do. You know them: Every Saturday they usually do something."

"That's true," Willie conceded. "Man, I hope they work it out. But I'm glad you're being a good sister."

"It's me and Toya. We have to take care of each other."

They made it home and instead of identifying a movie, Willie put the TV on the Golf Channel, which was great for Stephanie; she had no interest in the sport and it would help put her to sleep. The sooner she dozed off, the sooner she could wake up and be closer to seeing Charles.

When the morning came, she was exuberant. Lively. Excited. She anticipated an involved conversation with Charles, the attention he offered, the compliments and his touch.

They had planned to meet at noon at the Fisherman's Wharf in San Francisco. Willie left the house first, which solved a big concern Stephanie had: How she was going to get her overnight bag out of the house without Willie noticing. But he made a Home Depot run before Stephanie went into the shower.

"I might not be back before you leave," he

said. "So tell Toya hello for me. Keep me posted on how it goes."

"I will, honey."

She rushed out of the shower, got herself together, packed the small bag and headed to the city. When she arrived, Charles was already there, leaning against the rail and looking out toward Alcatraz.

"I'm taking a chance being out in public like this," Stephanie said. "You live in L.A. You're safe here. But I'm not."

"But you love the rush, being on the edge, don't you?"

Stephanie wanted to act offended, but she couldn't help but smile.

"I knew it," Charles said.

"You don't know me. You only know my body."

"Well, I know you a little. I know your body a lot. But we still have to get better acquainted."

Stephanie shook her head in amusement.

"But, seriously, if you see someone you know, give me a sign and I will play the role, move away, act like I'm a family friend, whatever I need to protect you."

Charles earned points with Stephanie for his willingness to deceive. She knew it was silly because she was cheating, but she felt protected with him, the way she wished she felt with her husband.

"Thank you. And I believe you."

They made it through the line and onto the ferry to Sausalito without seeing anyone who knew them. The water was a little choppy, so Stephanie sat much of the twenty-five-minute ride across the Bay to the quaint town.

She felt better the last ten minutes and joined Charles outside to soak up a gorgeous, partly cloudy day that offered flashes of sun, warm temperatures and picturesque clouds.

"I don't mean to talk about my husband, and especially to you, but this is crazy," she started. "He has never, not once, taken me here, suggested we come. He never told me he even knew it existed."

"Let's not worry about that. Actually, let's count it as a blessing that we can be together now. I mean, if he had taken you here in the past, maybe you wouldn't be here now. Or maybe you wouldn't feel as you do now. We get to experience it together. We're taking each other on a journey away from our home lives."

Stephanie pondered those words as Charles checked in at the front desk. He got the keys to their room overlooking the bay. He spared no expense, and Stephanie appreciated that he was willing to extend himself to help create the most comfortable environment for them.

"This is beautiful," she said, opening the drapes and looking out on the massive water that was highlighted by sailboats. "So beautiful. I'm almost sad."

"Sad? Why?"

"Because I can't stay. I have to leave at some point, and I really don't want to. I'd love to spend the night here with you and enjoy the peace."

"Then stay."

Those three words convinced Stephanie to do that. But how? She was up to her earrings in lies as it was. What could she come up with that Willie would accept?

"That's easier said than done. I already said I'd be home tonight and he questioned me about that."

"I'm not putting any pressure on you."

"I know. I'm just saying . . . But maybe I will call my sister."

"The sister you said has been on your ass about us? The sister who obviously hates me? The sister who wants you to end it with me? That sister? Why would you call her?"

"To cover for me. I already told him I'm with her today. I don't need her to lie for me. I need her to not make herself available to my husband."

"She has a husband, right? Won't he call him if he can't reach either of you?"

Stephanie's shoulders dropped. "Yeah, he will. He wanted to call him today."

"So, it's hard for me to say this, but don't risk the drama. There will be other times. In fact, you should come to L.A. for a weekend."

"Let's not talk about any of that right now. I want to enjoy all of this."

Charles nodded his head and pulled out a bottle of champagne, brie and crackers, two small plates and a knife. "This is perfect for a day like today," he said.

Stephanie set up the small table on the balcony and they enjoyed the snacks and bubbly, the view and each other, hardly saying a word for several minutes.

"This peace right here, I love," she said, looking out at the elements. "Gorgeous and relaxing."

"This is how life should be, really," Charles said.

"What are we going to do? I'm not trying to get heavy, but we're having these wonderful experiences together, but you have someone at home and I have someone at home. I think all the time now: Am I brave enough to leave?"

"Do you really want to leave? I'm trying to be pragmatic or play the devil's advocate. Do you want to leave? Are you ready to leave?"

"I don't know — but I think about it. A lot of it would depend on you."

"Me?"

"If you are strong enough to leave, I can be strong enough."

Charles was not ready to hear that from Stephanie. He poured more champagne in both glasses and took a sip of his.

"You're right: We'd have to be strong to leave," he finally said. "Do we have that strength? Should we walk? It's not cut and dried."

"It may not be, but, when all the bullshit is washed away Charles, it's only me and you left. That's how I see it."

"I see it differently. I see my wife and your husband and agony. I see us hurting people we actually love and have built a life with. That's not something I want to envision."

"You think I want that? You think I don't have a heart, that I don't love my husband? I do. But, at the same time, I'm in a place now where I should be living. My daughter is gone and making her way. She's happy. Willie is happy, apparently. Everyone's happy but me. I want more. But you're say-

216

ing I should stay so I won't hurt other people's feelings?"

"That's not a small thing, Stephanie. Think about your daughter. I know she's a young lady and doing things. But her parents are her rock. Her parents *together.* A divorce can be harder on older children than younger. You don't want to do that to her."

"Sounds to me like you're skirting the issue. I've heard you speak, remember? You're good at being passive-aggressive and —"

"What? Passive-aggressive?"

"Yes. You address stuff without taking it head-on. You're trying that with me right now."

"I'm trying to stay patient here. Tell me what you're talking about."

"You're giving me all the reasons to stay, but no reasons to leave. You're not saying what you really want to say."

"Which is what, since you know how my brain works?"

"You don't want me to leave because you want to stay."

Charles finished off his champagne and took a deep breath.

"You're right, Stephanie. You're right. You're right because I don't have a reason to leave. And I have said you shouldn't leave because you don't have one, either. Listen, what we're creating, it's great. I look forward to seeing you and sharing thoughts on what's going on in the world, with public education, you name it. I enjoy our passion. A lot.

"But we're just getting started at this. Do we turn our worlds — and our spouses' worlds — upside down when we don't know what *this* will turn into? I say we don't. I say we continue to spend time together when we can, communicate every day as we have, and build on this. But to talk about it now, after less than two months, that's too fast.

"Think about it this way: If we both were single, would we be talking about moving in together or getting married? After two months?"

"People do it all the time after less time than that."

"So, you're telling me you're ready to leave your husband to be with me?"

"Yes. I think so."

"See, it would be stronger if you said you were ready to leave for a better life, for peace, to regain your sense of self. Almost anything would be better than leaving for me . . . or any man. I'm flattered that you feel so strongly about me. But I'm a little sad that you aren't looking for more. You can't look for a man to solve your problems or to save you from your life."

Charles' logic embarrassed Stephanie, who was smart and rational on most days. But her emotions ruled.

"You've got me all twisted up," she said. Charles looked at her and she smiled.

"You're right. I'm getting carried away." She took a deep breath and recalibrated her emotions and expectations. "See, this is why I like you so much. You give me the balanced, honest view. I need that sometimes, especially when emotions are involved."

"Here," he said, pouring more champagne and then raising his glass. "Let's have a toast and then take a nap."

"Oh, yeah. A nap sounds great," she said, unbuttoning her shirt. "All of a sudden I'm getting so sleepy."

Charles feigned a big yawn. "Me, too."

They then took a final gulp of the bubbly and went inside to the room, taking off their clothes in the process.

"All that talk made me horny," Stephanie said.

"Don't even try it — you were horny when you woke up."

"That's true. See, you're getting to know me."

They kissed and helped each other finish undressing. They did not bother to pull back the sheets. Stephanie lay on her back and Charles ravaged her body with kisses and passion. And when they were done, about a half-hour later, they fell asleep in each other's arms, a deep sleep that took them far from their real lives.

Chapter Sixteen: Closing In

Juanita

Maurice grew increasingly concerned about Juanita's behavior. She kept her cell phone closer to her and regularly used it for texting purposes. She seldom was available during the day when he called her at work. And she had stopped taking the occasional ride into the office with her husband.

He had a golf trip scheduled for a weekend at Pinehurst in North Carolina, but was reluctant to go. He was suspicious of his wife's fidelity, and it left him feeling sick to his stomach.

He was not sure how to deal with his turmoil. If he addressed it with Juanita and was wrong, she would be aghast. If he were right, he'd be crestfallen. Either option made him more convinced to say nothing and to observe more closely than ever.

It ate him up that he had no one to share his uncertainty. His family adored Juanita and would think he was paranoid . . . or worse. Her family praised her existence in every way. He could not tell his friends — it would be humiliating to tell them he thought his wife was cheating on him.

Finally, though, after three vodka and tonics and two beers, he woke up Juanita one Saturday night. He surmised that the element of surprise would catch her off guard and reveal something. He could not go on any longer feeling so uneasy.

"You sleep?" he said as he shook her out of her slumber.

"Huh? What's wrong?"

She could smell the alcohol on his breath.

"Are you cheating on me?"

Juanita was prepared for that question. She had rehearsed her answer to the inevitable question more than a dozen times.

"Yes," she said. "I have two boyfriends. I see one as you're eating dinner that I cooked after I leave work and come straight home. The other one I see in the church basement, during Sunday School."

Maurice did not expect that answer. He expected her to be outraged at the accusation.

"Now can I go back to sleep? I'm meeting my boyfriend at the playground with the kids tomorrow. I need my rest."

She plopped her head back down on her pillow and turned her back to Maurice, who felt so silly that he got up and left the bedroom.

Juanita lay there with her heart pumping. She expected him to question her at some point, but the reality of it frightened her. She also knew that the questioning was not over. Maurice, when sober, would explain his question.

She decided then to take the lead, to bring up the subject in the morning, to put Maurice on the defensive. She thought of many ways to protect her secret. She did not consider leaving Brandon alone.

So after breakfast, she got the kids settled in their room in front of their Xbox, and addressed her husband.

"Can you explain why you insulted me last night?" Juanita asked. She felt like an actress. "I mean, really Maurice."

"Well, first off, I'm sorry," he said. "I wasn't trying to insult you. I was trying to get some answers."

"You question my faithfulness?"

"I don't. I had questions because you don't seem to be yourself. I call you at work and you're never available. Even after our last session with Dr. Fields, I tried to surprise you by taking you to lunch, but when I went to your office, you weren't there. And no one knew where you were."

Juanita's heart rate climbed and her mind raced. "I went and got a massage that day, in Bethesda," she said. "I called in after the session and my meeting was cancelled, so I tried to get some tension relieved with a massage. Does that make you think I'm cheating on you?"

"I didn't know where you were. And then there's this talk with the doctor about sex. It makes me feel like you're not satisfied."

"And I'm the type who would go and get satisfied somewhere else? Maurice, I'm so insulted. We have a family. I've lived my life doing the right thing. And that's what you think of me?"

"Baby, I'm sorry. I want you and us to be happy. When things aren't right, my mind goes crazy places. Please forgive me. I won't do any of this again."

"Any of what?"

Maurice looked away briefly and took a deep breath. "I won't accuse you anymore and I won't go through your things."

"What things? What are you talking about?"

"I'm only admitting this because I want you to know how concerned I was . . . I looked through your cell phone."

"You what?"

"I was trying to figure some things out. And . . . I'm sorry."

Juanita walked to the kids' room, checked on them and closed the door. Then she stormed back to Maurice, who was in the family room.

"That's unacceptable, Maurice. You have no right to go through my phone, through my anything. What's wrong with you? That's a violation I cannot accept. Keep your fucking hands off my phone."

It was rare that Juanita used profanity. In fact, Maurice had not heard her curse since before they got married, when she was upset over a grade she'd received in business school.

"I'm sorry. I was panicked and I . . . I just did it."

"I don't have a lock on my phone because I don't have anything to hide. At the same time, it's my phone. I don't go through your things, Maurice. Never have. You're entitled to your own space and what's yours is yours. I'm so angry right now. Shit."

"I sincerely apologize, 'Nita. I do. It won't happen again. I promise."

Juanita was mad, but she put extra on it to make her point. She realized that if she had not deleted her exchanges to and from

Brandon, there would have been chaos and her family would be in jeopardy.

"I hope you found something that made you feel better."

"I found nothing, and that made me feel better. Well, there was this one phone number I didn't recognize. You called it a couple of times."

"And you want me to answer questions about numbers I dialed from my phone? Are you serious?"

"No, I don't. I already called the number." Juanita held her breath. "It was the massage place you said you went to."

"Maurice, do not go through my things again. I can't believe you."

She was relieved. And to avoid showing it, she turned her back to her husband and left him standing there, feeling foolish. And while he felt somewhat embarrassed in exposing himself, Maurice also was relieved. He had successfully investigated if Juanita had any questions about his infidelity. By raising his questions, he knew she would raise hers as a counter if she had any. She did not do that, so the cheating Maurice was engaged in was not under scrutiny.

Months before Juanita called Brandon, Maurice had met Gloria Wright, a Capitol Hill attorney who was walking to the parking lot toward her car as Maurice headed the same way. He'd offered to help her with a box she carried; she was moving from one job to another.

He'd asked her if she had celebrated the new job, and she told him that her closest friend who would normally celebrate with her was out of town. Gloria also had shared that she was going through a divorce and was not in a celebratory mood anyway. But Maurice had offered to treat her to a cocktail, and she had accepted.

After two drinks, they'd moved from the bar to a small booth and had wound up kissing and groping each other. "I can't believe this is happening," he'd said to her.

"Why? Because you're married?"

"No. Well, yes, that too. But because you're beautiful. I didn't expect this."

"I didn't, either. We kind of hit it off, I guess. But I'm sorry. I don't mean to disrespect your marriage."

"By all means, disrespect it," he'd said, laughing. "I'm not going to lie to you: I love my wife. But you're like . . . not even a breath of fresh air. You're a tsunami of fresh air."

Gloria had laughed and blushed at the same time. "Well, I'd like to see you again, if you'd like that," she'd said.

"I sure would."

So, every other Saturday, when he dressed for golf, Maurice would take a trip to Annapolis with Gloria. Or he'd go to her Capitol Hill home and they'd make each other cocktails, cook together and make love. The sex did not happen until his third visit, but once they got started, it was a consistent part of their relationship.

Often, since she lived so close to where they worked, they would rendezvous at her house for lunch. They'd eat whatever leftovers she had made for dinner the previous night and then delight on each other. And then go back to work, thoroughly satisfied.

Maurice was almost overwhelmed with the situation. "Please don't think I'm crazy to ask this — and if it's the wrong question that might mess up what we have, please ignore it — but why would you be interested in me? I'm not that handsome. I'm married with two kids. I'm comfortable but not rich. What's the deal?"

"You're a gentleman. You were a gentleman to me when I needed a gentleman in my life. That allowed me to look at you and eventually to open up to you. Let's face it: My life isn't the greatest right now. I left my job because one of the partners wanted sex with me — and didn't even have the decency to offer me a promotion. I wouldn't have had sex with him under any circumstances, but he thought I should want to sleep with him or would sleep with him because of his position. So I finally took a job making less, but I'm not in fear of getting raped at any moment.

"I'm going through a divorce that's pretty unseemly. He's mad that I don't love him anymore, so he's being an ass. He's a lawyer, too. And that's another reason I like you: You're *not* a lawyer. I've been with three lawyers and that's three too many for me."

"I get it," Maurice had said. "You're using me. And guess what? I have no problem with that."

They'd laughed and their relationship was in full swing. He believed he covered his tracks so cleanly that Juanita had no idea. The reality was that she was so caught up in her own cheating that she was not paying attention.

Chapter Seventeen: Claiming the Claimable

Rhonda

By the time she arrived to Lorenzo's, Olivia had called him.

"What's up with your girl?" he said as Rhonda took a seat at the kitchen bar.

"Who? Olivia?"

"Yeah. She called me. Was all aggressive about getting with me. What brought all this on? What did you say to her?"

"What did I say? I didn't say anything. I *wouldn't* say anything — to anybody. Are you kidding me?"

"Well, I had to ask. You told me she was super-interested all of a sudden and then she calls me."

"*She* brought you up out of the blue. She said she had been in contact with you and decided she was going to give you some coochie."

"I wonder why."

"She's bored and desperate."

"So, that's what it takes for a woman to want me: bored and desperate? That's why you're here?"

"No, it's not."

"Then why are you here? I'm glad you are; no doubt about that. But what's broken at home that can't be fixed?"

Rhonda was not sure how transparent she wanted to be with Lorenzo. But the combination of the drinks from earlier and her desire to be truthful about something combined to open her up.

"My husband — we've been married fourteen years — is either depressed or doesn't care anymore because he has let himself go. I think I'm like a man in this way: I'm more of a visual creature than most women. I like a man's body, how he grooms himself, how he dresses, how he smells. Those things are very important to me. My husband used to hit all those marks. But in the last few years, he has blown up. And what makes me really angry and disappointed is that I've told him about it and he still won't do anything about it."

"So I'm your release, your outlet?"

"I didn't expect for this to happen. But I saw you walking by my house and I was impressed that you were in shape and was taking care of your body. You eat right.

That's a turn-on for me. What's crazy is that I saw you — right? — but didn't get to meet you. Then I go out with Olivia, and there you are.

"I will admit: When I saw you that night, coming over toward us, I thought you were coming to speak to me. But you went right by me to Olivia. I was disappointed."

"Really? I saw you, but I knew Olivia. So I had to speak to her. We had gone out a couple times. But I noticed you, for sure."

"So why me now instead of Olivia?"

"You know Olivia is cool. I like her. Wasn't a real chemistry, a real connection. But with you . . ."

"With me what?"

"With you, it was different. It *is* different. Sometimes it's hard to explain. I felt something. I feel something."

"Maybe because I'm married you thought you could take advantage of that."

"Wait, don't even try it. Nothing happens unless you want it to happen. I didn't make you do anything. Women . . ."

"What do you mean, 'women'?"

"Women kill me. You act like you don't know that you control what happens with a man. We can try hard, try to influence you, romance you, whatever. But if you don't say 'go,' it's not going."

"But where are your morals? I'm married."

"My morals are wherever yours are."

Rhonda got angry, but only for a second. He was right. She knew, as the married one, that the burden was more on her than Lorenzo.

"What does it say about me that I'm doing this?"

"It says you're unhappy."

"But is it shallow to be so disappointed because I'm not happy with the way my husband looks now?"

"Yes, you could call it 'shallow.' But here's the thing: It's *your* life. I'm not saying that to get you out of your clothes — you *do* look good, though. I'm trying to be impartial. What's important to me might not be important to the next person or to you. Who can judge if you're being shallow? You like what you like."

Rhonda nodded her head in agreement.

"So how long could we do this? How long could you do this? You don't think you'd want more from me than sex?"

Lorenzo was stumped. He had not given much thought to how long he and Rhonda would keep up their tryst.

"I get more from you than sex," he said. "I get conversations of substance, which isn't the easiest thing to get out there. As for the sex, as I said, I'm not in control of that. You are."

"But you don't think you'd reach a point where you'd want more from me, to be in a relationship with me?"

"That could happen, sure. I'm trying to stay on an even keel. I know you could end it right now, so I'm, like, mentally ready for it. I have to be this way to protect myself."

Rhonda was impressed that Lorenzo expressed his vulnerability. Men were more likely to accept their fingernails pulled out with pliers than admit they could be hurt. She was turned on.

"So, you can keep this up as long as I want to?"

"I guess we will see, huh?" he said. "If you're good to me, I may be hard to get rid of."

"What if you found another woman? What if Olivia throws herself at you?"

"We can play the 'what if' game all day. The real question is: Can you handle it if I start dating someone?"

He was right. Rhonda had forced herself not to think of that scenario. But when Olivia said she was interested in Lorenzo, her territorial gene kicked in.

"I know I have no right to ask you not to

see anyone else . . ."

"But . . ."

"But I don't want you to see anyone else."

"Why?"

"Because. I mean, you know. It's like, I mean . . ."

"You haven't said anything."

"I'm looking at it like we're in a relationship. I realize how crazy that sounds. I'm being totally honest. When most women have sex with a man, she looks at him as her man. Or she wants him to be her man. That's how we are.

"So with you, considering I'm, you know, married, I have no right to say that. But it's how I feel. I know I have some nerve to ask you to be faithful to me. But I don't want you to see anyone else, especially Olivia."

Lorenzo was flattered but also conflicted. He did not have a desire to date various women, but the beauty of what he had with Rhonda was that he had the freedom to see as many women as he liked — without the concern of having to account for his actions or whereabouts.

And he lived in Atlanta, meaning there was an abundance of women within his reach. He happened to have "cleaned house" right before meeting Olivia, meaning the three women he juggled were cast aside. "Time for a new crew," he'd told his boys. "Time to reload."

They'd laughed about it, but he was serious. He considered Olivia a prospect and even considered bouncing between her and Rhonda, but thought better of it. He still, though, had an interest in seeing other women.

"I don't know how to respond to that, Rhonda. I'm single — you're married. Why should I agree to see only you? That makes no sense."

Rhonda knew the only leverage she had was her body.

"We're doing too much talking," she said. "I came over here not to talk, but to . . ."

"To what?"

"To do whatever you want. I'm not going to try to fool myself about my life. My marriage has lost steam. Eric's weight issues were the latest and greatest problem. But it's been lacking steam for a while. We don't do anything. We don't have any fun. We're going through the motions. I don't want to go through the motions anymore."

"So take off your clothes then."

"Excuse me."

"You heard me. That's why you came over here."

Rhonda was too tired to put up a fight,

mostly because Lorenzo was right.

"I know this is a mistake, but —"

"Mistake? A mistake happens once. If it happens more than once, it's a decision."

Rhonda smiled. She realized, on one hand, that Olivia was right — Lorenzo was all over the place in terms of what he wanted to do with his work life. But he was smart in a quirky kind of way. Clever. And he was straightforward in a tactful way. She liked him. And she liked the bulge in his pants.

"You're right — this is my decision," she said, turning her back to Lorenzo so he could unzip her dress. She let if fall to the floor, never turning around. Again, she wore no panties or bra. She bent her naked body over the counter, inviting Lorenzo to take her from behind. Rhonda did not want to face him; she wanted him to please her — no kissing, no romance. She wanted only pure force and passion.

He had no problem providing her that. In seconds, he dropped his pants and kicked them off from around his ankle. He eased his way into her moistness and Rhonda arched her back and challenged him to give her all he had.

Lorenzo accepted the challenge and held her firmly by her waist and pulled her toward him as he thrust his hips forward. The sound of their bodies smacking filled his home, along with Rhonda's increasingly loud moans. Sweat formed on his brow and after several minutes of sustained pounding, rolled down the side of his face and back.

Rhonda enjoyed the action. She took the pain/pleasure as long as she could. In fact, she took it as a challenge not to break down and buckle under the power of his lunges. It was not until the buildup of pleasure collided in ecstasy at the point of his force, did the pounding cease.

They both collapsed to the floor, breathing heavily, pleased in different ways, but pleased nonetheless. "I needed that," she said as they lay on their backs, looked at the ceiling. "I really needed to be taken advantage of, to feel the aggression of a man I'm attracted to who desired me. I'm not sure you understand that, but that's the truth. I needed to be fucked."

"Wow. Such language," Lorenzo said, laughing. "I will give you this much: You're clear about what you want."

"I gave you all that and that's all you give me, that I'm clear about what I want?"

"Think back over the last fifteen minutes and you'll realize I gave you much more than that," he said.

"That's true. Know how I know? My body tells me so."

Chapter Eighteen:
Trauma Drama

Stephanie

When she woke up from her afternoon delight with Charles, it was almost six o'clock. He was still asleep. He had driven up from L.A. early that morning, and needed to catch up on his rest.

She slid out of the bed without awaking him and slipped into a nightshirt. After a trip to the bathroom, Stephanie stepped out on the balcony, leaned on the rail and pondered her life.

The thrill had abandoned her marriage for some time. The more consumed Willie was with work and building a successful business, the less she was a priority to him. She blamed herself mostly because she felt herself easing away and said nothing about it to her husband and did nothing about it. It was a classic case of the proverbial growing apart.

A huge part of that was her smoldering

animus with Willie. Early in their marriage, she had learned he'd had an affair with a former girlfriend. It was not a lingering thing, he'd insisted and she believed it was a one-night fling. But it had happened nonetheless and it broke their marriage for a year.

She had found out about it in the most unique way: Willie had told her. They had celebrated their third wedding anniversary. After a weekend in Reno, Nevada, where they'd won $800 gambling, fished in Lake Tahoe and generally had a beautiful time together, Willie had told Stephanie they needed to talk.

They were on their couch in the first home they'd bought together in Alameda. He had been drinking much of the unusually chilly November evening. When Stephanie had asked him, "Are you as happy as I am?" he'd spoken his truth.

"I'm more happy than you are probably," he'd said. "I was in a place with our marriage last year where I didn't think it would last. I'm only being honest."

"I remember when we had our issues, our growing pains," she'd said.

"To be where we are now after being where we were is pretty crazy."

"It wasn't that bad, was it?" she'd asked.

"Maybe not for you. But I was being pulled all different directions."

"By who? By what?"

"We weren't getting along that great and then Theresa, my old girlfriend kept nagging me and —"

"What? You were talking to her? Why?"

"Because we weren't getting along that well. So she and I would talk and then one night —"

"One night *what*?"

"That one night when you were upset with me because I said I'd rather not spend Thanksgiving with your mother, and —"

"Yeah, I remember the night. What about it?"

"That night I thought you overreacted when you left me in the house, sitting there like a fool. So I called Theresa and one thing led to another."

"And? What the hell does that mean, Willie?"

"I called you that night, if you remember, but you wouldn't answer. So I ended up going over to her house."

"You what?"

"I know, it was stupid. But I can tell you about it now because we've overcome the early troubles and now we're great."

"What did you do at her house, Willie?"

He had looked away from his wife. He knew in every symbolic "man code book" there is never a mention of telling the truth when it came to infidelity. In fact, it says to "never admit" to an affair. And yet, in his drunken state, Willie went against the No. 1 code.

"It didn't mean anything," he'd said, which in the "man code book" is a sentence never to utter to your woman, along with the other one he'd told Stephanie: "It just happened."

The joy they had found in their relationship was shattered like a Christmas ornament falling to the floor. Stephanie had screamed and cursed. Willie had cried and begged for forgiveness. They went to counseling every week for a year. It wasn't until Willie comforted her with attention and love as she dealt with her mother's death that she finally saw beyond his indiscretion and truly forgave him.

As Stephanie came to grips with her mother's death, she and Willie came back together as a couple. Still, while she forgave him for putting their marriage on the line, she never forgot that he hurt her and dishonored her. She moved on from it, but somewhere in her mind, it was always there.

She believed she had payback to get, if

she ever was so moved. He'd cheated on her and she'd forgiven him. If he ever caught her cheating, Willie had her actions when he cheated as a blueprint on how to respond to it.

Charles was Stephanie's payback, more than a decade later.

She understood all this time later her cheating would jeopardize her marriage if Willie found out. Men were less tolerant of infidelity, their pride more times than not unable to take knowing another man had been with his woman.

But it felt right to Stephanie, not wrong, to be with Charles. She had refused to consider the feelings of his wife. She did so because she knew it would bother her. So, she kept her head down, focusing solely on her needs and desires.

That focus drove her to the idea that she would stay with Charles at the hotel. She would figure out something to tell Willie. The room, the view, the feeling, Charles . . . all felt too good to end.

She went back into the room to tell Charles just that. He had awakened and was sitting on the side of the bed.

"I'm going to stay," she said. "Can I stay with you?"

"You're joking, right? Is that a trick question? I dreaded having to be here by myself, sitting at some bar, eating dinner, the whole time wishing we were together."

"That was the perfect answer."

She then retrieved her cell phone from her purse. It showed three missed calls from Terry, her sister Toya's husband. "Oh, shit."

"What?" Charles asked.

"My brother-in-law called three times. Why is he calling me?"

"Could it be about us?"

"It has to be. What else could it be?"

"Call him back."

Stephanie used a few minutes to craft a story before she called. She stepped on the balcony and waited for Terry to answer.

"What's going on?" she asked.

"We're at Highland Hospital on Thirty-first."

"What happened?"

"I'm still not sure. Toya passed out. We were headed to the movies and she collapsed. She hit her head and is unconscious. She's with the doctors."

"Oh, my God. I'll be there fast as I can. And don't worry about calling Willie. I will call him. She's going to be all right, Terry. She has to be."

She returned to the room with teary eyes.

"He found out?" Charles said.

"No. That was my brother-in-law. My sister is in the hospital."

"What? What happened?"

"They aren't sure yet. She passed out and hit her head. She's with doctors now. I've got to go."

She hurriedly got dressed, brushed her teeth, packed her bag and teased her hair. Charles hurriedly dressed and walked with her to the dock, where the boat was boarding back to San Francisco. He bought tickets for both of them.

"I know I can't go to the hospital, but I can spend this time with you on the boat."

"That's so nice of you. Charles, if something happens to Toya, I won't know what to do with myself."

"You've got to put positive vibes out there. You can't think the worst. All good vibes help."

They took a seat on the ferry and he hugged Stephanie as they both sat in silence. She prayed a consistent silent prayer.

When they got to Fisherman's Wharf, he walked her to the parking lot where she had left her car. "I'm praying all is well," he said. "Please call or text me to let me know what's going on. But stay positive."

They hugged and kissed and she sped off. She waited until she got onto the Bay

Bridge before she called her husband.

"Willie, meet me at Highland Hospital. Toya fainted and is in emergency."

"What?"

"Yes. Terry cancelled golf and he and Toya went to the movies. He called to tell me."

The combination of the alarming news and the panic in Stephanie's voice had the impact she wanted: Willie did not question where she had been all day. That gave her some relief, but she remained riddled with worry about Toya.

They had their obvious differences about her affair with Charles. But they were each other's keepers. As kids, they slept in the same room and talked to each other in the dark about everything imaginable until they fell asleep. They kept that up even as adults, when they took trips without their husbands.

When Stephanie, who was two years younger, was a senior in high school, her family had struggled to raise the money for her to go to college. Toya did not go to school past twelfth grade; she had worked as an executive assistant in a law firm in San Francisco. She had saved money for two years and when it was time for her little sister to enroll in college, Toya had provided the money for Stephanie to advance her education. That's how close they were.

And when Toya had married Terry, Stephanie had planned the wedding, hosted the bridal shower and the bachelorette party and served as matron of honor. And when they lost their mother, they drew on each other for strength. They had myriad friends between them — none of them closer than the sisters.

All those thoughts ran through Stephanie's head as she weaved through traffic to get to the hospital. She was scared.

Terry spotted her before she saw him. He hugged her.

"What did they say?"

"The doctors put her in a coma, a drug-induced coma," he said.

"What?"

"When she fainted, her head slammed on the edge of a concrete step. So there was trauma and stress to her brain. The way they explained it to me, the medically induced coma relieves stress off her brain and they can take her out of the coma when they need to, after the swelling goes down."

Tears flowed down Stephanie's face. "Can I see her?"

"Come on," Terry said, leading her to her room.

Before going in, Stephanie wiped her face

and gathered herself and took a deep breath. She walked in and immediately burst into tears again. The sight of her sister hooked up to tubes and machines horrified her. Terry hugged her and whispered into her ear.

"You have to be strong. They say she can't hear us, but they don't really know. So we have to talk to her, let her know we're here for her."

Stephanie nodded her head and composed herself again. She went to her sister's bedside, as Terry left the room.

"Girl, it's me. I'm here and I know you're just getting your rest. Your behind loves to sleep. I didn't know you'd go to this length to get more sleep."

She laughed, although tears seeped through her eyes.

"I gotta tell you, though. It scares me to see you like this, in here. But you'll never be alone. Between me, Terry and Willie, you will always have someone by your side. I'll tell you about Charles, too. Probably tomorrow. If anything will wake you up, that will do it, I'm sure. But I want to tell you this right now: I love you, Toya. And I need you. So get as much rest as you need. But you get better. Fast. You are the only person on this earth I cannot live without."

She sensed someone was in the room and looked up to see Willie.

"She's the only person, huh?" he said.

Stephanie left Toya's bedside and walked over to Willie. "That's what you have to ask me as my sister lays in a coma? I don't think so."

She stared at her husband for a few seconds and returned to her bedside, where she held her hand and rubbed it. Willie stood back, near the foot of the bed, his arms folded. Stephanie did not acknowledge his presence.

Chapter Nineteen: The *Real* Me

Juanita

"Is it only about sex for you?"

That was the question Brandon asked Juanita as they sat at the bar at Marvin's at Fourteenth and U Streets. It was a simple question, on its face. For Juanita, it was complicated.

"I never thought about it. I'm not trying to use you for sex, if that's what you're asking."

"Then what do you want from this? You're not leaving your cushy life. You have a good job, a husband who loves you, a BMW, two great kids. What are you doing fucking around with me? Seriously. I need to know this."

Juanita knew Brandon deserved the truth, especially after asking such an honest question. She wanted to answer, but she had to wait until the bartender moved to the other end of the bar.

She leaned into Brandon's left ear. "These fucking bartenders are eavesdroppers. He's fooling around down here for no good reason. Just trying to hear our conversation. Ever notice that?"

"Damned right I noticed it. Happens all the time. I don't say shit around them. And watch, he's going now, but he'll be back to try to catch something we're talking about."

Juanita smiled for two reasons: One, she could use the word "fuck" with Brandon without hesitation or concern of being judged and, two, it was funny to her that he noticed how bartenders tend to hang near people involved in deep conversation.

"Anyway," she said. "you know why I'm messing around with you, as you put it? Because I can be myself with you. You're the *only* person I can be myself with. Literally. I can use profanity and listen to rap and go-go music and drink hard liquor and I can give you head while getting a massage and you don't judge me. You know that's me and you're okay with that.

"Now, that said, I'm not being fake about anything in my life. I'm the person my husband knows and I'm good to my kids and kind to people and friendly and all that. I go to church and teach Bible study and I believe in God. I volunteer at PTA meetings and with my sorority. I *am* a good person. I am the person people see and know.

"But if people see you a certain way, they judge if you show them more than who they *think* you are. In a relationship, I am passionate and sometimes wild. I'm not a lay-on-my-back-and-give-it-to-me wife. I'm not, but that's what I have been. I'm trapped inside this perception that I'm a prude who's delicate and so proper. And I'm not that at all.

"I don't blame my husband. Everyone's different. He's not an exotic kind of lover. He's just, 'Let's do this and keep it moving.' As you know, I'm more than that. *Way* more than that. But since I've been so stale with Maurice all these years, if I come out of my bag now, he'd feel some way about it. He has me in the boring-ass box that I just can't take anymore."

"Trust me, he will like it if you busted out of that box. I promise."

"With most men, I would believe that. But I have tested it over the years. Told him once at a restaurant: 'Come to the bathroom with me.' You know what he said? 'Why?' We saw some movie where the woman was demanding her man fuck her good — see, I can't even say 'fuck' around Maurice; he'd think something was wrong with me — and he was mortified that the woman, in the heat of the moment, used profanity.

"So, I've created this mess for myself because when we first started dating, I followed his lead and that made me reserved and in a shell. I wouldn't be here with you now if I had a husband I could be sexually free with — someone who is what you might call 'a freak.'

"I certainly wouldn't call you or me a freak. That's an overused and inappropriately used description of someone who has an open sexual identity and sexual freedom. You know what I mean?"

"Sound like you read that out of a dictionary. But I get it. Listen, my boy Larry and I talk about it all the time. I know guys who meet women, date them for a while and finally have sex and come back calling her a 'freak.' So, I'm like, 'What makes her a freak?' And he'd say, 'Man, she was trying to have sex in the movies.' And I'd say, 'And what's the problem? That doesn't make her a freak. It makes *you* a freak that you think there's something wrong with that.'"

"That's my husband. He's so conservative about sex and passion. I made the cardinal sin women make: I thought I could change him. I thought, especially when we first got married, that I could wear little outfits for him and slowly open him up to being erotic. Shit, I danced for him and he told me to stop. Said I looked like a stripper. I said, 'That's the point.'

"I hinted around going to a strip club when we were in Miami one time, before the kids came. I said, 'You know, men go to strip clubs with their significant others now.' I was hoping he'd ask me if I would go. Instead, he said, 'That's ridiculous.' So I knew not to bring it up again.

"Obviously, he's my husband and he has great qualities. But I'm thirty-four years old. I'm more sexual now than I have ever been — and will only get more sexual as I get older. So, what am I to do? Deny myself my whole life?"

Juanita also liked Brandon because he was honest with her and did not shape his opinions to benefit him.

"If you had married me, you wouldn't be in this situation," he said, laughing. "I know I was a fuck-up, though, not really sure of where I wanted to go with my life. You were always focused. So, while we were a match in some areas, others we weren't."

"But, Brandon, people don't seem to put enough importance on sex in a relationship, especially women. I didn't even do it. I put it down the list of important factors as I was deciding on a husband. I figured it would get better and it would be okay. How fucking wrong was I?"

"What I was going to say," Brandon added, "was two things: One, men are usually the ones who choose a wife that ain't what he wants her to be sexually. I know because I almost did it. I almost proposed to a chick I liked because she had a good career and would be a great mother and I could trust her. But the sex was not what I needed. I have listened to guys talk about the fact that they cheat on their wives because the wives weren't, to use that word, 'freaky' enough. It just goes to show, like you said, it's important and can make or break a marriage.

"The other thing I was going to say is this: You don't have to deny yourself, but you don't have to be with me, either. You're going to have to talk to your husband. I know who you are, and cheating isn't you. Well, I guess it is since we're doing what we're doing. But you are the most complete and pure woman I know. I see all the things in you that your husband sees. You've got to make him see the passionate side, the erotic side, too — and make him understand there's nothing wrong with it.

"I don't know how you do it. Shit, just seduce his ass. Just dominate him. He'll be uptight at first, but after a few minutes, he'll start enjoying it. I'm sure of that. And if that fails, go to counseling."

Juanita had a lot to ponder. Brandon's point about having a heart-to-heart with Eric registered with her.

"But wouldn't he, as a man, be embarrassed? Wouldn't he feel like, I don't know, less than a man if I told him sex with him was boring?"

"He would, yeah. His ego would be bruised. But he also would step up his game. You know why? Because a man who knows his wife isn't happy sexually, knows she could step out on him. And that's the last thing any man can handle."

Juanita decided in that moment that she would tell Eric of his performance shortcomings. She did not want to continue cheating on him. But her body called for much more than his tentative and uninspired effort.

"I'm going to do it," she told Brandon. "You know what that will mean for us if he gets his shit together?"

"I do, and I will miss you. But I understand. You have a family. You want to keep it. Fucking me in the long run would not help you keep your family."

"So what do we do now?" she said. "I thought you had a room at the Renaissance."

"I do."

All that talk about sex made Juanita horny.

"We shouldn't just let your money go to waste, should we?" She gave Brandon a sly smile. He knew what it meant.

He turned to the bartender, who had come back and forth during their discussion countless times. "Check, please."

Juanita laughed.

"I guess this is like the drug addict who has committed to going into rehab the next day, so he decides to get high one last time before checking in," Brandon said.

"Yes," Juanita said. "So bring me that crack pipe."

"Yeah, I got you."

"You're the only person I can talk to like this, so I just have to get it all out when I see you because I'm back to being Mrs. Goody Two-Shoes once I'm at home. And don't get me wrong: I love being her. I love the respect she commands.

"But it'd be nice to get my ass smacked every once in a while. Just saying."

She and Brandon burst into laughter.

"You're sick," he said, still laughing. "You

need help."

The laughing continued. "You know something else? I don't have these kinds of laughs with Maurice. We used to laugh a little. But the more bored I have gotten, the more frustrated I have gotten, which has made things not so fun-loving. I was just trying to get through the day without exploding. Then you came along."

"You called me, remember?"

"Same difference."

"Okay . . . but not really."

"Let's go to the room."

"Fine, Juanita, but this is the last time . . ."

"Wait. We can't make that commitment yet. This may take some time."

Brandon shook his head and led Juanita out of the restaurant. When they got to the hotel, they encountered an older couple, in their eighties, on the elevator.

"You're a handsome couple," the woman said.

"How do you know they're a couple?" the man snapped at his wife.

Brandon and Juanita looked at each other and laughed.

"I know people. Don't be mad because you don't."

Brandon grabbed Juanita's hand.

"See, I told you," the woman said.

"Being a couple doesn't mean they're married," her husband said. "She has a ring, he doesn't."

"Maybe left his ring at home."

The man asked, "Who's right?"

"Well, both of you, actually," Juanita said. "We are a couple. But we're not a couple."

The old man knew what that meant. "The trouble with trouble is that it starts out as fun."

"Well, I hope you're working on fixing things," the woman said. "But *you* can't do it. You can't solve a problem with the same minds that created the problem. I would call on God. Or a man of God."

"You *would*," her husband said sarcastically. "I see what's going on here."

He looked at Juanita, down at her ring and back into her eyes. "It's hard to resist a bad boy who's a good man, isn't it?" Then he glanced over at Brandon. "I know this: You can't run from a problem because wherever you go, you take yourself."

"Okay, that's enough out of you, old man," his wife said. "You lovely kids live your best life."

They reached their floor and exited the elevator. Brandon and Juanita were quiet for a few seconds. "Old people speak their minds, don't they?" Juanita said.

"And they speak the truth, too," Brandon added.

When they got into the room, their urge for passion had significantly decreased. They thought about the observations of the older couple.

"What did he say? 'The trouble with trouble is that it starts out as fun.' I'd never heard that before, but he's right," Juanita said. "All the buildup to that night at the St. Regis and the actual night of the St. Regis . . . it was all trouble. I knew it was trouble to go to your room, but I went anyway. And you know why? Because trouble felt good to me. It was exciting. It was fun. I'm not even talking about the sex. I'm talking about sneaking around talking and texting you. That was trouble, but it was fun. I hadn't had any real fun in a long time — too busy being the perfect mother, wife, daughter, friend, and on and on. That shit takes a lot out of you. To do something daring is fun."

"What's the movie? Arnold Schwarzenegger and Jamie Lee Curtis. The one when she's a bored housewife and becomes a spy."

"Oh. It was called *True Lies*," Juanita said. "Exactly. I can relate to that movie, how the wife felt. The need for adventure can drive you to some places you'd never expect to be."

"Well, we know what we've been doing was a mistake," Brandon said.

"You know what, Brandon? I'm not going to say it was a mistake. It was wrong, but not a mistake. I don't regret any of it."

"You're a bad — dare I say it? — *bitch,*" Brandon said, laughing. Juanita was hardly offended. Indeed, she accepted the moniker as a confirmation that she had not gotten so far from her complete self. She deemed it a compliment.

"So, what's up, Juanita? We're here in this room. Came here for a reason. But we don't have to do anything. I think we shouldn't do anything. And you know that's hard for me."

"You're the shit," she said. "You could easily take advantage of me, but you're actually trying to do right by me. I appreciate that. More than you know."

"Of course. But let me squeeze that ass before you leave."

Juanita laughed uproariously. "See, some people . . ."

"Nah, it's all good," Brandon said. "I want to see you happy. You deserve that. Want me to talk to your husband. I'll tell him, 'Dude, wake up. You got the freak of the week. Who doesn't want that?' "

"I'm sure that would not go over well, especially coming from you."

Then Juanita stood up, turned her back to Brandon and bent over. "I'm leaving. But go ahead. Squeeze it one last time."

Brandon smiled and grabbed two handfuls of her ass cheeks. "Damn, I'm gonna miss this," he said.

"Ummm," she said. "Me, too. Me too."

CHAPTER TWENTY: STEAL AWAY

Rhonda

After cleaning up and putting on her dress, Rhonda decided she'd chat with Lorenzo for a few minutes before going home. It was almost one in the morning — the time she told her husband she would be home.

They sipped on water. "That was good," she said, "and I'm not talking about the water."

Lorenzo smiled.

"Tell me something: Are you really going to open a restaurant? I ask because Olivia said you've been a photographer, created websites, worked as a personal trainer, was a host at a restaurant and on and on. She seems to believe you were lying."

"Wow," he said. "She told you that? Well, I have had a lot of jobs. Not because I'm flighty, but because I have a lot of interests. I like the restaurant business the best.

"The host job she mentioned was actually

the general manager at a four-star restaurant in Buckhead. The photographer and website jobs she talked about are companies that I still have. And I never worked as a personal trainer; I told her I *had* a personal trainer at one point."

"Really? So what about the restaurant?"

"You know where P. Diddy's restaurant, Justin's, used to be? That's the space we're considering."

"We?"

"I have four partners — all friends who have their stuff together. They have owned spots before in Birmingham. I'm on board and we have the backing, the money. We're just looking at the best location. So, Olivia . . . I really don't know about her now."

"So, why me? You have so much going for yourself, Lorenzo. I'm married."

"I can see beyond that. I can see *you.* I can tell that you're not necessarily a woman who would cheat. You believe you've been driven to this. This is out of character. I could be wrong. I've been wrong once or twice. But I don't think I am in this case."

"Thank you for that," Rhonda said. "But —"

"Rhonda, you don't have to continue to question me. You can if you need to, but

I'm not only with you for sex. I'm not."

"What else could it be? I'm not leaving my husband."

"Sounds like you want to end it. Is that it?"

"I never have been in this position and questions keep coming up."

"I don't mind the questions. I don't. But maybe you should really think about this. I respect your questions. I would feel some kind of way about you if you did this without questioning yourself or me. So, think about it over the weekend and let's talk on Monday."

"See, that's what I mean. It's Friday. Now that we've had sex, you don't want to talk to me again until Monday."

"I'm not going there with you. You're taking something thoughtful and making it something sinister."

"Sinister? You and your words."

"You get my point. You're making it sound like I don't want to talk to you now that we've had sex."

"I'm sorry. That's not fair. You deserve the benefit of the doubt, especially after not taking advantage of me that night when I was so drunk . . . You're a gentleman, so I will give you the benefit of the doubt."

"You need to go on home," Lorenzo said,

laughing. "Get some rest. Clear your head. Call me on Monday — unless you want to stop by during one of your walks. But don't answer that. Come on, I'll walk you to your car."

Rhonda hugged him and whispered into his ear, "Too bad I'm taken. I'd let you be my man."

Lorenzo said, "If I wanted to be. You might not be as sexy single as you are married."

That comment made Rhonda step back. "Please tell me you're joking. Don't insult me like that."

"I truly was joking," he quickly responded. "I'm sorry. I thought it would lighten the mood a little more. Too much heavy stuff. Come here. Let's hug again."

They embraced and Rhonda made sure she did not look like she had just gotten sexed.

At the front door, Lorenzo wanted to kiss Rhonda goodbye. "Let's hug," she said.

They did and he opened the front door. Rhonda's face turned flush when they stepped outside.

"Lorenzo! Where's my car? I parked it right there. Where's my car?"

"Oh, shit. Damn!"

"Somebody stole my car. This is so messed up."

"I can't believe this. Look, there's no glass on the ground. They had to be professionals."

"What am I going to do? I can't tell Eric my car was stolen from here."

"Where did you tell him you were going?"

"To Whisky Mistress in Buckhead."

"Shit. We have to go up that way, report your car stolen, and then you can have him pick you up from there. It doesn't matter where your car was stolen. You need the report to say you were in Buckhead."

"What about video cameras up there? It will show that I left."

"Trust me, for a stolen car, they won't go to those extremes. They'll file a report, put the car on a list, and that's about it. If they happen to find it, you're lucky. It's important to you, but the cops will say there are more important crimes for them to pursue."

They went back inside, where Lorenzo went upstairs to change clothes. Rhonda texted Eric.

We'll be leaving in a few minutes. You want something while I'm out?

A few minutes later, Eric returned her text.

Nothing to get out this late but into trouble.

That text made Rhonda uneasy. She pondered how to respond, but came up with nothing. So she didn't.

On the drive to Buckhead, she and Lorenzo were quiet for a while. Her mind was all over the place. It bounced around from her car being stolen, to her infidelity to her husband and marriage, to having to purchase a new car, to Lorenzo and how much more she liked him.

Lorenzo's mind raced, too. He thought of what his neighborhood was coming to that a car could be stolen from his driveway, how he had the ideal scenario with Rhonda — sex with no ties, how, as much as he enjoyed that and liked Rhonda, that she was another man's wife and how dangerous that could be.

"Is your husband the type to go off, to shoot me if he saw us together?"

"What? No. Eric is calm — too calm, if you ask me. But he did go crazy that time I spent the night at your house. I hadn't seen that look in his eyes or heard him yell and curse like that in a *long* time. He scared me."

"That's great to hear."

"I'm sorry, but you asked."

"That's part of the downside to this, Rhonda. If he found out, he could lose it and come looking for me with a shotgun, a knife, a bow and arrow. Anything."

Rhonda laughed. "A bow and arrow?"

"I'm just saying that he could put all this on me and want to take me out."

"That's not Eric. And he's *not* going to find out. I can't have that."

They arrived at Whisky Mistress and found a parking lot in a nearby strip mall that looked plausible for a car theft. Rhonda called police and it took about twenty minutes for a cop to show up.

"Damn, that's how they take car thefts? They take their time coming out? That's crazy."

"On the crime meter, it's on the low end."

Rhonda shook her head. She called Eric.

"Eric, you're not going to believe this, but my car was stolen . . . It's gone. I had some drinks, but I know where I parked . . . No, they wouldn't tow it. It's a parking lot. Other cars are still here . . . The police came and I filed a report. I can catch Uber home . . . You will? Okay . . . It's lit over there . . . There are a few people here, but not many . . . Okay. Thank you."

She turned to Lorenzo. "He's coming to get me."

"You can sit with me for about ten minutes. He should be here in fifteen or so."

"Do you think they will find my car?"

"A better question is whether your car being stolen is a sign that we shouldn't be doing this."

"I should be asking that question, not you."

"Why didn't you?"

"I don't want to think about that right now. I'm hoping they find my car. I paid it off two months ago. I have no interest in another car note any time soon."

"I understand that and insurance will cover that if it comes down to it. But do you believe in omens? Karma?"

"Not really? If I did, I'd be scared to death of what's going to happen to me. And it would be something bigger than having my car stolen, I'm sure of that."

Lorenzo smiled. "I guess that could be true, huh?"

"I'm going to get out. You should go. I don't want Eric to see me getting out of your car."

"I would try to hug and kiss you, but you didn't seem to want that earlier. So, I'll simply say good luck."

Seven minutes later, Eric pulled up in his Lexus truck. The music was blaring. He had a drink in his hand.

"Are you drunk?"

"Just having a drink, that's all. Want some?"

"I've had enough. Turn down that music."

Eric obliged. "So, where was your car parked?"

Rhonda pointed. "Over there."

Eric drove up to the spot. She pointed again.

"Right there?"

"Yes."

He got out of the car and inspected the parking space she'd identified.

"No glass on the ground. Must have been a real pro."

Rhonda nodded her head and thought, *That was the same thing Lorenzo said.*

Eric got back into the car. "I guess this spoiled a good night for you."

"We had fun. But, yeah, my heart dropped when my car wasn't where I left it."

"Well, you have the police report. And it's insured, so finally we can get some value out of that. But they'll likely find it somewhere abandoned nearby in a day or so. Thankfully you didn't have your laptop in there."

"I know, right? I'm frustrated you had to come here. And if they don't find it, I really don't want to have to shop for a new car."

Eric did not respond to her comment. He

had a buzz.

"I've been thinking about your problem with my weight and I've decided that it shouldn't matter," he said. "I've been a good husband to you. I have given you everything I could, except a child. I wanted to do that, but you didn't want kids. We've had our issues, gotten past them and been strong. I'm that same guy who paid for you to get your master's degree and who took you on your first trip out of the country to Paris.

"You've spent the last several weeks making me feel bad about myself, when I don't have anything to feel bad about. I've been reliable. We don't have any bills. We're comfortable. But you're not happy? But I'm not good enough?"

Rhonda felt guilty. And foolish. Eric's points were on point.

"I didn't say you were not good enough for me," he went on. "And I didn't say I wasn't happy. I've been trying to say that I want us to be like we were. I have gained maybe some weight since we've been married. But so have you. You don't hear me complaining."

"I want you to be attracted to me. I want you to desire me. That's the number one reason, Eric. I work at staying together.

That's important to me. I need you to have the same attitude about me, about being attractive for me, about me desiring you. I know how hard it can be to maintain the interest when you see someone every day. That's why I try to look good for you. That's why I wear a nightie to bed every night.

"At the same time, Eric, you don't do anything to make me feel attracted to you."

"I'm here."

"But honey, that's not enough. We've been in a rut for a long time. Let's face it. And I don't think it's shallow to want my husband to look good and to be healthy. You eat crazy, and you know it. To eat healthy is self-respect. I don't think you're respecting yourself."

They pulled into their subdivision. Eric did not respond for a few seconds. When they turned on their street, he said, "And you're respecting me?"

"I'm not disrespecting you."

"Oh, you're not?"

Rhonda did not hear Eric because her attention was elsewhere. As they pulled up to their home, she noticed a car in their driveway. The closer they got, the more the vehicle came into focus. It was *her* car.

Eric pushed the remote control to the garage door, drove past Rhonda's Audi

5000 and into the garage. He turned off the car and sat there, looking straight ahead. Rhonda's heart pounded out of her chest.

She was shocked and mortified — and scared. She did not know what to say, so she sat there in silence.

Eric got tired of hearing nothing. "Isn't that your car in the driveway?"

"How did it get there, Eric?"

"I thought you told me it was stolen from Buckhead."

"Eric . . ."

"What? I really want to hear this."

"How did my car get here?"

"I drove it here, that's how." Eric's voice rose. "What the fuck is wrong with you?"

Rhonda jumped out of the car and lowered the garage. She was sure Eric's voice would carry so loudly that the neighbors would hear. She didn't want that.

Eric followed her into the house. She was not sure how to play it, so she tried to flip it.

"Why are you playing games? Why would you take my car? That's so childish."

"No, actually, it was brilliant. I needed to see who I was dealing with. If you told me the truth about where your car was, then I'd know you weren't up to no good. But you lied, which told me everything. You're a cheating bitch!"

"Don't call me a bitch."

"I didn't. I called you a *cheating* bitch."

"I'm not dealing with you. You're drunk and you're evil."

"You're half right. I'm evil because that's how I need to be to deal with a devil. You're fucking some guy who lives in the same neighborhood. Fucking him while I sit at home waiting for you. And I'm the bad boy fat guy?"

"Who said I fucked anybody? How did you make that leap?"

"You told me by all the lying you're doing. You would not go all the way to Buckhead to stage a car theft if you weren't fucking him. He's the same guy you probably were with that night you claimed you spent with Olivia."

"What? Where did you get that?"

"From you. Just now. You didn't deny it. Plus, Olivia told me you haven't been to her place in months."

"You called Olivia?"

"Right after I used the spare key to drive your car home."

"Eric . . ."

"I'm listening. But I don't know if I should because everything that comes out of your mouth is a fucking lie."

276

Rhonda was not prepared to address the onslaught of questions Eric had. All she had were lies.

"Look, I'm not trying to get out of control here, Rhonda. I know everything. Now it's about if you can be honest with me at all. You tell me the truth right now or it's over. Period."

Rhonda had no other recourse. She did not have a lie that would save her as a last resort. The truth, though, was ugly. Her only option, she believed, was to be forthcoming. But she needed an answer to a question first.

"Well, Eric, please tell me how you got my car."

"I shouldn't tell you shit. But I will, just because. I was headed to the grocery store around eleven when I saw you coming into the subdivision as I was leaving. I thought you saw me; I waved at you. You didn't see me, I guess. I whipped a U-turn, expecting you to be headed home. But you turned right instead of going straight.

"By the time I got to the street and turned, you were walking to the door of some house that was not ours and some dude opened it. I was so angry and so . . . hurt. I couldn't believe it. I was going to knock on the door. But I decided to text you, which you ignored. I sat in front of that house for at least thirty minutes. Then I decided to go home, walk back over there with the spare key and take the car — and then see what you would do.

"So I came home and waited. I made me a drink. Then another and another and another . . . I think. I lost track. Just when I was about to come over there, you texted me to say you were headed home. I knew it was about to get interesting. And then you called back with the lies. That's it. Your turn."

Rhonda felt helpless. There was nothing left to tell but the truth.

"I met this guy —"

"What's his name?"

"His name doesn't matter. And please don't do or say anything to him."

"Look at you — trying to protect your boyfriend. Listen, you cheating whore, I may be drunk, but I ain't stupid. Why would I attack him? It's not his fault. He did what he was supposed to do, as a man. A married woman offers him sex, nine times out of ten, he's going to take it. It's stupid for the spouse to get upset with the person your husband or wife is cheating with — unless it's a friend or relative. If it's a stranger, that person should not be your target. You're my wife. *You're* my target. Now tell me the truth."

"Eric, I don't know what to say. I told you I was upset about your weight and I got *really* upset when you basically told me it didn't matter how you looked or if we did anything exciting. I thought that was wrong and it created a divide.

"I met this guy one night out with Olivia at Suite Lounge. He knew Olivia. Then I saw him again a few weeks later and —"

"Saw him where?"

"Uh, I saw him in front of our house. He was walking. That's it."

"That's it? No, that's only the beginning. What else?"

Rhonda just looked at him.

"Were you with him that night you claimed you were mad at me and with Olivia?"

"I *was* mad at you . . . But yes."

"I knew it. Giving me that bullshit about staying with Olivia. Worse than that, you've been making me out to be the bad guy, the loser. If you really love someone, it's easy to stay faithful. I've had my chances to step out on you, and I wouldn't do it. I wouldn't because I love you. Loved you."

"Oh, you don't love me anymore? Just like that."

"Ah, yes, just like that. You can go to fucking hell as far as I'm concerned."

"You said we were going to try save our marriage."

"If I did, I lied. I needed confirmation before I finished packing my shit so I can get out of here."

"Eric, let's be reasonable. We have a lot of years to just toss aside like that."

"You should have thought of that before you started fucking someone else, before you humiliated me and defiled yourself. Once you opened your legs for another man, our marriage was over."

Rhonda felt stupid, humiliated and hopeless. Her shoulders slumped. But she could not cry. It came to her that Eric knowing was a relief. She hated the sneaking around. She hated the dishonesty. She disagreed with his position that if she truly loved him, it would have been easy to be faithful. She loved Eric, but she was unfulfilled. She had envisioned herself with other men, men who were not overweight and who cared about their appearance. It *was* shallow, she concluded, but she couldn't help it. It was who she was.

The end of her marriage was not such a bad idea for her. She did not want it to come this way, with Eric hurt and hating her.

So she mustered some resistance. "Eric, don't make an emotional decision about us. We have a lot of history."

"And we'll always have a lot of history. But our history ends now."

CHAPTER TWENTY-ONE:
VISITING HOURS

Stephanie

The doctors would only allow one person to spend the night in the room with Toya, and it was difficult for Terry to get Stephanie to understand that it would be him, not her. She finally acquiesced, after ten minutes of heated discussion, but refused to go home. She stayed in the visiting area downstairs.

"We can relieve each other," she told Terry. "You're going to need a break in the middle of the night."

"Why don't you go home and get some rest and come back in the morning?" Willie told Stephanie as she claimed a space downstairs.

"Go home? You ought to know I'm not leaving my sister. Period. Not until she wakes up and smiles at me."

"What about me?"

"What about you? What does that mean?

Who's going to cook for you and make up the bed? Is that what you mean?"

"I mean, shouldn't you be home with your husband?"

"I'm so scared right now for my sister and so angry with you. My sister's life is on the line. And you're worried about me being with you at home? You should be talking about staying here with me, if anything. How selfish can you be?"

"I'm not trying to be selfish. I know how you are. I'm trying to get you to take care of yourself. You won't eat. You won't get any sleep. And you'll end up in one of these hospital beds yourself."

"I don't care. Do you understand what sacrifice is about for the people you love? I don't think you do. That's why your whole life is work and your business and not our marriage."

"Wait. Where did that come from?"

"It came from my mouth — and my heart. I don't want to talk about it now. I want to concentrate on Toya. But we will talk about it."

"You bet your ass we will talk about it — and other stuff, too," he said with anger. He pointed at Stephanie and walked out.

She was glad to see him go. The guilt of being with Charles coupled with her anger at him was too much for her to deal with at that time. Stephanie wanted to be alone with her thoughts and prayers.

She purchased a blanket and pillow in the gift shop and got as comfortable as she could in the waiting area. The sun had gone down and she hadn't eaten since she'd shared cheese and crackers with Charles. But eating was not a priority for her. She wanted to pray. She went up to Toya's room and asked the nurse if she could say a prayer and leave. The nurse gave her five minutes.

She and Terry joined hands and they each held Toya's.

"God, I'm so scared right now. Toya needs you. Terry needs you. I need You, Lord. Only You can make this situation right. It says in the Bible: 'If two or three are gathered together in My name, there am I among them.' We're here in Your name now, God. Heal Toya. Wake up my sister. Wake up Terry's wife. She has a lot more to offer the world. Bring her back so she can continue Your work. Bring her back and I will be the servant I should have been all along. I know I have fallen short of Your desires for me. But please, God, do not hold that against Toya. We pray that You bless us with Your grace and mercy. She deserves to be okay, Lord. We have comfort in knowing

You will do what's best and that You do not make mistakes. In the precious name of Jesus, we pray. Amen."

She wiped away tears and leaned over the bed and delicately hugged her sister.

"We've got to stay positive," Terry said.

Stephanie nodded and left the room. She hardly remembered walking up the hallway, past the nurse's station and onto the elevator. She made her way to the chair with her blanket and pillow. There were three people not far from her — a couple and a man. They all looked sad.

She dug into her purse and pulled out her cell phone charger and plugged it into the wall. Then she folded herself into the chair, wrapped the blanket around her shoulders, hugged the pillow and lost herself in her fear.

When their mom had died in a car accident six years earlier, Willie had been supportive, but she had survived because of her sister. They'd cried together, prayed together and ultimately pulled each other off the figurative floor.

It was Toya's words that changed their inconsolable spirit. She'd said, "Look at me. Wipe your face. You know Mom. She wouldn't have this from us. If nothing else, she taught us to be strong. We've mourned her for almost two days. We've got to get up and honor her now. We are her daughters. We have to show who she is by getting our shit together."

That rationale turned things. The sisters hugged and then gathered themselves. They remained grief-stricken. But they displayed strength, especially at the funeral, that they believed their mother admired.

Recalling those moments alerted her that strength was required as her sister lay upstairs fighting for her life. Inducing a coma was not a fail-safe procedure. The hope was that there was no major damage to Toya's brain. They could not determine that until the swelling went down. Even then, it would not be until she woke up and showed cognitive indications that they could be assured of a full recovery.

All that scared Stephanie in a way that made her tremble. She wanted to be strong, knew she *needed* to be strong, but could not shake the reality of what could happen. Then she started talking to herself.

"It's not the reality of what could happen *until* it happens."

"God would not take her from me now. It's too soon."

"How could I plan her funeral? It would be too much."

"Brain damage could make her unable to walk or talk. How could I handle that?"

Only the chime from her cell phone, indicating a text message, pulled her from her sullen place. It was Charles.

I'm sure it is an intense time for you. Please send me an update. Even if it's brief, I'd like to know something.

In all her panic, Stephanie had forgotten about Charles. If none of this had happened, she would have still been with him in their romantic hotel room on the water, even at the risk of her husband being over-the-top upset. Toya's situation changed things — for that night and long term. Stephanie's focus had to be on helping her sister recover from the traumatic brain injury. Not Willie. Not Charles. Not even herself.

Instead of texting Charles, she called him. "Hey, how are you? How's your sister?"

"Thank you for texting me. It's a nightmare, to be honest. The short version is they put her in a coma, hoping to reduce the swelling in her brain — she collapsed and now they're waiting for the swelling to go down. After that, they can determine if she had any brain damage."

"Oh, my goodness. I am really sorry to hear this, Stephanie. Anything I can do?"

"Just be supportive, please. Pray for Toya. Pray for me. That would mean a lot."

"That goes without saying. Where are you?"

"I'm staying at the hospital, in the waiting room. Just gonna stay here until Terry, my sister's husband, needs a break from her bedside. I'm not going anywhere. I'm not going home, to the store. Nowhere. But, Charles, I'm so scared."

"You're supposed to be scared because you care so much," he said. "But you also need to be faithful, positive. Put uplifting vibes in the air, vibes that your sister can draw from and get better. I believe there is something to the power of your mindset, what you put into the universe. Stay positive that the best will occur. When you believe, you feel less helpless. You believe."

Charles' stock in Stephanie's eyes increased exponentially. Her husband, in her time of need, provided drama instead of support. Contrasted against Charles' steady and supportive disposition, Willie seemed like a loser.

"You don't know how much you mean to me right now, how important you are," she told Charles. "I probably shouldn't say this, but you're more supportive than my husband. He isn't here, hasn't offered a word of encouragement. Wanted me to go home."

"He didn't get that you needed to be close to your sister?"

"Sad, but he didn't."

"Well, I wish I could be there with you. This room is not the same without you. If I hadn't paid for it already, I would just go stay in Oakland to be closer to you."

"I'm glad you feel that way. I'm trying my best to stay positive. It's not easy."

"Make it easy. Focus on what you want to happen. Focus on what you're going to say to her when she comes out of it. Focus on making your friendship with her even better. And when in doubt, think about me."

Stephanie smiled, which was something she had not done since learning of Toya's condition. Brownie point for Charles.

When they hung up, Stephanie tried to stay positive. But she began to ponder her life as her sister clung to hers, and her mind took her to various places. Some of them were pleasant places. Others made her feel bad about herself. She especially focused on her judgment. When she thought about her affair with Andre earlier in their marriage, she felt embarrassed. Now Charles.

What's wrong with me?

She married Willie because he was opposite of her father, who had cheated on her mother with her mom's friend. Stephanie was nineteen when she'd learned of the infidelity that broke the family. She and Toya had their image of the ideal man wrecked. Their mother was devastated. The relationship Stephanie had with her dad was never the same.

She began calling him by his first name. She saw less and less of him. And the things about him that she once admired — his leadership within the family, his history with the Black Panther Party, his business acumen, his wisdom about most everything — diminished. She did not lose total respect for him because she understood how he provided for his wife and two daughters, even if Toya was not his birth child, and they benefitted from the life lessons he taught. But she looked at him differently and often with disdain.

What bothered her as she sat in that hospital waiting room was that she had to admit that she was her father's daughter. Many family members had told her that she was like her father in more than looks, and Stephanie admitted that they were right, and not just about the positive parts of his personality or character.

While Toya had their mom's personality and disposition, Stephanie had her father's, and the fact that it manifested itself in her extramarital relationships made her feel low. She was there when her usually stoic, calm mother howled like a wounded animal at the revelation of her dad's affair. She and Toya sat with their mom for five hours trying to console her as the pain tore through them, too. For her to have stepped out on Willie made her equal to her father, which was hard for her to accept.

She managed to prevent crying at the revelation, but it got her down. She considered herself honorable, but she had done dishonorable things — just like her father.

Stephanie crawled up in the chair and covered her head with the blanket. But no matter how dark she made it, there was no escaping that she mirrored her dad, even in ways she did not want.

There were times when she told Willie that she was more like a man in certain areas of life, especially in dealing with the opposite sex. She wasn't the dreamy, romantic type of woman. She was not the kind of woman to have a lot of female friends; she got along better with men than women. And, when she was single, she juggled men as men did women.

The sins of the father.

Over time, Stephanie was able to forgive

her dad, but not like Toya. Stephanie never called him "Dad" again. Instead, she called him Nick. Conversely, he and Toya talked regularly and often went out for lunch or dinner in San Francisco, Marin County or Napa Valley. Their relationship was solid, which meant a lot because Toya's natural father was a phantom.

Stephanie pulled the covers from off her head. She realized she had not called her father about Toya. It was half-past midnight, and it was a call she did not want to make. Not because of the hour, but because Nick doted on Toya in a way that belied the side of him that Stephanie abhorred. So, she knew he'd be just as troubled as she about her condition.

But she *had* to make the call. Toya would want him to know.

"The sky must be falling for you to call me," Nick said when he answered the phone. "I can't believe it."

"I only called because you should know that Toya is in the hospital."

"What?"

"She, for some reason, collapsed today and banged her head on the side of a cement stair. They've put her in a coma to take the pressure off her brain . . ."

Stephanie gave him more details, including the hospital. And even though she told him he could not see her until the morning, he said, "I'm on my way."

This did not make Stephanie feel good. She knew she'd have to spend time with her dad. At the same time, despite all animosity, she still longed for his approval. That was the hold a father could have over his daughter.

For all she had done, including raising a beautiful, accomplished daughter, Stephanie still believed her father looked at her as less than what she should have been. She knew it could have been, was more likely, her insecurities; Nick loved his girls with equal passion. When they learned of his infidelities, he was equally concerned with their reaction to it as he was his wife.

What incensed Stephanie was that he showed little remorse when it all came crashing down. He was flippant, arrogant and dismissive. "At this point, it is what it is," he had said to his family.

If that was not hurtful enough for Stephanie, Nick was her natural father, but he seemed, in her mind, to favor Toya, whose father fled to Seattle never to return when he learned her mom was pregnant. Nick's closeness to Toya always bothered Stephanie, no matter how little she discussed it or how vehemently she denied it.

Nick might have been overly attentive to Toya to make up for her father not being there, but for Stephanie, it took something away from their relationship. Then his cheating all but ruined it.

All those thoughts filled her head as she struggled to get comfortable in the chair in the waiting area. Between the dilemma of Charles, Toya's condition and her father, Stephanie was exhausted. So, she nodded off while saying silent prayers.

When she woke up nearly an hour later, she was astonished to see Charles standing over her. She thought she was dreaming.

"I thought you could use a hug," he said.

Stephanie instinctively looked around to make sure Terry — or anyone she knew — was not around. "Oh, wow. Charles. I can't believe you."

He held out his hand and helped her out of the chair. They hugged.

"I can't believe you're here. I can't believe it."

"I just couldn't sit in that room, knowing you were here by yourself, at a time like this, and not come over. I was worried, but I'm glad no one was here. How are you?"

"So much better now. It means a lot that you're here. I didn't realize how much I needed a hug from you."

"Good. But I'm not going to stay long. Any new word on your sister?"

"Not yet. Last I heard was that they will keep her in the coma for at least a day or two. Nothing much has changed yet. A few days and the swelling should go down . . . Hopefully."

"Remember, you have to stay positive. Trust the doctors. Shoot, trust God."

She hugged Charles and he kissed her on the top of her head.

"Stephanie?" came the voice.

She opened her eyes and pulled back from Charles to see her father.

"Nick."

"Baby girl."

She stepped away from Charles. "Come here," Nick said. They hugged.

"This is Charles, one of my colleagues from the school system. This is Nick."

"I'm her father. Nice to meet you."

"Father? Oh, wow. Nice to meet you, sir."

"I'm going to leave now. But I'm glad I was able to come by for a few minutes, Stephanie. Nice to meet you, sir."

They shook hands and Charles left.

"Why was he kissing all on you?"

"Don't start. He was comforting me. Isn't that why you're here?"

"You look good, Steph. Tired, but you look good. Where were you before you got here? Nice dress."

"I was gonna hang out with Toya, but they had other plans. You're not here to talk about me, are you?"

"We don't have to have limits on what we talk about, do we?"

"This time is about Toya, Nick."

"Nick? Still won't call me 'Dad,' huh?"

"No need to. Anyway, you want an update on Toya or did you come here to quiz me . . . Nick?"

"Tell me what happened. Everything."

It was nearly two in the morning and Stephanie was emotionally drained. Going through everything was hardly appealing.

"Can we just relax here? I've told you everything. Go up to the sixth floor, Room six-zero-six. Tell the nurses you're her father. Maybe they will let you see her. Maybe Terry will take a break and you can go in there for a while."

"I just got here and you're trying to get rid of me."

"Toya would love it if you went to see her. You surely didn't come here to see me."

"Did — what was his name? — Chris —"

"His name is Charles."

"Did Charles come here to see you or Toya?"

"Your daughter is upstairs in a coma. And you want to talk about me? *Really?*"

"You're right. Where is the elevator?"

She pointed and off went Nick.

Stephanie sat back down, picked up her phone and called Charles.

"Just wanted to thank you again for coming to see me. I wish my father hadn't come. You could have stayed longer."

"You never mentioned your father. Seems like there's some tension between you two. Am I wrong?"

"We have our issues, yes. Well, actually, I have issues with him and he doesn't seem to understand why, which is an issue. But I don't want to talk about him. My sister is the apple of his eye, so he's where he should be.

"But let me ask you something. I don't talk much about my husband, but you *never* mention your wife. Why is that? Why are you seeing me?"

"The same reason you're seeing me: Home isn't right. We've been married twenty-two years. What I haven't discussed with you is that I had prostate cancer about six years ago. It was rough going for a while. But I got through it.

"There were times when I thought I was going to die. When I got through it, I knew I had to live my life, *enjoy* my life. My wife is a good person. But the only reason I have not gotten a divorce is because she was there for me at my lowest point. She hardly left my side. She kept me from emotionally giving up. So, there is some loyalty I have to her."

"Loyalty? You don't consider seeing me behind her back loyalty, do you?"

"I mean staying married to her. I can't leave her. For her and her family, the marriage means something, even if it is a farce. I wouldn't be surprised if she's seeing someone."

"And you wouldn't care if she was sleeping with someone else?"

"I'd care. I guess I just don't want to know about it. And that's the same position she's taking. We basically have an arrangement: Always be respectful. It's worked so far."

"Wow. I don't think I could do that. I couldn't share you."

"You wouldn't have to. You're right up my alley. Passionate, fun. You're in education, so we have a great professional connection, too. It's ideal."

"It *would* be ideal, yes. But we're both married, so . . ."

"I'm thinking we should talk about this in person."

"I don't know when that can be. I have to be here for Toya. And there's no telling how this will play out."

"Well, I'm introducing a program in San Jose all week, so I'll be able to come by again when the coast is clear."

"Maybe I'll find us an empty room so you can take care of me," Stephanie said. "I'm almost ashamed to be thinking like that at a time like this. *Almost.*"

Chapter Twenty-Two:
It's a Small, Small World

Juanita

Maurice sat in the family room with his children and their sitter in a suit and tie, waiting for Juanita to get dressed. They were going to an Inner Caucus semi-formal party at the Omni Shoreham hotel. It was Juanita's suggestion.

Part of weaning herself off of Brandon was to immerse herself in her husband. Dressing up and going out to a nice event was something they did frequently before the kids had arrived, and would be a good way, she thought, to have fun together.

But Maurice was not happy. The more time he spent with Gloria, the more time he wanted to spend with her. Worse, he was irritated that Juanita took an extra forty minutes to get ready.

Finally, she emerged downstairs, looking beautiful, but not enough to ease Maurice's ire.

"Finally," he said.

She had not taken any more time than usual, but this time, Maurice expressed his frustration. Juanita was not sure how to react to it at first, but quickly decided to keep things light.

"Aren't I worth the wait?"

"You look great. I'm just ready to go, that's all."

They hugged their kids, gave the sitter some last-minute instructions and headed to the car.

"You didn't used to mind waiting on me, no matter how long I took," she said as they pulled off.

"I always minded. I just didn't say anything."

"Well, why are you saying something now?"

"Because I didn't really want to go to this thing — and then you had me waiting? What do you do for ninety minutes anyway? Bake a cake?"

"You're a man. It's a woman thang."

Juanita laughed. She was intent on having a good time with her husband. Her rationale was the more fun and adventure they had, the more she would accept not having the wildness she believed she needed. It was not the ideal way for her to live. She knew that. But it was the best way to keep her family — and to not hurt her husband, who she knew worshipped her.

When they arrived at the party, there were hundreds of young-to-middle-aged professionals nicely dressed and in good spirits. But not Maurice. He seemed uptight.

"Baby, what's wrong?" Juanita asked.

He took a deep breath and smiled at his wife. "Nothing. I'm okay. Let's get a drink."

In the ballroom, the longtime popular D.C.-area band, Spur of the Moment, played songs that packed the dance floor. "You look handsome, husband," she said.

"Thank you. You look pretty good yourself."

She smiled at him, and he grabbed her hand and led her to the dance floor. They found a small space away from the speakers and danced to two songs before Juanita asked, "Can we get that drink now?"

On the way to the bar, they encountered friends and colleagues, and exchanged small talk.

"There are two seats at that table. Why don't you get them; I'll get the drinks. You want red wine, right?" Maurice said.

Juanita thought it was an ideal time to test her husband. She passed on having the heart-to-heart in favor of just being her full self. When she wanted to use profanity, she decided she would. When she wanted to have something other than wine, she would.

"I'll have a Woodford Reserve."

"What's that?"

"A bourbon."

"You don't drink bourbon."

"Actually, I do."

"I'm not getting you a *bourbon.*"

"Why can't I have what I want?"

"Since when did you start drinking bourbon?"

"Since before I met you. I stopped, but I want to have bourbon tonight."

"This is crazy."

"What's crazy is I'm arguing with you over what I want to drink. You know what? Fine. I'll get it myself."

Juanita turned and walked to the other side of the ballroom, where there was another bar. There were two people in front of her. She ordered her drink, "Woodford. Neat, please," but realized she did not have anything in her small clutch other than lipstick, cell phone and mints.

"Shit. I don't have my money," she said to the bartender.

The man behind her stepped in. "That's a cheap trick to get someone to buy you a drink," he said. She turned around to see

Brandon. Her heart fluttered and pounded at the same time.

"What are you doing here?"

"I told *you* about this party, remember?" he said.

"Oh, my God. I really need this drink now. This is twice I have run into you while I'm out — after years of not seeing you at all. You know I'm here with my husband, right?"

"I'm on a date, too. She went to the bathroom."

"Can you pay for this for me? Then I'm going to find my husband."

Brandon pulled out some cash and paid the bartender. She thanked him.

"No hug?"

She smiled. "Not on your life. Well, at least not here. Have fun. You know I have to go."

She could see Maurice headed their way. Before she could leave, Brandon's date arrived. He introduced them. "This is my friend from way back, Juanita. Juanita, this is Gloria."

The women shook hands. Juanita successfully masked her jealousy. "That's a beautiful dress," she said to Gloria.

"Yours is beautiful, too."

Just then, Maurice arrived with tension in

his face. "You're really drinking bourbon?" he said.

"Maurice, this is Brandon, a friend I haven't seen in a long time. And his date. I'm sorry, tell me your name again."

Maurice shook Brandon's hand and turned to his date. The tension in his face intensified.

"Gloria," she said, extending her hand. "Nice to meet you."

Maurice was stunned to see his mistress standing beside his wife. He felt awkward.

"Uh, umm, hi. Nice to meet you, Gloria," he managed to get out. He turned to Juanita.

"How do you know — I'm sorry."

"My name is Brandon. I've known Juanita for about fifteen, twenty years."

"Really? She never mentioned you."

"We hadn't seen each other in at least fifteen years," Juanita jumped in.

"Oh, I see. And, uh, Brandon, this is your wife?"

Gloria's and Maurice's eyes met. "My wife? Not yet."

"Really?" Juanita asked. "You're considering marriage?"

"Never know," Brandon said.

"Well, you have a beautiful candidate," Maurice said. Juanita looked up at him.

Then he added: "Like me."

For the next minute or so, a mix of anxiety and tension filled the space the four lovers shared. Brandon basked in it. But Juanita, Maurice and Gloria felt stifled.

"Husband, let's dance."

"We just danced a few minutes ago. Hey, why don't you dance with Brandon? I want to get a drink."

Brandon turned to Gloria. "Only if you don't mind."

"Go ahead. I'm going to get a drink, too."

Brandon smiled and Juanita begrudgingly downed the rest of her bourbon and followed Brandon to the dance floor.

"This is so fucked up," she said before they got one dance move in. "After this dance, you take your date — how old is she, anyway? — and go to another part of this ballroom, please."

"Am I bothering you? I'm just here at a party I told *you* about. I should be mad at you for closing in on my space. You knew I was going to be here. That's why you came."

"You're so arrogant to believe that. And it's not true."

"Well, we're here now, so make the best of it. It's pretty ironic that your husband offered you up to me. Why would he do that?"

"I have no idea. And if he knew about us . . ."

"Well, he doesn't, so let's make the most of it."

He grabbed Juanita's wrist and led her to the middle of the dance floor, where Maurice and Gloria could not see them. Then he moved in, pressing his body up against hers.

"If you don't stop."

"What are you going to do? Tell your husband. He asked me to dance with you. I'm just doing what he asked."

He grabbed her waist and moved his hands slowly around to her ass. Then he squeezed.

"You're so bad."

"Bad like you want me to be."

Juanita looked up at him and smiled.

By the bar, Maurice eased over to Gloria. "I'm surprised to see you. But happy to see you, although I wish you were alone."

"What are the odds that my date is friends with your wife? This is spooky."

"For sure. I want to hug and kiss you right now. But who's this guy you're with?"

"You're jealous?"

"I am. Maybe I have no right to be, but I am."

"I understand because I'm jealous, too.

Your wife looks good. But it makes me feel — I don't know — funny to see her, to meet her. It was easier knowing she existed but not seeing her."

"If I could have prevented it, I would have. You can believe that."

"Want to leave them? Let's go back to my place."

"I wish you were serious."

"Me too. That would be wonderful."

"But I'd like to dance with you. We've only danced in your living room."

"I don't want to raise any suspicions, Maurice. If we're too familiar, she will notice. I'm a woman. I know these things."

After a few songs, Brandon and Juanita made their way back from the dance floor.

"It's too crowded out there," Juanita said, sidling alongside Maurice.

"You have a delightful date," Maurice said to Brandon.

"So do you."

"I'm going to go to the bathroom," Gloria said.

"Again?" Brandon cracked.

"Just to freshen up, if that's okay with you. Juanita, want to come with me?"

The last thing she wanted to do was leave her husband and her lover alone. But she trusted Brandon. "Yes, I will," she said.

Maurice's heart dropped as the women left.

"So, how long you all been married?" Brandon asked.

"Going on fifteen years."

"How long you've been dating Gloria?"

"We met a few months ago and have gone on a few dates. She's a rock star, though."

"Yeah, seems like it. What kind of work do you do?"

"I'm a massage therapist."

Maurice's antennae went up. "A massage therapist. Really? Where?"

"I used to work at some spas at hotels downtown. But I've been at Massage Envy in Bethesda for about four months. It's a little more casual and relaxed."

Maurice turned into private detective then. "It's amazing you've been here all this time and just seeing my wife for the first time in almost twenty years. This is the first time you've seen her, right?"

Brandon was intent on protecting Juanita. He quickly thought back to their introduction, when she had said, "We hadn't seen each other in fifteen years." So he answered, "Yes. She still looks pretty much the same, too."

Maurice nodded his head and looked off. "What kind of work do you do?"

"I work on Capitol Hill in the Rayburn Building and —"

Brandon did not hear the rest. He knew Gloria had worked at the Rayburn Building, and she told him she had been dating a man who worked there. It was one of the things he liked about her; she was transparent. When he inquired about why she was single, she'd told him: "I'm quasi-single. By that, I mean, I'm going through a divorce and I date a man who is not divorced. I'm not proud of it, but I own it. That's why I can tell you."

Further, Brandon drove Uber on off days, and he met Gloria when she was a passenger in his car one afternoon. They exchanged numbers. When he dropped her off at her house, there was a man standing out front, waiting for her. He believed in that moment that man was Maurice. That reality stunned him.

In the line outside the women's bathroom, Juanita and Gloria clicked. They admired the fashion of the women, chatted about the D.C. social life and learned a little about each other.

"So, you and Brandon — how did you meet?"

"I live on Capitol Hill and sometimes I drive to work, sometimes I catch the bus and sometimes I catch Uber. One day, I went with Uber and he shows up in, like, three minutes. When I got into the car, he insisted I sit in the front and said, 'I've been waiting for you all day.'

"He got my attention right away. We chatted and I felt intrigued enough to give him my number. He called me and invited me to get a massage — you know he's a massage therapist, right? — and I was sold. I had just gone through a divorce and I'm open to new things. He's a lot of fun so far."

"I bet he is," Juanita said.

When they returned to the men, Maurice's disposition was different, and Juanita noticed. Juanita knew then she had to separate from Brandon and Gloria.

"Husband, let's find a table where we can sit down. I don't want my feet to start hurting."

"Sure," he said. Then he turned to Brandon. "Nice to meet you, Brandon. I may have to send my wife to your location. She loves massages."

Juanita's heart pounded. She had told Maurice she had gone for a massage. *Now he knows Brandon's profession? Did he put it all together?*

"Nice to meet you, too, Maurice. Maybe I'll see you around the Rayburn Building when I pick up Gloria."

Maurice swallowed hard. *Does he know about Gloria and me?*

Juanita caught Gloria staring at Maurice. She thought: *How could he not know or at least have seen this woman if they worked in the same building? And why is she looking at him like that?*

Brandon gave Juanita a strange look as he and Gloria went one way, and Juanita and Maurice went another. They were walking in different directions but headed on a collision course.

CHAPTER TWENTY-THREE: AFTER THE STORM . . . A TSUNAMI

Rhonda

As Rhonda sat on the couch with her head spinning, Eric packed a second bag and stormed toward the garage. He had calmed down, but was resolute in his plans.

"I felt like I was failing you. That's what you made me feel like with all that crap you said about me. And it turns out that you didn't just fail me. You failed yourself. I remember you going off about marriages falling apart because of cheating. *Hypocrite.*"

Rhonda wanted to offer a substantive response, but all she had was: "I hope, when you calm down, you will come back home so we can talk about it."

"Yeah. I wouldn't bet on that."

And then he left. Rhonda felt a confluence of emotions: She was miserable that she had hurt Eric. She was embarrassed that she had been caught cheating. She was relieved that she could do as she pleased.

She was scared of being single again.

Lorenzo did not dare text her, knowing she would be under so much scrutiny from her husband. But with Eric gone, presumably to their unoccupied townhouse they owned on the other side of town, Rhonda texted Lorenzo, despite it being nearly two in the morning. She needed to let him know what had happened, just in case Eric went to see him.

Can you call me? My husband knows.

Her phone rang twenty seconds after sending the message.

"What?"

"Yes. He is the one who moved my car. He saw me coming into the subdivision when I was coming to see you, and followed me. He saw you let me into your house."

"Oh, shit. What did you tell him?"

"He asked your name, but I wouldn't tell him. I told him it was about us, not you. He said it was over, packed two bags and left."

"What? He left? To go where? Here?"

"I don't think so. He said he wasn't. Said he has no problem with you — you were doing what a man would do. We have a townhouse in DeKalb County that he said he was going to. But he's so angry, I don't know."

"Damn. This is crazy."

314

"I know. I'm sorry."

"It's not your fault. Not anyone's fault. What's up now?"

"I don't know. I feel bad. And I feel relieved. I feel free. And I feel scared."

"I understand. This might sound superficial, but it's going to be all right."

"I hope so. I have a headache. I'm going to take something, take a shower and try to get some sleep. I will call you tomorrow."

Rhonda ingested some Tylenol, decided on a long, hot bath with a glass of wine and got into her bed alone for one of the few times in fourteen years. Her mind and heart were too torn to get much sleep. The overwhelming thought was the hurt she'd caused her husband.

She'd seen him angry at her for various reasons. She'd seen him scared early in the marriage when they both lost jobs two weeks apart and financial troubles threatened foreclosure on their home. She'd seen him regretful when he overacted and lashed out during arguments. She's seen him empathetic and thoughtful and kind and tender.

But Rhonda had never seen the pain in Eric's eyes during the three years they dated and fourteen they were married. Knowing she'd caused him such anguish crushed her.

She slept a few hours and woke to an empty home. It was eerie — and sad. Even as Eric had gained weight and lost interest in doing anything outside their routine, he was always there. There was comfort and security in that. Not having it left her feeling empty.

The temptation to call Eric mounted, and finally became too much.

"What do you want?"

"I want to talk to you, Eric."

"Talk."

"Shouldn't we do it in person?"

"Talk."

"Okay, well. I just want you to know I understand that you hate me and that you're disappointed in me and don't want anything to do with me. But I'm so sorry, Eric. I made a mistake. It wasn't a little mistake. It was huge. I wish I could take it back. I really do because I love you. We've been together for seventeen years. We have a lot of memories between us. We shouldn't throw it all away over this."

Guilt made her take that position. Her issues with Eric were real, and they were beyond his weight. His lack of interest in doing things and going places with her — "exploring life," is how she put it — made her angry and feel as if her life was wasting

316

away. That bothered her and made her consider a life without him for a few years.

Encountering Lorenzo took her interest in leaving to another level. He was attractive and interesting and fun. She saw the possibilities in him. Rhonda had told Eric she wanted to work on their marriage, but the reality was that she was tired of trying to prod him to show interest in enjoying life differently from the way they had for so long.

"You threw it away, Rhonda. Not me. You think I would ever trust you again? I don't think so."

And then he hung up.

The abrupt end to the conversation led Rhonda to a Sunday morning in a fog, unable to focus on one thing. She did not eat. She wanted to pray, but was not sure what to call on God for; after all, her sins created her drama.

She did not think about what a divorce would feel like: the loneliness, the responsibility. The *failure*. What would her friends think? There were three couples they would visit or have visit them to play cards or watch sports. Rhonda didn't like cards and wanted to go out into Atlanta to enjoy the myriad social options, but she always gave in to Eric, who argued, "What's the point of spending money and being around strangers? We can drink as much as we want and have fun with our friends here, at home."

After a while, she stopped fighting it and gave in. But she was not happy. She felt trapped. But while being free gave her new oxygen, she also felt embarrassment, especially if Eric was transparent to friends about why the marriage would end.

In an effort of damage control, she called her mother, who lived in Fort Pierce, Florida. She had married a retired Navy officer and fled south. Elizabeth hardly visited Atlanta. "It's too much like New York, too much going on, too fast."

But she and Rhonda talked regularly and often; she was her daughter's sounding board.

"Mommy, how are you?"

"I was okay. But you call me 'Mommy,' so I know something's going on. What's wrong?"

"That's not true. I call you 'Mommy' all the time."

"You don't even realize it. When all is good, you call me 'Ma.' Not 'Mom' and not 'Mommy.' I know my child. Now what's wrong?"

"Are you sitting down?"

"I'm literally sitting on a swing at Jetty Park with David."

"Oh, I don't want to interrupt your day."

"You know we walk either here or Pepper Park Beach almost every day. It's not a big deal. What's going on?"

"Well, I think Eric and I are getting a divorce."

There was silence on the phone.

"Mommy . . ."

"Hold on . . . David, excuse me a minute."

Elizabeth walked out of David's earshot and went off.

"What are you talking about? You all got past the seven-year itch and are going on fifteen years of marriage. It should be easy now. What's going on?"

"I haven't been happy for a long time. Eric's a good man, but he's resigned to doing the same thing every day. There's no excitement, no adventure."

"You want an adventure? Being single in 2017 will give you an adventure you wish you didn't have."

"I'm not afraid to be single."

"Well, you should be. You're forty-one years old. You think there are men waiting around for you to be in a relationship, to build something. You're my child and I love you, but your thinking sometimes is too

319

extreme. You end up single now and you'll be single the rest of your life. You think single is the greener side? Think again."

"I've already met a nice man and —"

"Ah, ha. So that's it. You think you're hot shit because some single man was interested in a married woman? I might be old, but I ain't out of touch."

"You're not old, Mommy. What's your point?"

"My point is even down here, where there are less distractions and people are more civil, women face the same problem: Lack of good men. Shoot, in most places it's a lack of *any* man. But you think you're such hot stuff that you're going to get single and have this swinging lifestyle that you fantasized about?"

"I just want a life that has something interesting going on in it. That's all. And I deserve that. That's not asking too much."

"Well, you already tried it and look what you got for it — you're losing your husband and marriage."

"You think I should stay in a marriage that is bland? Yeah, I'm forty-one. But I don't have any kids tying me down. I have a good career. I don't have to live the life of Laura Ingalls Wilder."

"Who the hell is Laura Ingalls Wilder?"

"Laura Ingalls Wilder, *Little House on the Prairie.* I live in modern times in a city with a lot going on. And yet I'm cooped up in the house with a man who's grown so fat that he wheezes when he climbs the stairs. Doesn't want to do anything. We hardly go to a movie. And I'm supposed to be okay with that?"

"You're supposed to make it work, child. You don't know what it's like to be single."

"Well, looks like I'm going to find out. And thanks for having the confidence in me to make it."

"My job isn't to disillusion you, Rhonda. My job is to tell you the truth."

"That's not the truth you're talking. Excuse my language, but the truth doesn't give a damn about your opinion. You should know me as well as anyone. You raised me. And you think I can't make it in the world without a husband? You don't know me at all."

Her mom had unwittingly inspired her to find whatever she had in reserve to make it as a divorced woman, if it came to that. By the time she hung up, she was charged to make her way. There were countless areas to shore up, but her mom indirectly issued her a challenge that she would accept.

She started by texting Eric:

321

I'm really sorry things are like they are, Eric. It's my fault. Totally. I accept responsibility and I understand that you don't trust me. You're a good man who deserved better. I'm ashamed that I have hurt you like this. Please forgive me.

She spent much of the afternoon and evening thinking and planning and worrying. She made a meal of toast and a boiled egg and texted Lorenzo. He did not respond before Rhonda decided to go on a walk around the subdivision. She needed the fresh air and to stretch her legs.

Walking also allowed her to think. In this case, she thought about Lorenzo, which made her feel good. All of her thoughts the previous eighteen hours had been difficult to digest and made her feel bad about herself. Something encouraging did come out of the madness: She could be with Lorenzo as much as she pleased, which was something she really wanted. In fact, with all the turmoil that came from cheating with him, she needed his attention, affection and presence.

She knew Lorenzo wanted the same. That was the redeeming element she was able to grasp. Rhonda felt the need to speak to Olivia about what was going on with her and Eric and her and Lorenzo. She knew that would be a tough conversation, but she was at a place that required honesty.

Olivia did not answer, so Rhonda left a message: *Girl, a lot is going on. We need to talk. Call me back.*

The idea of sharing her world with her closest friend put a bounce in her step. The air felt good on her body and the doldrums she had placed herself in seemed less burdensome. In fact, she picked up her pace as she got closer to Lorenzo's. Maybe he was home and she'd get to see him. *That would really make me feel better.*

When she got to Lorenzo's house, however, there was a car in the driveway. She did not want to ring his doorbell unannounced — until she noticed the car.

It was Olivia's white Mercedes C230. She knew it was hers because the frame around her license plate read: *"Hotness."* Realizing Olivia was there made her feel threatened — and she was not sure why.

Was it because Lorenzo had told her he was not interested, and yet invited her over? Was it because she had, in one sense, considered Lorenzo hers, and therefore off-limits, especially to Olivia? Was it because Olivia had told her she wanted sex with Lorenzo? Was it because she had blown up her world messing around with Lorenzo and he was entertaining someone else?

Her mind would not allow her to stop creating scenarios, so to save herself from herself, she went to his front door. She had to ring it twice — and she was willing to ring it all night until someone came to the door — before she could detect someone approaching.

Rhonda turned her back so she could not be seen through the peephole in the door. When she heard it open, she turned around to see Lorenzo, whose expression did not denote that he was happy to see her.

"Rhonda, what's going on?"

"You tell me. I texted you a few minutes ago. You didn't respond. What's going on? Is that Olivia's car?"

"Rhonda? Girl, I knew that was you," Olivia said, as Lorenzo stepped aside. "I know your voice. What are you doing here?"

"What are *you* doing here?"

"Was about to do *something* before you rang the doorbell. Why are you here?"

"Can I come in, Lorenzo?"

He looked at her with a curious expression.

"Why not?" he said as he walked toward the kitchen, shaking his head.

"Girl, I was on my walk and I looked up and saw your car. I said, 'Let me see what

324

this diva got going on up in here.' "

The women, sitting at the kitchen table, laughed. Lorenzo didn't.

"So you remember Lorenzo, right? From Suite Lounge?"

"Oh, I remember him. I've seen him walking in my neighborhood."

"Our neighborhood," he said.

"When he gave me the address, I put it in my GPS and I was like, 'This is taking me to my girl's house.' I had no idea you lived in the same subdivision."

"Surprised me, too," Rhonda said. "But am I interrupting a date or something?"

"I'm a woman, he's a man. We're together at his house — I would say you're interrupting a date, yes."

Lorenzo tried to hold back a laugh, but couldn't. That infuriated Rhonda.

"Oh, that's funny?"

"Actually, it is funny. But that's not the question. The question is: Who comes to someone's house uninvited?"

"You all bickering like y'all a couple or something," Olivia said.

"I'm just saying that she doesn't know me, but she rings my doorbell because she sees your car? That's inappropriate."

"I apologize; you're right. I got caught up in the moment, because I noticed Olivia's car. I'll leave shortly. So what's going on, girl?"

"I just got here about thirty minutes ago. I saw you called. I called you early this morning. Do you know Eric called me?"

Rhonda glanced at Lorenzo.

"He left a message saying he wanted to talk to me, ask me a question. What's up with that?"

"You have to ask him, Olivia."

"Your husband called her?" Lorenzo asked.

Rhonda nodded. Lorenzo smirked and headed to the fridge. "Want something to drink? Oh, but you're leaving, right?"

"I was walking, but I'd like something to drink, since you're offering. Whatever you guys are having."

"So, Lorenzo finally called me back this afternoon," Olivia said.

"And you're over here today? He doesn't mess around, I see."

She gave Lorenzo a look he hadn't seen from her, but he knew it was hardly pleasant.

"Why were you playing hard to get with my girlfriend, Lorenzo?" Rhonda asked. "Do you have a girlfriend?"

"I wasn't trying to play hard to get," he answered. "I didn't know she was trying to get with me. Just been busy. And to answer the other part, no, I don't have a girlfriend."

"Why don't you? I don't understand. You're in Atlanta, home of the beautiful women. Here's Olivia, all smart and elegant. What's up with you? You gay?"

Olivia nearly spit out her drink.

"Well, gay technically means happy, so I'm happy to be single," Lorenzo said. "And you're right about Olivia; she's a catch."

"You're a catch, too."

Olivia quickly chimed in. "Yeah, but she's married, so . . ."

"For argument sake, why couldn't I have a husband and a piece on the side? Y'all men do it — brag about it, the conquests. I don't see any reason why what's good for them ain't good for us."

"Maybe you should try it."

"Rhonda? *Please,*" Olivia said. "She loves her husband. She ain't on the market."

Rhonda pondered if she should give some version of the truth, an edited version that would not include Lorenzo. She decided against it because it was not the time or place.

"So since I'm here, I'm gonna get all up in y'all's business," Rhonda said. "So what do you think of my girl? You must have some feelings for her since you invited her to your house."

"I don't think that's something you should be concerned about — unless you're her momma," Lorenzo said. "Otherwise, I'll deal with Olivia on this."

"I don't think I should have introduced you two. Seems like you have beef over me. You know me, Rhonda. I won't let a man take advantage of me. But Lorenzo is a sweetheart. I *think.* I'm trying to find out.

"But what did you want to talk to me about? I got your message, but it would have been rude for me to call you while I'm sitting here with this fine gentleman. Plus, we were about to do something a little more fun than talking to you."

Rhonda could not tell if Olivia was exaggerating or playing or what. But she took her seriously, which made her uneasy. *Was Lorenzo going to sleep with her? And a night after sleeping with me?*

"Oh, really? I interrupted your fun, Lorenzo?" Rhonda asked.

"Since nothing happened, I don't know if it would have been fun or not."

"Oh, baby, you can believe when I'm involved, it's fun," Olivia cracked.

"Well," Rhonda decided, "I'm going to finish my walk. I'm clearly interrupting. But come over to my house when you're finished

328

here, Olivia. But don't be too late. Lorenzo, good to see you again."

And then she left. Her stomach was unsettled, but she was hopeful that Lorenzo would reject Olivia's inevitable advances. *But why would he invite her over in the first place?*

Rhonda's walk back to her empty house was wrought with guilt and doubt and questions. She figured quickly that Eric lied about talking to Olivia, in effect fooling her into admitting she had not spent the night with her as she had told him. But the potential for him to get confirmation of his thoughts remained, and Rhonda was in full damage control mode.

Over the forty-five minutes between when she got home and when Olivia finally rang her doorbell, she struggled with what to tell her girlfriend. The full-blown truth was too much, she decided. Telling her about Eric leaving would open the avenue to many questions. Not telling her, though, would leave open the possibility of Eric giving her the news, which surely would be a problem for her relationship with Olivia.

First, though, she needed to hear more about what had happened with Lorenzo. Rhonda tried to remain casual as she sought to pry information out of her friend.

"Girl, that was a trip," Olivia said as she walked in.

"How did it go?"

"It went good. I wasn't gonna have sex with him or anything like that. I talk a good game. I just wanted to see how he would handle the situation. And he handled it probably too well."

"What's that mean?"

"I think he might be gay."

"That man is *not* gay, Olivia. How can you say that?"

"Easy. There are obvious tendencies that I saw, with number one being he turned me down."

Rhonda was relieved: "I thought you weren't going to have sex with him?"

"I wasn't, but I was seeing where his head was."

"Well, him rejecting you doesn't mean he's gay, Olivia. That's how bad rumors get started. Maybe he has a girlfriend or maybe he thinks it's too soon."

"See, that's what I'm talking about, not about me being irresistible. I'm talking about a full-fledged man would have been down for whatever, whether he has a girl-friend or not. That's what men do. No real man I know would turn down a chance for sex the way I offered it."

"Damn, what did you do? Throw your pussy on the table?"

The women laughed. Rhonda laughed harder because Lorenzo did not give in to Olivia.

"Yeah, whatever. What I did was I talked to him — directly. I said, 'Look, we're adults. I don't have anyone and you just said you're single. So, maybe we should fill in the gaps for each other.'

"He was like, 'Olivia, you know I like you. That's why you're here. But when sex is involved, all kinds of feelings start coming into play. If we go there, let's at least try to prevent drama in the long term. If you get to know me, you might not even want to get with me.'

"Now what man talks like that? If anything, a man wouldn't say anything. He would have led me to the bedroom. Now, I wasn't going to sleep with him — I don't think. But I did want to see where his head was."

"So now you know."

"I do. But what did you want to talk about? What's your drama?"

"Who said anything about drama?"

"You did in your message."

"Oh, I did, didn't I? Well, come on in here

and take a seat. I think you'll find all this very interesting."

Chapter Twenty-Four: Daddy Issues

Stephanie

The fact that she could feel sexually aroused while she was so scared about her sister and frustrated about her father told her all she needed to know about her life.

A man who was interested in her and displayed his interest meant more than she realized. Charles showing up at the hospital was not only thoughtful and caring, but a turn-on. She had told Willie that a man who showed his affection by his actions was a man women appreciated.

Charles resonated with Stephanie. She, however, knew that a divorce was a step not to be taken lightly. Above all, she had a daughter who loved her parents and surely would react emphatically to a divorce.

She thought: *Where is the line between my happiness and making other people happy?* And she did not have an answer.

Before she could get too enthralled in that

question, her father and Terry emerged from the elevators.

"You left her alone?" Stephanie asked. There was almost terror in her voice.

"It's okay. She's okay," Terry said.

"I don't want her to be alone. Ever," Stephanie snapped. "And I hope you were talking to her and not just sitting there sleeping."

"We came down to stretch our legs," her father said.

"Stretch your legs. I'm going to be with Toya."

Immediately, she headed for the elevators, without looking back. When she got to outside Toya's room, she took a deep breath. Then she went in.

Her sister lay there lifeless, as if she were asleep, save for the connections to her head and mouth and the machines humming ominous sounds.

Stephanie stood over her at her bedside and surveyed Toya's body. The image made her sad. But in her heart she believed she could hear her, so she pulled up the chair closer to the bed, clutched her right hand through the bed railings and talked.

"Nick is here. I know you want me to call him 'Dad,' but I'm still struggling with it. He met Charles. Don't get all upset; he doesn't know about us. Charles came over because he was concerned about me, said he knew I needed a hug. He was right, Toya. Willie went home and I was all alone in the visiting area downstairs, worried.

"When he came, it brightened up my outlook, my world, really. Isn't that how it should be? You always talked about how Terry was made for you and always felt like he was with you, not against you. I think the way you put it was, 'He's the captain of my team.' I liked that. But to be honest, I was a little jealous, too.

"Willie hadn't made me feel like he's even on my team. Forget about being the captain. I'm not sure where it went south. That's what bothers me. I know it was gradual, like gaining weight. But also like gaining weight, one day you look in the mirror and realize, 'Damn. I'm fat.'

"That's how this has been with Willie. I realized one day that I'm not happy, that I often feel alone in the marriage. When people lose weight, the goal shouldn't be to lose weight because you can always find it again. The goal has to be to *get rid of it.* In my marriage, I have to get rid of feeling empty and alone. Charles has been that source to this point, but I know it's wrong. I *know* it's wrong. But I'm learning about myself after all this time.

"Toya, I need to feel loved. Not by every-body. But you and Willie, I need to feel that. Even as we argue about what I'm doing, I know it's because you love me. With Willie, the arguments happen because he's discon-nected from me and doesn't want to believe it, so he doesn't want to hear about it. And the business is his first love. That's what he really cares about, not me."

Stephanie took her other hand and placed on top of hers and Toya's. "I've used Charles to give me some of the feelings that I need to have. Even before we had slept together, communicating with him through texts and e-mail felt good. Someone was interested in me. That meant a lot to me.

"I know you're stronger than me and more pragmatic than me. I'm more emo-tional and my actions are tied to what I'm feeling. I have been seeing Charles because I needed it. I still do. Look at tonight. Willie doesn't see how I would need him here right now and goes home. And Charles who is visiting, who doesn't even live in the Bay, comes over in the middle of the night to give me a hug. See the difference?

"But I'm willing to make a deal with you. I will let Charles go if you wake up and be all right. How's that? You don't have to wake up now. Get your rest. But when you're ready, open your eyes, talk to me. And then we can go take that trip to Vegas we've been talking about for six months. Just me and you. No husbands."

Stephanie sat back in the chair, took a deep breath. She wondered to herself if God was punishing her by putting Toya's life in jeopardy. That scared her and made her pray.

Father God, I need my sister to be all right. That's all I'm asking. Please do not punish Toya for my bad deeds. She has tried to guide me away from sin. She has been faithful to You. She deserves to live. She deserves to be healthy. Please, God, bring her out of this and make her whole. I have faith that you will.

When she opened her eyes, her father was standing in the doorway.

"What sins you've been committing?" he asked.

"You're like in a soap opera, eavesdropping. I can't even pray in solitude?"

"That's not answering the question."

"You should take it as an answer because that's all you get. Why are you up here anyway?"

"I came to say I'm leaving and will be back soon."

"What's 'soon'?"

"I'm not sure. Probably tomorrow. But I need you to keep me abreast of what the doctors say about her condition."

"Why can't you be here to find out for yourself?"

"I can't be here every minute. I don't know how you can, either."

"Because that's the sacrifice you make for someone you love. I shouldn't have to tell you that."

"Don't get cute with me, girl. I raised this woman right here as if she were my own. So don't tell me about sacrifices."

"Yeah, and you sacrificed the family for your own good, too."

Nick fumed.

"Step outside this room."

Stephanie knew she was out of bounds, but she also believed she had the truth on her side.

"What?"

"I haven't seen you in several months and that's all right. You call me Nick instead of Dad, and I accepted that. But don't think you can disrespect me to my face and get away with it."

His voice rose and nurses at the station could hear the grumblings. "You don't know what the hell happened in my marriage."

"I know you got a divorce because you

338

cheated. And then you acted like it was no big deal."

"No big deal? My life was turned upside down. All our lives were. Because you didn't see me looking shattered doesn't mean I wasn't shattered. I was. I am. Still. Until you go through that — disappointing the woman you love, destroying your family — you can't sit in judgment of me."

Stephanie lowered her head. She *had* judged her father all those years, never talking to him about why he cheated or his feelings after the breakup.

"And if you don't want to feel what I feel," he added, lowering his voice, "you'd better tell that guy Charles to go someplace."

Stephanie raised her head and tried to act indignant. "What are you talking about?"

"I'm old, Steph. My vision gets worse every year. But I ain't senile and I ain't blind. That man kissed you on the top of your head with passion, not empathy. So if you're doing something, stop. If you're thinking about doing something, stop. That momentary pleasure you think you want won't be worth it — unless you want to be divorced."

"You think I would have an affair on Willie?"

"We've always said you're more like me

339

than your mother."

She was hurt because the truth often hurts.

"I'm not even dignifying that," Stephanie said. "If I'm like you in that way, I suppress it. My marriage is fine."

"I've said what I had to say about it. The rest is up to you."

He hugged his daughter, who did not hug him back, and left.

Stephanie returned to the room and told Toya: "I guess he told me, huh?"

The various emotions clashed against her brain and sensibilities, and she broke into tears. Her hands over her face, she wept a good cry, one that cleared her sinuses and her contact lenses. It also cleared her mind: She was resolute about being content in her life, not discontent or bored.

That notion became profound in the middle of her crying spell. The prevailing emotion was her fear and sadness about her sister, whose future was as uncertain as a butterfly's flight path. The delicacy of Toya's life was a resounding notice to Stephanie of how precarious life was, how short it can be.

How can I exist in a stale marriage when I believe in living a vibrant life?

Her answer was that she couldn't. Charles

was a stopgap, a filler, a case study of what it could be like to be with a man who moved her. Above all, he was married, so their affair had to end at some point. He had told her he was not leaving his wife. So, what they had was temporary, and she had no control over how long it lasted.

Worse, she began to think about his wife and her decisions: *What if she found out? Is it treason against women to serve as a mistress to someone's husband? How could she be so selfish as to disregard the morals instilled in her by her mother?*

She heard the words that her mom often uttered when Stephanie and Toya were kids growing up: *Do what you know is right.*

It was a simplistic, but profound statement when taken in its full context. *You know what to do. You've been taught and schooled and lectured on what is right. So do it.*

Falling back on that basic principle taught by her mother moved Stephanie to a firm decision on Charles: It was over. She didn't like not having control over that situation, anyway. At the hotel in Sausalito, before she got word about Toya, she had a moment of anxiety. Stephanie enjoyed Charles so much that she was becoming dependent on his attention and passion. She felt vulnerable, knowing that she would be crushed if he decided to end their affair when she was not ready.

Charles did not give her any indication that he wanted it to end, but knowing he could hurt her caused discomfort. But it was not enough for her to pull away. However, combined with her guilt and the idea of honoring her mother's words, Stephanie found the strength not only to extricate herself from cheating, but also to work on her marriage.

She leaned close to Toya's ear. "Remember when Momma used to say, 'Do what you know is right'? She used to say that so much, I guess because we were always doing something we shouldn't have been. Or when we went over to a friend's house or to a party, she'd tell us the same thing: 'Do what you know is right.'

"For my own selfish reasons, I have ignored that standard. Not anymore. Like you told me, I know better. So I'm ending it with Charles. I —"

"Ending what with who?" came the voice behind Stephanie.

She turned around to see her husband, Willie. Her heart dropped. She almost lost her breath. She hoped she was dreaming. She was not.

"We need to talk," he said, motioning with his finger for her to leave the room.

"I, uh, I don't want to leave Toya alone."

"Toya is fine. And Terry just got here, so he's coming up now. Come on."

The look on his face frightened Stephanie. Willie turned and went into the hallway. A few seconds later, Terry entered the room.

"How's it going?" Terry asked.

"It's . . . you know. Status quo," Stephanie said.

"Well, go get some rest. I'm here for the rest of the night. It's almost three in the morning. Get some rest and come back when you feel like it and then I'll get some rest."

"Okay," Stephanie said, "but are you talking to her?"

"Talking her head off."

She smiled, hugged Terry and entered the hallway, where nothing good was waiting on her.

CHAPTER TWENTY-FIVE: YOU ARE NOT ALONE

Juanita

They hung at the party for another hour or so, chatting with friends and enjoying the music. But there was a cloud over both of them. Juanita wondered if Maurice had an idea about her affair with Brandon and she was suspicious of if he knew Gloria.

Maurice got the feeling that Brandon and Juanita's relationship was more current than they led on — and was concerned if Brandon knew he and Gloria had their thing on the side.

Neither could hide their swirling emotions and thoughts on the ride home. There was silence. Not even the radio played. They were so consumed in their secrets that they didn't even notice.

At home, in the bathroom, Juanita texted Brandon.

Hey, please text me back. Does he know you gave me a massage? Did he question you? Tell me everything I need to know.

In the closet, Maurice frantically texted Gloria. *Gloria, are you OK? Did she question you about us knowing each other before tonight? Does your friend know about us? Give me all details.*

Neither of them was comfortable in their own thoughts. They acted guilty. After a quick shower, Maurice took his phone with him. "I'm going to check on the kids." Juanita was glad he left. "Okay."

That time apart gave them a chance to check their text messages.

Brandon's to Juanita read: *I don't know. He asked me my job and I told him. Does he know you came to me? Because you're my girl, I will tell you that I think Gloria knows him. I saw him standing outside her house the day I met her.*

Gloria's to Maurice read: *Brandon is a massage therapist. He said wife could vouch for his work. Then tried to backtrack and act like it was a long time ago. Not sure if he knows about us, but he's curious, asking questions. I'm telling him nothing.*

Neither Juanita nor Maurice knew how to respond to the messages. He went back to their bedroom and finished undressing. He took his cell phone to the bathroom with him.

Juanita erased the string of text messages and got into bed. It was nearly three in the morning, but she was not sleepy. She was scared. Her squeaky-clean reputation — and her marriage — hung in the balance of how Maurice took the information he had. And now she wondered about her husband's activities, too. Maurice, in the shower, placed both his hands on the wall and let the water pour on him as he tried to figure out a reason why he would act as if he did not know Gloria, if asked by Juanita.

He finished his shower, and entered their bedroom, which was only lit by the moonlight gleaning through the blinds. He slid into bed as quietly as possible, curled up with his back to Juanita and closed his eyes.

They lay there in quiet, wide awake. Juanita wanted the night to be over, but decided it was best to take the offense, to act as if everything was fine. So she turned over and sidled up against Maurice's body, which was rigid and warm.

"Maurice," she whispered into his ear, "I love you."

Those were the last words she uttered to her husband on most nights before they went to sleep. They were sincere words; her infidelity did not take away from her love for her husband. The affair was a separate entity — a separate account, so to speak, that had different deposits of emotions and purposes.

She liked being a different person with Brandon. She was the woman she wanted to be. Besides their hotel encounters, she would stop by his apartment after getting her hair done on Saturday afternoons, have sex, and go home feeling reinvigorated. She enjoyed being irresponsible. The "bad girl" behavior balanced out the goody-two-shoes life she lived.

She never considered ending her marriage, though. She also seldom considered the pain it would cause Maurice if he found out. That's what scared her — hurting her husband, losing his respect, her reputation, her *family.*

Maurice was equally fearful of the same things. But Juanita's perceived perfection impacted his self-esteem. He often felt inferior to her status as the sweetest, kindest, *perfect* woman. With Gloria, he had a no-strings-attached situation where he was not judged by how people judged her.

Whatever their misguided reasons, Juanita and Maurice faced potential revelations that could implode a marriage that meant a lot to them.

"I love you, too," Maurice responded to

his wife.

She kissed him on his shoulder and he slowly turned from his side to his back. Juanita put her arm around him, and he kissed it. She raised her head and their lips met. They kissed deeply — more passionately than they had in several weeks.

He caressed her body and she closed her eyes, trying desperately to take in the passion between husband and wife. They kissed again before she turned her back to him and lifted up her nightgown and pulled down her panties. She did not want him to see the shame on her face.

Maurice entered her from behind, and she cried as her husband made love to her. There were tears of guilt and regret — *and* because she wished it was Brandon in bed with her.

She hoped making love would close some of the intangible distance between them and push aside any concerns Maurice might have had about her and Brandon. Yes, she used sex to divert attention from her misdeeds. She was that desperate to keep her reputation and live up to her image, while averting a crisis in her marriage.

She wiped her face as he did his business and waited for him to finish. When he did, Juanita pulled up the covers, curled up in the fetal position and cried herself to sleep. Maurice had no idea.

In the morning, they agreed to pass on going to church and to spend the day at home with the kids. They had the same idea: To reinforce the value of family to deter bad behavior.

They both slipped away to text Brandon and Gloria, respectively, but they were mostly holding their breath that the other would not bring up what they learned at the party.

It was not until that Sunday night that Maurice indirectly addressed the situation. "I think we should have another session with Dr. Fields tomorrow, if we can. Can you make yourself available around three?"

Juanita tried to seem unfazed. "Yes, I think. If you confirm the appointment in the morning, I will make sure I'm there."

She was interested in going because it was eating her up not to share what she had been doing with anyone. Juanita was not an open person, but she was a talker who liked to share her world with those closest to her. She often was mindful not to come off as boastful when she talked about her family or career.

There were two of many girlfriends she was close to, but would not dare share with them her activities with Brandon. In fact, she had not returned a call from Sandra because she was too busy running around with Brandon.

That thought inspired her to text her friend before putting the kids to bed. Sandra responded immediately.

So, you are alive, huh? Good. Let's do lunch tomorrow. I have some news.

Juanita wrote back: *OK. Noon at Fiola. Is it good news?*

Sandra: *It's juicy.*

The next morning, Maurice called her on her job to tell her the first available appointment was Thursday — four days away. They agreed to take that appointment. "Do you think we need to talk before then, among ourselves?" he asked. Wondering if Juanita knew something was getting to him.

"We can always talk, Maurice. So maybe we will."

They hung up and she confirmed her lunch date with Sandra, which was good because Brandon texted her a few minutes later asking to see her.

I made plans with my girlfriend. And after Saturday night, I shouldn't be missing in action any time soon, if ever again.

Brandon texted her back: *Good. You're going to try to make your marriage work?*

Instead of texting him, she called.

"You know how much I enjoy being with you. But we talked about it the last time I saw you — I can't see you anymore. Not like that. I want to. I do. But I can't afford for Maurice to find out. I have to protect my family."

"I understand, 'Nita. I'm good."

"But your text after the party said you had seen my husband with your friend?"

"Gloria. Yes. I met her when I was driving Uber on an off day. Picked her up at the Rayburn Building. Dropped her at her house. On the way, we connected and she gave me her number. But when she got out, the guy standing there waiting for her looked like your husband. I didn't know at the time. And I could be wrong. I'm only telling you this because you're my girl. I don't hate on someone else doing their thing. And I'm not telling you so we can keep doing what we've been doing. My allegiance is to you. You should know."

"Are you sure it was him?"

"Not one hundred percent. But if I had to bet on it, I would say it was him."

"Okay. Thanks. I gotta go."

It was one thing to read a text from Brandon while under duress. It was another to hear the conviction and certainty in his

351

voice. And she was immediately angry and hurt and disappointed.

How could Maurice cheat on me? I have been all he could ever want.

Still, as mad and hurt and disappointed as she was, she had done the same to Maurice.

If this is true, if Maurice really is cheating on me, then maybe it's what I deserve.

By the time she met Sandra for lunch, Juanita was confused about what to do and what to say to her husband. She worried: Would accusing Maurice of cheating spark him to counter-accuse, forcing her to defend an indefensible position? And she questioned: *Would it all just go away if none of it was ever discussed?*

She placed her swirling thoughts aside when she saw Sandra waiting for her at Fiola. They hugged and smiled and complimented each other on how they looked after they got to their table.

"I'm trying to figure out why you disappeared for about a month," Sandra said.

"It's been crazy at work and home, really. But everything's good."

"Of course, it is; you have the perfect life."

"Don't start."

"You *do*. Be glad for it. I'm about ready to kill the men in my life every other day."

"Anyway, what's going on with you?

What's this juicy news?"

"You're not going to believe this."

"What, Sandra?"

"Alexandria is having an affair."

Alexandria was the third member of their close-knit group, a realtor in Northern Virginia. She was a stylish, dignified woman with a middle-school-aged daughter and a husband of twelve years who owned four McDonald's.

"*Stop.* How do you know this?"

"She told me."

Juanita looked at her with a strange expression.

"That's right, she told me. We were at Busboys and Poets on Fourteenth and she blurted it out. Said she had this client who moved here from L.A. She showed him properties for a week. She said the attraction was immediate, but she didn't think he had any interest in her. But when he found the house he wanted to buy — a place over in Old Town — he hugged her and then kissed her. She said she kissed him back.

"This was almost a month ago. She's been seeing him ever since."

"Seeing him is different from sleeping with him."

"She screwed him that day — right there in the house he decided to buy. Said they 'blessed the house.' And here's the crazy part: She said she's so happy."

"I'm stunned. I thought their marriage was rock-solid. She never complained — well, not to me — about any problems they were having."

"Me, either. But apparently something major was going on. For her to sleep with this man she knew for a week is not what I would have expected out of her."

"Does she know you're telling me?"

"She called you herself, but you didn't call her back. She was going to tell you. We're the only ones who know."

"I guess you never know what's really going on in people's lives. I could have sworn Alexandria would never cheat."

"I know. She said it could be a midlife crisis. But she also said she and John have been arguing a lot over small stuff and it's worn on her. You know he likes to drink and go out without her a lot on Fridays after work. She got tired of complaining and did something to make herself happy. That's what she said."

The server came over and took their orders. Juanita thought about the news she had heard, and it made her feel better about herself. It was the misery loves company thing. Learning someone else had done wrong validated that she's not a bad person, someone who made amoral decisions. It didn't take away from the person she was. She believed that because her opinion of Alexandria did not change with learning of her infidelities.

After they ate, Juanita considered telling Sandra about her life. But only for a second. That news would go to the grave with her. But the belief that Maurice was having an affair would be a stunner to Sandra — and it would help her to get out in front of what could come out about her affair.

But Juanita was fiercely private and protective of the reputation she built. Her husband cheating would be a reflection on *her.* Plus, what if he was not the man Brandon saw at Gloria's house? If he denied it, there would be no way to prove the accusation. *Why muddy the name of my husband on hearsay?*

So she kept quiet.

"I will call Alexandria tonight. I can't believe this heifer. I hope she doesn't allow it to mess up her marriage."

"That's always the risk. I never told anyone," Sandra said, "but I had an affair on Thomas when I was married way back —"

"What?"

"I did. I never told anyone. Well, I told Alexandria when she told me about what's going on with her. But before then, I kept it to myself. The thing about it was, I wasn't looking to cheat. I went to one of my high-school reunions and saw one of my old crushes. We started talking and kept in touch and the next thing I knew, we started this fling."

"I had no idea."

"Good. I didn't want you to have one. It lasted about four months. I won't lie: There was something really exciting about sneaking around. It was wrong and I would never recommend someone put her marriage on the line like that, especially a woman. But I did enjoy it."

"How did you end it? Why did you end it?"

"It got to a point where I was getting too reliant on it. It was hurting my home life. I was seeing him every week, so that means I was lying every week and putting my marriage in jeopardy every week. Turns out, the marriage failed, anyway, but not because I was cheating."

It was not lost on Juanita that Sandra's story sounded like hers. In fact, Sandra identified something that Juanita had not — she was becoming dependent on Brandon.

"And I tell you what; I still miss that thrill sometimes. I can tell you and Alexandria this, and no one else. I would never encourage someone to cheat. Never. But it worked for me for the time I was in it. And I felt bad about it. I'm lucky I didn't get caught. And I told Alex: 'You're a grown woman and you know what you're doing. But please be careful.' That's all I could say."

Juanita took it all in. Her two closest friends had cheated on their husbands. For her, it made them more human, more likeable because they were able to admit their mistakes. She was proud of them, in a strange way. But she was not proud of herself. She could not be that open with her dearest friends. She never seriously considered telling them.

And she knew at the session with Dr. Fields on Thursday she would not admit to any wrongdoing. She, at times, detested her impeccable reputation, but she coveted it, too — and would go to extreme lengths to protect it.

Juanita preferred she get back to her life as if Brandon never had happened. But he *did* happen, and that left her vulnerable.

Chapter Twenty-Six: True Lies

Rhonda

She decided to give it to Olivia raw, but less than truthful. She figured making up an elaborate lie to protect their friendship was better than telling her that she had been sleeping with the guy she had an interest in.

"I met a guy."

Olivia seemed stumped at first. Rhonda was among the last people she would expect to cheat. She saw her dote over her husband when he had the flu. She passed on many girls' nights out to stay at home with Eric. She seemed perfectly content in her life, her marriage.

"A guy? What?"

"I met a guy. A man."

"And?"

"And I like him. His name is Adam. He's a dentist. A nice man."

"Wait. I don't get it. What are you talking about?"

"Eric left me."

"What? Rhonda . . ."

"Yes. Last night. He found out that I met this guy and have been seeing him for about a month. And he left me."

"I can't believe what I'm hearing. What are you doing seeing another man? I'm shocked."

"It has been building for a while. I'm not proud of it. I have to say that. But Eric let himself go. You see the weight he's gained. And he doesn't seem to think that's a problem, that I should be okay with him swelling up."

"I'm not the most fair person; I'll admit that," Olivia said. "I'm selfish — but that's who I am. No kids, no husband. But you married Eric for a reason. I thought it would be forever."

"I know. I went into it thinking he was the man for my lifetime. But things changed. We grew apart. I know that sounds like a cliché. But it's true. We want different things out of life. I want a husband who's connected to me, who wants to do things and live life. Not someone who eats himself to death and has no concern about his appearance and has no interest in exploring the world.

"And don't tell me that's shallow. It's

what's important to me."

Her mix of truth and lies did not go down easy for Olivia, who liked and respected Eric. But she was among Rhonda's tightest friends, and her allegiance was to her.

"Girl, I want you to be happy. Simple as that. I'm surprised. Shocked, actually. I never would have expected this."

"I'm okay with it, I guess. One minute I'm fine. The next minute I worry about having failed my husband. I worry about living alone. I worry about being single."

"All that is legit stuff to worry about, especially being single."

"You seem to be doing fine."

"Yeah, like you seemed to be doing fine in your marriage. This single life is no joke. We ain't spring chickens no more; gravity took hold and our stuff is falling. Then you look at the number of men out here who think they're the bomb because women are so desperate that they put up with their crap."

"I thought you liked being able to date who you want to date."

"Half of that is true. But the other half is that there isn't a lot to date — a lot of quality anyway. Look at Lorenzo."

"What about him?"

"He's single and he seems like a good guy. But I'm sure he's running a bunch of women."

"Why would you think that? You said he was gay."

"Why wouldn't he have a bunch of women? It's wide open for single men. I'm not saying he's a whore — but maybe he is. He sure has the ability to be one. Or maybe he *is* gay. I don't know. But tell me about this guy you're seeing. Are you seeing him, like sleeping with him?"

In that moment, Rhonda realized she had made a mistake. She should have told Olivia the truth or nothing at all. The lie was about to get bigger, and that made her feel sick to her stomach.

"I don't want to say too much more, Olivia. I can say he's a single, respectable man and we will see how things go."

"You know you're going to have a problem with him trusting you, right?"

"Why?"

"Why? Because you started seeing him while you're married. In the back of his mind, he will always wonder if you'll do it to him, too. It only makes sense. His ego will allow him to believe you cheated because he's so wonderful, but only to a point. And the point comes when you're not where he thinks you should be at a particular time. That's when your history will come in. He will always believe you are capable of cheating — and that's hard for a man to swallow."

Rhonda had not given that position any thought. It all had happened so quickly. Olivia's words forced her to focus and at least begin thinking about a plan. But she wanted to know something else first.

"So, back to being single. You don't like it?"

"I'm forty-three, never been married, no kids. For some women, that's okay. They're fine with it. Not me. I always wanted a husband and family. I'm not unhappy with my life. About four years ago, when I broke up with Tony, I gave up on having a husband and family. Well, I didn't give up. But I settled in my mind that it might not happen, so I could be okay with it. And I am.

"But you know how many events I don't go to because I'm tired of showing up alone? The Forrest Johnson Christmas party. The Rod Edmunds holiday party. The Mayor's Masked Ball. The Trumpet Awards. I have access to all those events and passed. I have met some good men. But the good men have many options and usually explore them. I have met some of the world's biggest assholes, too; guys — I won't even call them men — who are so dishonest that it's sickening."

Rhonda thought for a second.

"I wonder if anyone is really happy," she said. "Most of the married women I know complain about their life. And the married men I know say they aren't happy, either. When you think about it, it's sad."

"There are some people who are happy."

"Who?"

"Single men."

Olivia laughed, and Rhonda mustered a chuckle, too. But she was concerned. She thought about her mother's comments. "You know what I'm going to do?"

"What?"

"Not worry about men. I'm going to live my life and see what that brings me. I haven't been single in a *long* time. So I'm going to enjoy it. It's not like I'm some old maid. I got a little looks and a little body and a lot of sense. My mother told me I was crazy to get a divorce. But she doesn't know what it's like to be married to a man that you have lost attraction for. It's awful. I began to resent him. And, when I really think about it, this is the best thing because I've known Eric for almost twenty years and I don't want to lose respect for him. That's what it was heading toward."

"Wow. You're saying you'd rather be alone

than with someone you don't care for?"

"I care for Eric. I do and always will. But we literally have different ideas about how we should live. I want to do things, take advantage of all the concerts and events that come to Atlanta. I want to travel. I want to party. He wants to play cards in the basement with his fat friends and their lame wives. I know that sounds mean, but I was so tired of it.

"You know that I won the raffle for two tickets in the office to see Kobe Bryant play in Atlanta for the last time, and this man who loves sports didn't want to go? Said, 'Too much drama getting in and out of the arena. It's more comfortable to sit here and watch it on TV.' "

"What did you tell him?"

"I said, 'It's not about comfort. It's about the experience.' I was pissed. So I gave the tickets to the young guy in the office from L.A. He was thrilled. I should have gone by myself. But that was almost the last straw. So, yeah, I'd rather be alone and lonely than with someone who makes me miserable. I would be stuck at home and truly become an old *married* maid messing around with Eric."

"Was he always like that?"

"No. I wouldn't have married him if he

were. He liked to go to Chastain Park for concerts and Falcons games. It's like he hit a midlife crisis and shut down. And whatever was going on with him, he tried to eat his way out of it. You see how big he is? He's not the fit, muscular man I married. And that was important to me. I know myself. I need eye candy. Call me vain if you like. But that's reality. Instead of eye candy, he looks like the whole candy store."

The women laughed. When they settled down, Rhonda tried to cover her tracks.

"Listen, you're the only person I've told this to, other than my mother."

"You don't even have to say it. I won't say a word to anyone."

They rose from their seats and hugged.

"It's going to be all right, trust me," Olivia said. "I have experience in helping girls get back on the horse after divorce. You're the seventh friend, I believe, in the last eight or ten years going through this."

"And how are they?"

"Fine. Still single, but fine."

"I'm nervous; I'm not gonna lie. But I hope Eric and I can remain friends when all is said and done."

"Good luck with that."

"Why do you say that?"

"It could happen, but only after some

time. It's too fresh now, especially since he had the reason to leave. You know men; they hold shit against us like crazy. Their egos can't take certain things, and cheating is number one."

Olivia received a text message and said she had to leave. "Here is a single woman lesson right here," she said. "This guy texted me, asking for a date. So, I know he has no future with me. He has no manners, no chivalry. We haven't gone out yet, and yet he's texting me about going to dinner? And at this late hour? I have to set him straight. So get ready for a lot of that. Always command respect. Lesson number one."

Olivia left and Rhonda felt alone. The house was silent. She had become conditioned to Eric's snoring or wheezing or the TV constantly playing or him playing video games. And she thought: *Damn, I miss my husband.*

It was a fleeting feeling, though. The reality was she missed what she was familiar with, not Eric. But she was concerned about his feelings. So, she called him.

To her astonishment, he answered.

"Hi. How are you? I'm calling to say hello."

"To say hello? That's it?"

"Yeah . . . Can you hear me? There's a lot

of noise in the background."

"Yeah, I'm at the comedy club about to see Paul Mooney."

Rhonda literally pulled the phone from her ear and looked at it.

"You're at the comedy club?"

"Yeah."

"I couldn't get you to go anywhere, and a day after leaving the house you're out at a comedy club?"

"I don't have to answer to you anymore, Rhonda. I can do what I want."

"You always could do what you wanted. You always *did*. But you didn't want to do anything I suggested."

"Well, things change. Just like things changed when you started fucking buddy."

Rhonda did not have a retort. Tired of the silence, Eric said: "Gotta go. Will be by over the next few weeks to pick up the rest of my stuff. We can talk then about how this is going to go down."

All she could say was, "Okay."

She suddenly felt jealous and silly. Eric was out having fun, seeing *her* favorite comedian, and she was in an empty home pondering her life. She did as she always had when he made her upset: She reached out to a man. She frequently kept open opportunities with other men of her past by staying in touch, mostly whenever she felt stifled in her marriage. In this case, she texted Lorenzo.

You still up?

She waited several minutes, but got no reply. That was strange. He always responded to her texts in a timely fashion. But it was close to midnight, so she chalked it up to the late hour.

After a shower, she stood at the bathroom doorway, looking at her empty bed. By this time, on a normal night, Eric would be either snoring or lying on his back wheezing, with the remote control resting on his ample belly. Those sights did not bother her at first, but they grew to make her cringe. She smiled to herself at the quiet.

But Rhonda hardly was at peace. She was lonely. And for the first time in fifteen years, she was unsure of herself and her life.

Chapter Twenty-Seven: Mano Y Mano

Stephanie

"Who the fuck is Charles, Steph?"

"Lower your voice."

"Answer the question."

"Let's go downstairs. People are trying to sleep up here."

When they got onto the elevator, Stephanie said, "Charles is a principal in the Los Angeles area that I met a few months ago."

"Why are you talking about him to your sister?"

"Because I'm talking to her about everything. I'm trying to connect with her."

"But I heard what you said."

Before she could respond, the elevator doors opened. In the distance was Charles.

Stephanie's heart dropped. She intuitively knew it was him, but her eyes couldn't stay focused. The closer they got, the more into focus he came, and the more fear covered her body.

"Hi. I left my jacket. It has my wallet in it," he said, retrieving his blazer.

He turned to Willie, unaware of who he was, and extended his hand. "Hi. I'm Charles, a —"

"Charles? You're Charles?"

Charles looked at Stephanie, who looked at the floor.

"Charles, I'm Willie, Stephanie's husband. Why are you here in the middle of the night?"

"Oh, well, I, uh, I came by earlier to support your wife. I'm in town for a conference."

"The conference ain't here, man," Willie said.

"Yeah, I know. Like I said, when I called, she told me what had happened with her sister and that she was scared and alone, so decided to come by."

"You have on a wedding ring — you have your own wife, don't you?"

"I do. Eighteen years."

"Well, comfort you own fucking wife. Leave mine alone."

"Willie," Stephanie said, with fear in her voice. She knew her husband was a proud man and was not above engaging in a fight, even at forty-six years old.

"It's okay," Charles said. "I understand. I

370

would feel the same way. No disrespect intended, Willie. I was only trying to be a friend. I went through cancer a while back and my wife was there for me the entire time. But no one was there for her. So I know what it's like not to have someone there for support."

"As you can see, I'm here. And let's step over here for a minute."

"That's not necessary, Willie," Stephanie pleaded.

"Yeah, it is," Willie said. "Stay here."

The men walked about twenty feet away. "Aye, man, listen," Willie began, "if you came over here with a pure heart to support my wife, thank you. I appreciate it. But I'm a man and I'm not a fool. If you aren't fucking her, you're trying to — and I ain't cool with either one of them. So you best get a good look at her now because you won't be seeing her again. I don't give a fuck if you end up in the same elevator, you get off. 'Cause if I find out you didn't, I'm gonna come looking for you. And I won't be this calm; I promise you that."

Charles contemplated saying, "Okay" and leaving, but his pride wouldn't let him. "It's like this, Willie. You don't control anything I do, where I go or who I see. Period. You have, from what I can tell, a nice wife. Be glad with that. But don't think you can talk shit to me as if I'm a child quaking in my boots. 'Cause I'm not. And I wear big boots. So if you come looking for me, as you say you will, I hope you find me. And please believe I won't be this calm, either."

The men stared each other down. It looked as if they were going to start throwing, and Stephanie hurried between them.

"Charles, please go. Thank you for coming earlier."

Charles diverted his eyes from Willie's and into Stephanie's. "I wish your sister the best, Stephanie."

He picked up his jacket, glared at Willie, turned and walked away.

Stephanie's shoulders dropped. She was relieved . . . for a minute.

"If you're not fucking him, you should have been because that's what I believe," Willie said. "And that's a real problem."

"Willie, how can you think that?"

"No man who isn't fucking a woman or trying to would come to a hospital to support someone he met a month ago. In the middle of the night. Period. So either he's the nicest guy in the world — which he is *not* — or you're fucking him."

"I'm not even going to dignify that."

"Yeah, I'm sure you're not."

She believed the best defense was a good offense, so she went on the attack.

"Look, I'll be honest with you," she said. "You have some nerve being upset with someone — a man — being nice to me. You are the one who cheated and put our relationship, our marriage, on the line. But I guess cheaters believe everyone is capable of doing the same thing."

"So you're going to throw that in my face. That was *seven* years ago. We went to counseling and the one thing we took from it was that it wasn't going to be used against me."

"Well, that's bullshit, Willie. You weren't the one who was betrayed. You think I'm supposed to *ever* forget it? *No.*"

"I'm saying we got way beyond that. And that has nothing to do with what happened. And I answered for a year straight about that situation. I'm not going to get back into it, seven years later."

"We may be way beyond what happened, in terms of time, but it still hurts."

Stephanie was being honest. She had stayed in the marriage because she loved her husband and family. But the anguish she'd suffered when she learned Willie had been sleeping with an old girlfriend had devastated her. And so, part of her wanted

Willie to know that she had cheated, too. She thought to herself: *Two wrongs don't make a right, but they sure make it even, and that's all right with me.*

She was not sure if she would reveal that she had crossed the line with Charles. But she felt like she had regained some power in her marriage by Willie believing that she could or would cheat. At the same time, she was turned on by how jealous he was.

Their marriage had rebounded after Willie's infidelity but made a downward turn when he became so engrossed in work that his attention to Stephanie dwindled. It was especially noticeable after their daughter went away to college. When she was home, especially her last year of high school, they'd spent a lot of time together as a family. When she'd left to go to San Diego State coincided with Willie's business blossoming, his commitment to it grew.

He paid the mortgage and the utility bills and the car insurance, so he believed he was compensating for not being there. But that did not work for Stephanie, who coveted attention. She passively had complained, but Willie always countered with a persuasive argument: "This business is my dream come true. I have to be at the business to make the business work, Steph. You have to understand that."

She did not want to squash his dream; indeed, she wanted to support it, so she'd acquiesced. Over time, though, her desire to have a man's attention grew to a fantasy that she told herself would come true at some point. Charles came along at the right time, saying the right things, and Stephanie felt powerless against what she considered a prophecy she had put into the universe. She rationalized that "it was meant to be" because she had told herself it would happen.

Willie sat in a separate chair, staring off into the distance, and Stephanie was surprised at her emotions. She felt invigorated. She knew then that his cheating all those years ago really wore on her, even as she put on a contented face. But she was filled with anxiety when he worked late or went to the office on the weekends. Because he had cheated before, she knew he was capable of doing it again.

In reality, it had been stressful for her ever since she had learned of his cheating. She was often on edge about where he was, what he was doing and with whom. Because she wanted her family so badly, she had suppressed the constant anxiety and replaced it with relief when he finally called or came home.

Her pure side, the side that loved Willie, overtook her. She did not want him to live with the anxiety she had. She had gotten even with him after so long, and that was enough for her. He didn't have to know.

But since *she* knew, the anxiety that dominated for seven years washed away. The payback evened things. So, she went over to her husband and sat in his lap.

"I'm sorry, Willie. I made Charles feel comfortable enough to come here. I knew he was interested in me — or at least I thought he might be. I'm sorry. You're my husband and at this time especially, the family needs to be strong and together."

Willie nodded his head. It was not the "I'm-not-fucking-this-guy" declaration he desired, but he got enough to feel better about the situation.

"We've got some work to do once Toya gets better," he said. "I don't want you unhappy. And I don't want you seeking the attention of other men."

Those words penetrated Stephanie's heart. Willie sounded like the Willie she had fallen for almost two decades before. And so she leaned in and kissed him.

He kissed her back and she got comfortable in her husband's lap and they fell asleep together in the hospital waiting room. It was their most romantic night in some time.

Their sleep was disturbed by the sunlight — and people milling about the area. She looked at her watch; it was six thirty.

"Why did you say to Toya that you would leave Charles alone? I heard you."

Stephanie was perplexed. "I thought we moved on from that. I told you I encouraged him. I was telling Toya that I was going to stop encouraging him."

"I ain't too proud to tell you that I'm disappointed, hurt. You basically pursued this guy. No wonder he came up here last night. He's trying to close the deal."

"This should not be what we discuss the first thing in the morning. Can I brush my teeth and wash my face first? *Damn.*"

"You think you can tell me that, basically, you were flirting with someone and I should let it go."

"I let go of what you did."

"Yeah, that's what I thought. But after seven years, you brought it up."

"Oh, my God. I told you, Willie: I'm not a magician. I didn't hypnotize myself and forget what you did. So excuse me if I'm human."

"But you haven't brought it up in years. Now that I'm questioning you about your shit, you decide you've been traumatized by it for years and bring it back up. Pretty convenient. I'm just saying."

"You can say whatever you want. You don't know what it's like to have your trust broken like that. You don't."

"Actually, I do."

"How?"

"Who is Charles?"

Stephanie felt anxious.

"Who?"

"You heard me."

"I already told you."

"Sacramento teacher's conference. You met at the table. You've been texting and keeping in touch ever since."

Stephanie's heart pounded. *How could he know the details of her night with another man?*

"Where are you getting this from?"

"From you. Well, to be specific, from your e-mail. You liked e-mailing Charles and he, for some reason, liked to detail what happened. I give you credit. You did tell him that you loved me.

"Because I had hurt you, I didn't say anything. But I was devastated and hurt and felt betrayed and all the emotions you

378

shared with me. So, yeah, I do understand what it's like to be cheated on. And it's not a good feeling."

He had too many specific details for Stephanie to deny the tryst.

"Why didn't you say something, Willie?"

"I figured I deserved it. I wasn't fooling myself; I knew I hurt you bad. I was almost glad you did it because learning that lifted a burden off me. I felt like we were on an even playing field, even as I struggled with the actual cheating. It's complicated when you forgive your spouse for the ultimate betrayal. You want peace, but the distrust is powerful."

"We have to start over, Willie. I can't even believe this, any of this. I feel so bad and so . . . I don't know . . . embarrassed. Look, I never told anyone, and I wouldn't now."

"For the record, I stopped reading your e-mails because nothing good was going to come out of continuing to read them. And I didn't play tit-for-tat. I've been faithful. I know I work some crazy hours sometimes, but I have been faithful."

"That's all I needed to hear. I admit that I have had my doubts at times, all based on the past. But I trust you."

They hugged, but Stephanie wondered about her husband. She was angry that he

379

went through her e-mail, but confused as to why he would not confront her on what he found. She figured there was about a five percent chance that a man would learn his wife cheated on him and not say anything about it. Maybe not even that much.

He said the guilt from his cheating allowed him to feel like she was due to cheat on him. She understood that, but still struggled with him not saying anything — until now.

"How could you not let me know what you read in my e-mail, Willie? It's hard to imagine that you would be able to do that."

"It wasn't easy. I was hurt. But I felt guilty for years before I read the e-mail. I either had to accept it as getting what I deserved because of, you know, what I did. Or I had to blow up our marriage. You can believe the second thought was the strongest. But I went into our daughter's room. She was home visiting. I looked around the room and every photo she had either in a frame or on her wall was of the three of us. The family means everything to her. I couldn't do that to her. And it would have been hypocritical of me after I begged you for another chance and you gave it to me.

"So, I got over it . . . the best I could. Well, I guess I'm still getting over it."

Stephanie nodded her head. Slowly. All

that and she thought her cheating with Charles for months was a secret. She had deleted the text messages immediately, but was slow to trash the e-mails. They were there long enough for Willie to learn of her affair.

After their first encounter, the messages escalated from suggestive to salacious, including naked photos. Stephanie discovered she liked taking nude photos of herself.

She surprised Charles with a photo in her bra. His response encouraged her to send a topless picture the next week, then a full-body naked one and various poses in various stages of nakedness. Sending them excited her, made her feel free and dangerous. She assumed Willie had not seen those. They would have prompted him to explode.

Stephanie had stored the images in a Folder marked "Fashion" in her desktop in the office at home. She knew Willie had no interest in that. She appreciated the images so much that she could not bear to delete them. But her conversation with Willie let her know she *had* to get rid of them. Fast.

"This is not a place I expected us to come back together as a couple, but I'm glad we have," she said. "I'm grateful for you being here, for not tearing our family apart even though you had every right to. It says a lot about how much you love your family, how important it is to you."

"Yeah, let's not get so mushy right now that you don't forget something: I'm not having any more shit out of you. That Charles guy, I better not see him or hear his name ever again. It took everything in me not to punch him in his damned face. It's one thing to know he exists. It's another to see him right there lying to my face, like I'm a fool. I showed control last night I didn't know I had. I prayed on it — and you know I don't call on God for much — as you slept. I wanted to leave your ass. I wanted to hurt you. *Bad.* But I remembered how you felt, how I made you feel, and that's the only thing that kept me from believing I got what I deserved. It's the only thing that kept me here.

"You know my boy, Donald. He cheated on his wife at least twice and she caught him and he begged her to stay, and she did. Then a year later, he caught her cheating and divorced her as fast as Steph Curry gets off a jumper. Even though he was a consistent cheater, he couldn't take knowing she cheated once, and their marriage ended. I couldn't do that. Part of me wanted to, though. I can't lie. Bottom line: We've got some work to do to get back to right."

Stephanie promised Charles or any other man would never be a concern. But her immediate goal was to officially end it with Charles and to delete all traces that they had a relationship.

"Can you stay here for another hour or two?" she asked Willie. "I want to go home and shower and change. Then I can come right back."

"Yeah, go ahead. You probably need to sleep, at least a nap. You look tired. Between me and Terry, we'll keep Toya company."

"Okay. Thank you . . . for everything. Be back no later than two hours."

They hugged and she stepped into the northern California sunlight that forced her to scramble in her purse for her sunglasses. The ride home was bumper-to-bumper, but it allowed her time to think about how she would end it with Charles without hurting his feelings.

First, though, she had to erase all e-mail and photos. She cursed herself for not erasing all evidence. She was fortunate Willie loved her and was remarkably, almost unbelievably, reasonable. But she hated that he knew what she had done. She vowed to earn Willie's trust by working as hard as he had worked to earn hers. But she knew he would always have doubts about her, and that pained Stephanie.

At home, she dropped her purse on the couch in the living room and made a beeline to the office, where she logged into the computer and located the files that had damning evidence of her infidelity.

Before deleting, she read each e-mail and viewed each photo, and the reminiscing prompted her to realize she did not want to let Charles go. Their tryst was fun and exotic, and it made her feel good. But the revelations with Willie gave her hope that he could become the man she needed and their marriage could become fun and exotic.

She smiled at the thought of having two men truly interested in her for the first time since college. That case did not work out so well, with each guy finding out about the other — and walking, leaving her without anyone.

Stephanie admitted that Charles did the most for her physical and emotional needs, but he was unavailable. And the only way to move on was to say bye to Charles. That was not going to be easy.

Chapter Twenty-Eight:
The Lie Shall Set You Free

Juanita

They got through the early part of the week
without their issues or suspicions coming
up. Both were relieved. But both were wary
of what would come out of the meeting with
Dr. Fields.

At the session, she asked how they had
been.

"We're here," Maurice said.

"What's that mean?" Dr. Fields asked.

"Yeah, I want to know, too," Juanita said.

"It means that we are still together and
still willing to work on it."

"Is that it? There's nothing more to that?"
Dr. Fields wanted to know.

"Well, the truth of the matter is that we're
good, and we're wondering if we need to
continue coming here."

"You're the one who brought up coming
here again," Juanita said.

"So we can tell Dr. Fields to her face that

we're ending it."

"You surely can do whatever you like," the therapist said. "I think we've made some real steps, bumped up against some boundaries and have grown to understand each other better."

"That's what we have done more than anything: grow," Maurice said. "I won't speak for my wife, but I think we've matured with open conversation."

"Give me an example."

"Okay, like, we went to a big party last week. Got dressed up and had a good time. But while we were there, we ran into one of Juanita's old boyfriends."

"How did that make you feel?"

"Not so good, but probably because I didn't learn it from her. When she went to the bathroom with his date, he told me. Well, he didn't say the words. But he said the code words, like 'You've got a good one' and 'You're lucky. I'm still searching for my perfect lady.' Those kind of compliments were his attempt to tell me they were close and I shouldn't take her for granted."

"Isn't that a leap?" Juanita said. "You don't know the man, so you don't know if he was trying to tell you something or actually giving me a compliment."

"That's true," Dr. Fields said. "But why

did you come to that conclusion and not the alternative? There had to be something more than a feeling."

"I can answer that," Juanita jumped in.

"How would you know?" Maurice asked.

"I just do. And he felt that way because he *needed* to feel that way."

"Explain," Dr. Fields said.

"My friend was on a date with a woman I had just met, and Maurice acted like he had just met her, too. But he hadn't. I'm not guessing or insinuating what their relationship is or was or whatever. But it was enough for him to take leaps with my friend and me because he felt guilty about his own stuff."

Usually, Dr. Fields would interject. This time, she swung her head toward Maurice.

"How could you come up with all that? You're a mind-reader now? I found out that we worked in the same building, so I guess I have or could have seen her before. But you've taken it to another place."

"So, you're telling me you've never been to her house?"

"Her house? No, I haven't. Why would you say that?"

He knew, unless she had photos, she had no proof. Gloria certainly would not admit to it.

"How do you have him at her house, Juanita?" Dr. Fields asked.

"My friend told me. He dropped her off there several weeks ago and you were standing in front of her house on Capitol Hill."

"Ridiculous," Maurice said. And he was convincing, too. He had used the five days between the party and the session to devise a counter to Juanita's inevitable claims. "Impossible."

"Impossible, Maurice? Impossible?"

"I tell you what's not impossible; the fact that you saw your old boyfriend the other night for the first time in years. That's impossible."

Juanita had prepared for the inevitable, too. She was ready. "What? How do you get that?"

"He's a massage therapist at Massage Envy in Bethesda. You went to Massage Envy in Bethesda for a massage. And you're telling me you didn't have a massage by him? Too much of a coincidence. In fact, like Freud said, there are no coincidences."

"Actually, there are coincidences, as far as I'm concerned. And in this case, the coincidence is that I went to a Massage Envy and it turns out he works at one. But I did not go to the Massage Envy where he works. I went to the one at Potomac Yard. I told you I *wanted* to go to that one in Bethesda."

"Bullshit," Maurice said.

"Dr. Fields, is it okay if I make a phone call? I want to call the Bethesda location and have the receptionist check for Maurice to see if I have ever been there. They have the records."

"Maurice," Dr. Fields said, "do you need her to go through that length to believe her?"

"I know what I heard her say. She didn't say anything about Potomac Yard."

"I know I didn't. But I didn't say I went to Bethesda. Said I *wanted* to go there. But he doesn't believe me, although he cannot name one instance in all the years he's known me when I lied. Not one. But you can call on your own time the Bethesda location and the Potomac Yard's and get your answers."

Juanita had used a made-up name when she'd checked in at the Bethesda location. And she had Brandon that week put her in the system at the Potomac Yard location, where he once worked, for the same day. She believed Maurice would call for his own peace of mind.

"If you want to make those calls, Maurice, you can do so. But I believe we have to talk about this lack of trust that I'm hearing."

"I'm not saying I don't trust my wife. I'm saying that whole thing with her ex-boyfriend and not telling me seems fishy."

"Fishy? Why would I stand there while he's in my face and say, 'This is my ex-boyfriend'? That makes no sense. But here's also what doesn't make any sense: Instead of dancing with me, you suggest that he dance with me. *We* hadn't even danced, but you want me to dance with another man?"

"Why did you suggest that, Maurice?"

"First of all, we *did* dance. How can you forget that? And my wife loves to dance. I'm confident in who we are to each other, so dancing with another man wouldn't bother me. Since her friend was there — and I didn't know at the time that they used to date — I thought it was fine for her to dance a few songs with him. I didn't see the harm."

"As you say, bullshit," Juanita responded. "You had Brandon dance with me so you could spend time with Gloria, the woman you supposedly had laid eyes on for the first time."

"Again, you're acting like you're a mind-reader."

"I may be sweet and kind and innocent and all those things you've said about me over the years, but my eyes are open. I'm

390

aware of the things that are important to me. So as I danced, I also watched. And you all jumped right into some intense conversation."

"Of course, we talked — we were standing there together."

"Talked about what?"

"I can't remember now. It was small talk —"

"Looked like at least medium talk to me."

"Medium talk? What's that?"

"Something above small talk, a conversation between two people who are familiar with each other."

"So you're saying what, exactly, Juanita?" Dr. Fields asked.

"I'm not saying anything — except that I find it hard to believe that they worked in the same building for a long time and never saw each other."

"Maybe we did see each other, in passing. I don't recall seeing her. And she said the same."

"Again, this comes back to trust, doesn't it?" Dr. Fields asked.

"I have had no reason not to trust Maurice. I haven't. But that doesn't mean I believe what he's saying right now."

"So how would you describe where your marriage is at this very moment? I specify right now because couples tend to give an overview answer when I'm looking for your thoughts on things in this moment. Juanita?"

"I would describe it as tenuous. It's not rock-solid at this moment because we both have these ideas about each other that we're being dishonest. And it's not like lying about who drank the last glass of wine. It's about other people and presumed involvement with other people. I don't like how it feels right now."

"I don't either. I feel like I have been a good husband —"

"Wait, Maurice," Dr. Fields interjected. "Let's not get into an overview of your performance as a husband. Let's stick to this moment."

"Okay, well. I don't see the marriage as dire as she does. I don't see it as tenuous. I see it as challenged. We're definitely at a different place; talking to a therapist shows that. Not talking about our concerns until we get here shows that. But I don't see anything of the deal-breaker variety going on."

"Interesting," Dr. Fields said. "There was a potentially deal-breaking concern in a previous session — the subject of sex and passion. Anyone interested in taking that on?"

"I will," Juanita said. "Not a lot has been happening."

"Saturday night, remember?" Maurice said.

"First of all, Saturday night was four nights ago. Nothing since then. And the fact that he's okay with that is my concern. But not only that, on Saturday night, that was not passion. That was sex for the sake of having sex."

"Why would you say that? I didn't feel that way at all. I considered it us reaffirming things after a night that was sort of off-balance. We didn't talk about these things that bothered us, but we could both feel there was something going on. Questions. So, for me, it wasn't only sex. It was re-affirming."

"Okay, I'll give you that. But do you know I cried."

"What?"

"While we were having sex, I cried."

"What? Why?"

"Because I didn't feel any passion. We came in here and talked about my need for passion and what I have gotten is still not passionate. It's you getting our rocks off,

393

with no real effort or interest in pleasing me."

"Well, what do you want? A vibrator?"

"That would be nice. Yes, a vibrator during sex would spice up our love life."

"What? Dr. Fields . . ."

"What, Maurice? Your wife is telling you what she wants. I think you should be listening."

Juanita had had it with the prim-and-proper façade.

"Nothing wrong with toys to enhance our love life. And we can talk about other stuff at home. But the bottom line is that we have to spice this thing up. Let loose. Relax. Don't be so uptight. Don't treat me so delicately. Don't be afraid to ask for what you want. Do things we haven't done before. Do you know, Doctor, that we've been to exotic islands and never made love on the beach? Or at minimum on our balcony overlooking the beach? We've never made love on the floor in front of the fireplace. That's what I want, what I need. Adventure. Passion."

Maurice was embarrassed, and Dr. Fields could tell.

"There's no need to feel awkward about your wife telling you what she wants. It's —"

"Smack my ass," Juanita said.

"Are you *serious*?" Maurice asked.

"Hard," she answered.

"Seems like I might need to step out of the room and give you all some space," Dr. Fields cracked, and everyone laughed.

"But seriously," she went on, "this is a classic breakthrough. Juanita has been wanting to say this for a long time. Longer than you could imagine."

"Here's the thing, honey," Juanita said. "I am all of what you see and I am more than what you see. You understand?"

"I do now," Maurice answered.

"And I'll tell you this," Juanita added. "We have, for us, been through some stuff the last few months. And I guess I caused a lot of it. I'm sorry. But I'll tell you this: a passionate woman is worth the chaos."

Maurice smiled. Juanita let out a sigh of relief. She'd had her fling with Brandon, survived it without her husband knowing the full extent of it, and finally, it seemed, put a charge into Maurice to put more romance into their lives. She accepted there was no such thing as a perfect woman, even if she had tried so diligently to be exactly that.

But she was so relieved to share what she had been holding in for years that she could hardly contain herself. And she was relieved to see that Maurice did not mind that she was less than perfect or worse. Unleashing all that freed her up, and her husband's accepting of what she revealed combined to revive her interest in her vows.

For the first time in a long time, she felt the potential for fulfillment in her marriage. The expression of what she wanted, what she *truly* wanted, inspired her to embrace a life with her husband that could be fulfilling. That was short of perfect, but it was enough.

Chapter Twenty-Nine:
Harsh Realities

Rhonda

Rhonda was surprised at how well she slept. She had seen Diane Keaton in a movie say she slept in the center of the bed to make it feel less empty. She tried it and it worked.

She was disappointed to see that she had not received a return text from Lorenzo. She had come to know his schedule, and he rose each morning by seven. It was eight.

Her initial concern was his well-being. Then she wondered if that text Olivia received was from him and she went back to his house. She also guessed if he had another woman over and could not respond to her. Rhonda's mind played cruel games on her, so much so that she contemplated driving over to his house to see if there was a car in his driveway.

I'm better than that, she thought. Then she had a second thought: *No, I'm not.*

And so she freshened up and took a ride

over to Lorenzo's home. There was not a random car in the driveway, and Rhonda let out such a huge sigh. She went back home and this time called him.

He answered. "Why aren't you asleep?"

"I was asleep, but now I'm up and you're the first thing on my mind."

"So, what's going on with your husband? Did you work it out?"

"Work it out? I told you he left. I'm on my own now. I'm actually trying to see you. When are you available?"

"Well, that's hard to say right now. I have to work at the bar every day this week, which is good for me. The more experience, the better I will be."

"We live five minutes apart. There has to be time to see each other."

"I'm sure there will be. We have to figure out when. We're kind of working when the other person isn't."

"I need to get out of the house, so maybe I'll come down to the bar. I'll have one drink and watch you make drinks and talk to you in between."

Lorenzo did not respond.

"Hello?"

"Hey. I'm sorry. Doing some paperwork. Okay, you're coming to the bar tonight? That's what you said?"

"If it's okay with you."

"Sure. I'll see you down there."

"I *could* stop by for a few minutes before I go to work and get a little pick-me-up, if you know what I mean?"

"I do, but I can't this morning. Like I said, I'm doing some paperwork that has to be submitted to some lenders this morning."

"Oh, okay. One more thing: Did you get my text last night?"

"I did, but I got it in the middle of the night. And I would have texted you this morning, but I decided to wait until later."

"Okay. I would ask you about Olivia, but we can talk about her when I see you tonight."

Rhonda did not feel good about the conversation, but it was early in the morning and she let it go. She went through her workday morning without issue, but was perturbed when Olivia told her during lunch that she had heard from Lorenzo that morning.

"What did he want?"

"It was seven in the morning and he texted me about the weekend."

"Really?" She thought: *This man just told me he received my text and didn't text me because he was busy, but texted her at seven in the morning? I don't like this picture.*

"Yes, girlfriend. I think he's more determined to get with me since I rejected him. Men are a trip. They hardly have interest in you until you make it clear you're in control. They'll either do one of two things: Move on to the next one if they don't have an out-of-control ego; or pursue you like crazy because their ego cannot accept the rejection. That's what's happening with Lorenzo. He's not that interested in me. But since I spent all that time with him and would not give in, he's determined to make me his challenge. *Men.* It's so transparent."

"So what are you going to do? Since you know this, why not ignore him? Last thing you should do is go out with someone you have no interest in."

"Yeah, but I do have an interest. I don't know how much of an interest. Maybe I'm wrong about him and he's sincere."

Three days back on the market — and far from officially single — Rhonda felt competition. She was determined to go to the bar and turn Lorenzo's head and help him to continue to ward off Olivia.

So when she got home that evening, she did not bother to have dinner. She wanted to make sure she got into one of her formfitting, head-turning dresses that was sure to reel in Lorenzo. She decided to first watch

400

a little CNN to see what was going on in the world. She hadn't turned on a TV for three days.

When she got the television on, she was disappointed to learn the service had been suspended. It was Eric's job to pay the bill. And since he hadn't, Rhonda had to figure out how. First, though, she had to figure out where the bill was. She was that detached from it. Lorenzo handled that. It was something she decided she would figure out later.

Instead, she washed a load of clothes. When she came out of the laundry room, she screamed. Eric stood in front of her.

"What are you doing here? You scared the shit out of me."

"It's still my house. Came to get my things."

"Can we talk for a minute first? Please."

Eric gave in. They sat in the family room.

"Please don't apologize again," he said. "I get it. You're sorry."

"Can I explain myself? I don't want you to hate me. This might not make sense to you, but I'd like to try."

"I already know. You're upset — were upset — with me because I got fat and didn't want to do a lot of stuff you wanted to do. That's it in a nutshell. If it's something more than that, go ahead. Tell me."

"No, that's right. What I want to say is that I had never done this before. I could be wrong, but I didn't feel like you cared — about me, my needs, my wants. Anything.

"And think about this, Eric: When was the last time you called me 'baby'? When was the last time you called me anything affectionate? I'm a full-fledged woman; I need that."

"Are you blaming this on me?"

"No. Never. I will say that when you and that woman were about to have an affair — you would have if she didn't mess up and call when I was using your cell phone — I forgave you and stayed."

"You forgave me after texting the woman back acting like you were me. You forgave me after you made sure we hadn't done anything. But whatever the case, that was your decision. You stayed. I'm a man, and for me, I couldn't stay. I couldn't live wondering if you're not sneaking to see someone else. I love you, but I love myself more."

"I understand; I'm not trying to complain or talk you out of anything. I just . . . we've been friends for so long, Eric. It would kill me if we faded away. We don't have a child that would force us to communicate. I don't

want to lose you as a friend. That's important to me."

"I appreciate you saying that. And maybe
we can get there. Right now, I'm still
fucking pissed. My world — both our
worlds — are turned upside down. Now I've
got to try to make some sense of it.

"And the last thing I will say is this: I
won't tell any of our friends why we're in
this place. They like and respect you and I
don't want that to change. Besides, this is
our business. No one else's."

"You're a good man, Eric. Thank you."

"Yeah, apparently not good enough."

He struggled to get up from his seat, but
did — and headed upstairs. That last salvo
stung Rhonda. She stayed in her chair in
silence until Eric finished the last of two
loads to his SUV.

"You were, are, good enough. You have to
know that," Rhonda said.

"What I know is that you gave up on me.
I didn't have to get as big as I am. But I
did. And I could have done more things
with you. I'm trying to be fair right now.
Still, you broke your vows. You dishonored
yourself. Forget about me. I didn't expect
this from you. I didn't deserve it.

"I give you credit: You've inspired me to
live, to lose weight, to enjoy all Atlanta has

to offer. I hate that it came to this, but it is what it is now. I have to leave you because you don't want me. If you really wanted me, you never would have turned to someone else. And because you did, I could never trust you. I couldn't."

Eric shook his head and turned and left the house. Rhonda was sad, but relieved that he'd listened to her and hopeful that they could develop a friendship in the future.

Her immediate future, though, was to connect with Lorenzo. So, when the time came, she slipped into the beige dress that emphasized her figure and breasts, and after a long primping session in front of the bathroom and full-length mirrors, drove downtown to the Glenn Hotel to see the man she hoped would help in her transition to single life.

The bar was not busy, but there were a few tables of patrons celebrating someone's birthday in the lounge chairs. Only a woman and two men sat near the right end of the bar. Lorenzo was in front of them, laughing and conversing when Rhonda slowly made her way behind them and to the end of the bar. The heads of the men turned and followed her every step, including Lorenzo. Immediately, she knew the dress had the desired effect.

After a minute or so, Lorenzo excused himself and greeted Rhonda.

"Don't you look nice tonight," he said, placing a small napkin in front of her. "What can I get you?"

"Thank you. I will take a healthy dose of you."

Lorenzo offered a sheepish grin. "Okay, how about something to drink?"

"You," Rhonda said.

"Okay, how about I make you something I think you'd like?"

"Sure. You do know what I like."

She was embarrassed at how she threw herself at Lorenzo. The pressure of knowing she was competing against other women, especially Olivia, sparked her to overreact. But she enjoyed it. She hadn't openly flirted in years, and it brought her back to her youth.

Lorenzo presented her a drink and a few sips later, she found herself settling down.

But he worked the other end of the bar for several minutes at a time, leaving Rhonda alone. Finally, though, a man noticed her when he came into the lounge area and made his way beside her at the bar. He was tall, wearing a suit with the necktie undone, as if he were coming from a business dinner.

"Mind if I sit here?" he asked.

"Ah, no, that's fine."

"Steve Reese," he said.

"Hi. I'm Rhonda." She extended her hand to shake.

"Nice to meet you. But I don't shake hands."

"Really? Looks like you had dinner with business people. You don't shake their hands?"

"Only extreme cases. Otherwise, I tell them. Want to catch someone else's germs, shake their hands."

Rhonda was unimpressed. The guy stayed for five minutes and talked the entire time about subjects she had little interest in. Never a question about her. Finally, it became obvious that she was not interested, and he left. Three other men came with various levels of "game" that Rhonda came to recognize as the downside of being single: Lame, uninteresting men who could not hold a mature, intelligent conversation.

"I see you're not lonely tonight," Lorenzo said.

"I came here to see you. But you won't give me any attention. What's up with that?"

"I'm here now. What's up with you? Lots happened the last couple of days. You okay?"

Rhonda took a deep breath. "I'm okay. I'm going to be fine, in time and with your help."

"My help? I'm not sure what I can do. You're going through a divorce, last thing you need is to have me still in the picture."

She was taken aback. "What? What are you saying?"

"I'm saying that we both have a lot on our plate, so I'm not sure how much I'll get to see you."

"That sounds like a blow-off to me," Rhonda said. She didn't mean it, but she said it to be reassured. "If you don't want to deal with me, say so."

"I don't think we should be together — at least until your divorce is final."

Rhonda was stunned.

"Wait. Are you telling me that now that my husband has left me that you don't want to deal with me?"

"I'm saying something like that. Look, I will be completely honest with you. You know I like you. And one of the reasons I like you is because you don't make waves. You never asked me about other women, other than Olivia, because she's your friend. So that said to me that you only wanted sex. Why wouldn't I go with that program?"

"But now that I'm on my way to being

single, you're not interested?"

"Single? You're not single. Look, you're still wearing your wedding ring."

Rhonda, in the confusion that came with her husband leaving, never considered taking off her ring. It did not occur to her.

"I forgot."

"That's what I'm talking about right there. You're not in your right mind right now."

"I know exactly what I'm doing and exactly who I was dealing with, and I'm ashamed that I didn't see it earlier. You used me for sex."

"Hold up," Lorenzo said. "Don't play the victim to circumstances you created."

"Wow. So that's it? You're interested in me when I'm married, but the idea of me being single turns you off? What kind of shit is that?"

"Listen, it is what it was. I'm not trying to be a bad guy here. I'm preparing you for your new life."

"You could have done that by simply being a friend. Instead, you make me feel like shit."

"I'm gonna make you another drink. But don't feel bad about anything. We had fun, right?"

Rhonda felt stupid. Her mother's words

rang in her head. The look of Eric's disappointed face flashed into her vision. She sat there for a moment embarrassed and disgusted.

Her first instinct was to try to persuade Lorenzo to reconsider. But she found something in herself that she would need in her new life: strength.

She recalled something that she had read that empowered her: *A strong woman will stop trying if she feels unwanted. She won't fix it or beg. She'll just walk away.*

And so, Rhonda rose from her bar seat and headed for the exit. She turned to wave to Lorenzo, who waved back with a small smile. Rhonda then folded her fingers, leaving only the middle one upright, as she vanished behind the door.

CHAPTER THIRTY:
THE AWAKENING

Stephanie

After she deleted all e-mails to and from Charles, Stephanie exhaled at the computer. She then took a long, hot bath, falling asleep in the tub. She only awoke when the water finally began to get cold.

It was the bit of rest she needed to move on with a most important day: doctors called to say the swelling in Toya's brain had reduced significantly and she would be taken out of the coma; and Stephanie would have the tough conversation to end it with Charles.

The news of her sister gave her joy. But dealing with Charles would come first. She got dressed and called him.

"I'm sorry about that drama last night. Had no idea he'd be there," he said.

"I know. I know. I'm sorry, too. Listen, can we meet for a little while? I have to be back at the hospital in about two hours.

They are going to take Toya out of the coma, thank God. But maybe we can connect at the Terrace Room at the Lake Merritt Hotel."

Charles agreed. Stephanie had practiced what she would say, but never came up with anything that she thought worked. She decided she'd wing it.

She got there first and scored a table near the window, overlooking the lake. She was not hungry, but craved coffee. And after her coffee arrived, so did Charles. She rose from her seat and they had a long embrace. He kissed her on the top of her head.

"Thank you for coming and for supporting me last night. It really meant a lot."

"I wish I hadn't left my jacket."

"Me, too. I'm also glad you all did not get into a fight."

"We're men, you know? I understood his position. And I couldn't back down from him. Anyway, I'm glad to hear that it sounds like progress with your sister."

"Yes, the CT scans look good. She might have to go through some rehab, they're saying. She also might not."

"Yeah, they have to prepare you for the worst."

"So, Charles, a few days ago I was in that room in Sausalito, looking out at the water

411

as you slept and thinking about my future. *Our* future. I was so into that moment — and as soon as I felt really good about it, I got word about my sister to bring me back to earth.

"Being back to earth is not as much fun as the fantasy I have had with you. You really have put a bounce in my step and opened me up to new things. I'm grateful for you. But at the same time, just like you said you can't leave your wife, I can't go on doing this to my husband."

"Doing what to your husband? You told me you felt better about him because of me, because of what we've been doing."

"What I told you was I felt better about myself and was able to deal with him better. But that doesn't matter. What matters is I have to end this now."

"What? Why?"

"Because I love my husband and because he deserves much more from me."

"What about what I deserve?"

"Charles, I'm surprised at this pushback from you. You're married. I'm married. It's wrong. As good as it might have felt, it's wrong."

"It always has been wrong. What changed overnight?"

"What changed is that I don't want to do

this anymore. My husband almost found out about us and that scared the hell out of me. I don't want to do that to him."

"That's not acceptable."

"Excuse me?"

"That's not acceptable, Stephanie. I've fallen for you. I've been everything you need. And now you're going to end it? Just like that?"

"You told me you would never leave your wife. I understood. So what's the point of us continuing this?"

"Because it has been good — for both of us."

"What if your wife found out?"

"No way. She can never know. Never. That would ruin my life, ruin her life, and that can't happen."

"But the longer we continue this, the bigger the chances are that it becomes a setup for disaster. We almost saw it play out last night. I can't have that."

"We can be more careful, careful like we had been. Last night was no reason to stop seeing each other. No."

"Not for you, it wasn't. I know cheating on my husband doesn't make me a bad person. But it's not the best reflection of me. He deserves better. He deserves me working with him to make our marriage better. And I can't do that thinking about you and especially being with you."

"You were doing it before. Keep going as if Saturday never happened."

"But it did happen, Charles."

"It takes two to end it, and you only have yourself."

"What? 'It takes two to end it'? What are you talking about? It takes two to make a relationship. Why are you being so unreasonable?"

"Listen, this ends when I say it ends. Period."

Stephanie rose from her seat. "I don't know what's wrong with you, but I'm leaving."

"Sit down. You're not going anywhere. Sit down and listen to why it's not over."

"I can't believe you. What's wrong with you?"

"We have a good thing. It's made my life easier and exciting. I'm not ready to give it up. I've spent time and money on you. And if you think you're going to end a good thing for me, that's not happening."

Stephanie looked into Charles' eyes and she saw something she had not seen — desperation. That look made her scared, but she was even more convinced by his actions to move on.

"How can you prevent me? You can't make me see you."

He reached inside his jacket pocket and passed her an envelope. Inside were the naked photos of Stephanie. She was mortified.

"Why did you print these out? And why are you showing them to me, Charles?"

"Do I have to say it?"

Stephanie did not respond. Her eyes said it all.

"You try to end it, and these photos surely will end your marriage when they end up in Willie's hands. I know about his business and where it is. They could end up there easily."

Stephanie's anger was palpable. Her hands shook, she was so incensed.

"You would do that? You're telling me you're a lowlife? Really? I feel like I need to take a shower. How could I ever let you have even touched me?"

"You like my touch. Know how I know? You said it in these."

He pulled out a second envelope, a larger one that had the e-mails they had exchanged.

"Fuck you," Stephanie said so loud the waiter turned around. "You're a maggot. I spent the morning deleting all of this to protect us from exposure, and you have it all printed out? And you're threatening to send it to my husband? Oh, wow, that's a real turn-on, big boy. And how do you think I could ever be with you after you've blackmailed me? That's not exactly romantic."

"Don't be condescending. We can get past this moment. But you have to see the big picture. The big picture can be pretty or it can be really ugly. The good news is it's your choice."

"So you think you can extort me into having an affair with you?"

"*Continuing* our affair."

"I know you must think I'm cheap to deal with you now. But I'm worth something. I would have to be nothing to let you touch me again, much less sleep with you." She rose from her seat again. "Go ahead. Send them to Willie. I'd rather wreck my world than spend another second with you."

Stephanie took one step toward the door and turned back to Charles. Then she reached into her purse and pulled out an envelope and tossed it on the table. It was full of nude photos he had sent her, and his heartfelt e-mails, including comments about how his life was stale with his wife. And the envelope was addressed to Priscilla Richardson with her and Charles' home address.

"When you mail your envelope to Willie, be sure to drop that one in the mail to your wife. I'm sure she'd enjoy as much as Willie would enjoy your package. I read up on her. She comes from a wealthy, prominent family. I see why you won't leave her. I'm sure her family would love that package, too. The good news, as you put it, is that it's your choice."

Charles rummaged through the photos and e-mails and slammed the envelope on the table.

"And I know where you work, too. Maybe the superintendent of schools would like to see your inadequate penis and read about your love e-mails to me. And I hear she's somewhat of a prude, so I'm sure they'd get a real reaction out of her . . . Bye, Charles. Oh, and fuck you."

She left him sitting at the table, tearing up all the photos. Stephanie expected it to go much differently. But something told her to bring a little insurance. Still, it hurt her to know Charles was such a loser. She was so caught up in what she thought she wanted that she did not see beyond the surface and the physical, did not see beyond who he could be as someone who was cheating on his wife who had helped him overcome cancer.

She arrived at the hospital feeling secure that she had heard and likely seen the last of Charles Richardson. She could focus solely on Toya. She found Terry and Willie in the hallway outside Toya's room.

"I'm nervous," she said to Terry. "What if she —"

"We're not playing the 'what if' game," Willie said. "We're sending up prayers and positivity."

After several minutes, the doctor emerged. "Our patient is resting comfortably. She opened her eyes and began to cry. I told her what happened and that you all were here, down the hall. She didn't say anything. She went back to sleep, this time on her on volition."

"What about neurologically? Any damage?" Terry asked.

"She's fine. She showed movements in her arms and legs. Recovery to full strength will take about four-to-six weeks. She seemed cognitively fine and her brain waves are strong. She's going to be fine. Oh, and here's a piece of news you probably didn't know: The baby is fine, too."

"Baby? Baby?" Terry repeated.

"It's likely that's what caused her to faint," the doctor said. "Your wife was pregnant. Congratulations."

Stephanie hugged Willie and then Terry with tears streaming down her face. "I'm going to be an auntie. I can't believe it."

"I'm going to be a father," Terry said. "We had given up. We really had. This is a miracle."

Stephanie stepped away from the men and said a quiet prayer: "God, thank You. You have spared me my family and my sister's life. And You've given us new life in our family. I know You have forgiven me of my sins because You have blessed us with new life. Thank You, God."

New life meant the baby growing in Toya's stomach *and* the committed woman that had emerged in Stephanie. She thought to herself, while looking at Willie: *No relationship is all sunshine. But two people who love each other can share the same umbrella to get through the storm.*

ABOUT THE AUTHOR

Curtis Bunn is an *Essence* magazine No. 1 best-selling author of eight novels, including *Seize the Day, The Old Man in the Club, A Cold Piece of Work, The Truth Is in the Wine, Homecoming Weekend* and *Baggage Check.*

A Washington, D.C. native and graduate of Norfolk State University, he made the transition to author after a 24-year career as an award-winning sports journalist in Washington, D.C., New York and Atlanta. Curtis is the founder of the National Book Club Conference, an organization that hosts what has been called "Literary Bliss" for readers and authors, which marks its 15th conference in 2017.

You can visit Curtis at www.curtisbunn .com or on Facebook, Twitter, Instagram and LinkedIn.

5/1/17